LIARS' QUEST
The Enchanted Castle Archives
Book 1

By Michelle L. Levigne

www.YeOldeDragonBooks.com

Ye Olde Dragon Books
P.O. Box 30802
Middleburg Hts., OH 44130

www.YeOldeDragonBooks.com

2OldeDragons@gmail.com

Published in the United States of America
Publication Date: June 30, 2023

Chapter One

Dawn trickled over the rolling landscape of springtime fields and pastures surrounding Castle Fairhold. Mist billowed up from the streams and ponds that served the flocks and herds. In a sheltered dip in the landscape, a muffled curse rang out from a pond ringed by berry brambles already thick with a haze of green leaves and tiny white flowers. Splashing and sputtering, Ash slipped on the muddy bottom and submerged in the pond still icy enough to be her sole domain for pre-dawn bathing. She struggled a few steps into shallower water and stood up again, steady on her feet now. Gritting her teeth, she bowed her head as the billows of mist parted enough to give her a good view of the thin linen shirt slicked to her chest with water.

And the dreaded development made visible underneath.

"Traitor."

Bad enough her hips were widening, and her bottom had curves that would get her accused of eating too many sweets, or sitting down when she should be running errands. She was still the fastest messenger among all the castle servants. Now she had bumps on her chest. Tiny, but they would grow.

Bosoms. Why did she have to have bosoms? Yes, she was almost fifteen, although thin enough to pass for a boy of twelve. Most girls her age had bosoms, and proudly displayed them, by the time they were fourteen. She didn't want bosoms. She didn't want anyone to guess yet, and not for years and years, that she wasn't a boy. A prudish boy, granted, who didn't strip naked with the other servant boys to dance in rain showers to wash, and preferred to swim alone on hot summer afternoons when the castle taskmaster gave them freedom. And didn't sleep with the other boys in a pile with the castle dogs. The other servant boys had teased her about her prissy habits until she earned tasks serving the nobility that required clean bodies and pleasant aroma and neat hair. Jobs that came with privileges, such as eating in the kitchen while the food was still hot, or accompanying Lady Charlotte and Lady Beatrice on errands and even short journeys. Then Ash became very popular with the boys who wanted more than a bed in the hay and regular feeding when they became adults. They traded help with more strenuous chores for lessons on grooming, speaking properly, and reading.

Why did she have to start turning into a girl now? Lady Beatrice had sharp eyes. She would notice any blossoming under Ash's formal serving uniform. A bodice would tame her budding bosoms, but Ash didn't want to tame bosoms, she wanted to do without.

She needed to find something to flatten herself without looking like she flattened herself. Leather or cloth? Who of the kinder adult servants could she trust to help her figure out the mechanics of such a device?

Should she go to Granny Phlox? If anyone in Castle Fairhold knew Ash was a girl, Granny was hopefully the only one. She had been given charge of the orphans Lady Charlotte gathered up after the Great Flood that swept inland to Tippessee, destroying eight villages. Granny had tended the twelve children, ranging from toddlers to five years old. Ash thought she was the only girl. Still, if she had managed to hide under boy clothes all these years, who was to say another orphan wasn't also a girl disguised as a boy? Granny was nearly blind when Lady Charlotte set her up in the cottage on the other side of the cherry orchard and put her in charge of tending the orphans until they could report for service in the castle, but she was a clever old dame who never let her little pups, as she called the twelve, get away with anything. If anyone could help Ash find a way to hide the changes in her body at this highly inconvenient time, surely Granny could? But would she?

That was the crucial question. Ash shivered in the icy pond water as she considered who she could ask for help. Who would laugh at the secret and agree to help her just for the fun of mischief? Who would be furious she had deceived them so long? And who would betray her and force her to wear skirts and learn sewing and limit her reading privileges? Malchus, the castle scribe, thought girls couldn't handle anything more strenuous than herbology and poetry. Ash preferred history, legends, battle records, and anatomical discussions to bolster her growing repertoire of healing skills. She dreamed of traveling with Lord Dunstan when he headed out on the grand world-traveling adventure he had been planning since he was ten years old. Ash planned to be of great use to Dunstan, first as a healer, then helping him unravel magical riddles and stand up to illusions, should he encounter any bad-tempered enchanters or people or kingdoms under a magical curse. She was agile, and strong enough to scale crumbling fortress walls. She knew she could stand firm and stare down nightmare creatures with the boys training to be soldiers. Just one more year until Dunstan was old enough to leave Castle Fairhold, with a proper retinue of servants to set up camp and forage and record his adventures.

She had the skills to handle all those tasks. Plus, she had several characteristics sure to win the favor of the stray enchanter or faerie or talking animal. Most important of all: she was an orphan. Including her in an adventurous questing party would grant Dunstan other benefits. Not all her qualities and characteristics were magical, but according to all the books of adventures she had read, such things did seem to influence the chances of gaining magical help. However, she wasn't going to reveal them unless she absolutely had to. The first being she was a girl in disguise. Every legend indicated such a secret granted favors or advantages in tight spots. Second, she possessed a star-shaped birthmark in a rather embarrassing spot she could only see using a highly polished surface. She never would have found it at all, but the birthmark had an irritating tendency to glow silver at the dark of the moon, and blue at the full moon. She had employed a silver plate borrowed from the feasting hall to find it when she was seven, after too many nights waking up to an odd light in her sleeping nook. Ever since then, she made sure she slept alone, and wore trousers under her nightshirt.

"Just my wretched luck," she muttered as she splashed to the edge of the pond, and a gap in the thick wall of berry brambles. "The star will probably change color, or glow brighter, with all the changes in my flesh." She ducked through the gap, paused to look for inconvenient watchers, then darted to a clump of bushes where she left her clean clothes and a scrap of toweling to dry herself. "I need to go on a quest for a charm to wrap a permanent illusion around myself. This simply will not do."

The sun had risen to a finger's width above the horizon by the time Ash finished drying and dressing. She wrung out the thin overshirt and short pants she bathed in and shivered as a gust of chilly air penetrated the curtain of budding leaves and crooked branches. Thank A'theosius for a shorter winter than usual and an unusually warm spring. She had been able to shift from midnight basin baths to washing in the pond a good three weeks earlier than usual this spring. Winters were especially unpleasant in the castle, when too many of the inhabitants chose warmth over being able to breathe freely. Lady Charlotte, fortunately, valued Ash's sensitive nose and protected it. She regularly aided the elderly noblewoman in the stillroom, creating all sorts of potions and powders and salves for the benefit of the castle's population. When her duties kept her away from that olfactory refuge, Lady Charlotte supplied her with little spice balls to hang around her neck under her clothes. Still, the air cleared by the spice balls shrank as winter wore on and the gaps between laundry days grew longer. Her extremely sensitive nose and ears were another asset she held in reserve, to earn a place in Dunstan's adventuring party, when the day finally came.

Ash hurried through the garden gate into the castle and waved morning greetings to the dozen or so servants she passed in the halls on her way to the robing room, where the other morning serving boys were changing into their uniforms to serve breakfast. Petroc and Arto were there ahead of her, grumbling about something. The older boy gestured her over.

"Battle stations, Ash. Guess who arrived after sundown?"

She froze, her head filling with a long list of unpleasant distant relatives and government officials and inspectors who took advantage of the hospitality that Lord Digory's family was required to provide, no matter how little respect or affection they had for those unwanted guests. Considering how her day had started, she automatically thought of the worst possible choice.

"Lord Winston?" she whispered.

"Someone should check you for magical potential," Arto said, shaking his head in grudging admiration. Or maybe it was sympathy. "How do you always guess right?"

"Believe me," she said, and stepped up to the peg holding her surcoat and her polished formal shoes hanging by their laces. "I wish I was wrong."

Lord Winston was Lady Charlotte's cousin, twice-removed, with no estate of his own. He and his daughters, Lady Leena and Lady Lathia, traveled endlessly, visiting the estates of a shrinking number of increasingly distant relatives. Tradition and family honor forced those relatives to house his family, provide for their needs, and contribute to the tiny allowance granted him from their mutual ancestor's estate.

A few quick mental calculations startled Ash. Winston and his daughters had arrived an entire month earlier than usual. That meant yet another relative had died and the descendants of that relative considered themselves distant enough from Winston to refuse to host him. That meant Winston would stay several days longer at each of the remaining relatives' homes.

Lady Charlotte would have to die to free Castle Fairhold of the visits, and that was too high a price to pay. She set the standards of the castle's household. Serving in Castle Fairhold was a pleasure and a privilege because of her. She encouraged all servants to learn to read, and supported sensible things like regular bathing and large quantities of vegetables and fruit, instead of diets solely of bread and meat. Some of Lady Charlotte's generation dared to criticize her when they came to visit and saw the "new-fangled innovations" she and her son, Lord Digory, supported. Such mockery always died away when the semi-regular waves of diseases swept through the kingdom of Alfordia. Castle Fairhold always escaped the worst of the ravages and had enough resources and healthy residents to send aid throughout the kingdom.

Sadly, Lord Winston's disdain for Charlotte and Digory's "unhealthy passion for foreign philosophies," as he called them, wasn't strong enough to keep him from visiting every year. Ash wondered how far the alarm had spread throughout the castle, and which servants were already begging Hazel the local hedge witch to make them ill, so they could avoid encountering Winston and Lathia. Ash wished she had stayed longer in the pond and froze herself badly enough to start sneezing and be excused from serving breakfast.

Please, A'theosius, she silently prayed, *it's my birthday in three days. Will I be granted a wish of some kind? Could I use that favor to protect us from trouble while these guests are here?*

The moment she made that wish-prayer, Ash regretted it. She should really save her birthday wishes and whatever favor A'theosius granted orphans for more dire circumstances. Although right now she couldn't think of anything more dire than that vicious twit, Lathia, targeting her again. Hazel and Friar Ipswich and Granny Phlox had all, at one time or another, advised her to store up her blessings against the dreaded, tricky, disaster-poised-over-her-head seventeenth birthday. Two years was not nearly enough time to prepare. Her seventeenth birthday and all the possible terrible fates that could befall her, as an orphan burdened with that inexplicable star, made it imperative that she go adventuring and seeking magic with Dunstan.

Several traveling seers and portent-readers had given her odd looks over the last several years, when she encountered them while running errands or when they visited the castle. Being noticed by people carrying magical gifts was not a comfortable fate. Ash worked to avoid their notice. Even worse than being pinched or flirted with by Lathia was to hear whispered words of warning and omen, or magical, incomprehensible instructions that had to be followed to the letter if she wanted to avoid a dread fate.

That settled it. She needed to find some way to speed up Dunstan gaining permission to set out on his first adventure. Maybe she should spend more time in the castle library researching spells that would be useful.

First, she had to get through the breakfast service.

Ash said a silent prayer as she put on her surcoat, begging A'theosius that she be assigned to serve Lady Leena, the older of the two daughters. She asked for what she wanted instead of expecting servants to know her thoughts, and didn't pinch people under cover of the tablecloth, like Lathia.

Even better, Lady Leena was a maiden warrior in training. Now that was an option Ash hadn't considered. Maybe she could ask Leena for advice on restraining her badly timed blossoming. Maiden warriors couldn't be inconvenienced by jiggling anatomy in battle. Maybe she could ask to join the maiden warriors? She had all those questing skills to offer in service to a patron, and the magical benefits of that dratted star. Whatever it would do for her in the future. It hadn't revealed any magical qualities or benefits yet, other than disturbing her sleep.

Ash scrambled into her surcoat and mentally compared her physique to Lady Leena, on her last visit to Fairhold. Sadly, she didn't have the muscles or bone structure for a maiden warrior. They rode huge battle horses. The swords handed out to maiden warriors seemed to be twice the thickness and weight of the swords given to the soldiers under command of Captain Reginald. How strong did she need to be to merely lift one of those, forget about swinging it in battle?

The painful, inconvenient truth was that she was built more to be an acrobat and thief than a warrior astride a massive battle mount. Drat it, couldn't she find a better fate than to admit she was a maiden and endure lessons in singing and cooking and sewing and tending flowers, and yes, lose her reading privileges in the truly interesting parts of the library?

The depressing start to her day grew worse when the line of servants stepped into the dining room with full platters and pitchers, and Ash got her first glimpse of the people at the table.

Not only had Winston and his daughters arrived late enough in the evening that the serving boys hadn't heard, but Lord Advocate Justiciar Camwell had come to visit Fairhold as well. It couldn't be time for the circuit court to take place again, could it? Was everyone arriving earlier than normal this season? How had he managed to enter without waking the entire castle, demanding a welcome worthy of his status?

Ash wondered if this was A'theosius's answer to her prayer. The justiciar always put the serving boys through a little inquisition at meals to verify for himself that their education was progressing. Or so he claimed. Ash thought he asked the questions about history and laws and literature to show off his own education and not check theirs. Camwell claimed that book-learning and staying informed on events locally and around the kingdom and the world was beneficial to all levels of society. When Ash had graduated to mealtime service duties, she proved herself so agile at answering the justiciar's questions, all the other servants insisted she was permanently assigned to Camwell when he visited, just to give everyone else relief.

On the positive side, facing Camwell would keep her out of Lathia's reach. The odious girl found great amusement in pinching the backsides of every servant who came within her reach. No one dared yelp or flinch or worse, be so startled they dropped something at the worst possible moment. On her last visit, she had taken up the even more odious trick of constantly dropping napkins and utensils, to bring an unlucky servant within her reach. Leena constantly scolded her sister, but their father thought it was cute, and declared that Lathia was showing great favor to the servants when she played with them. He grumbled when Lady Charlotte and Lady Beatrice told Lathia that was not ladylike behavior, and they didn't appreciate the servants getting jumpy when they were serving food. Winston thought that was amusing. And grumbled more when Lady Charlotte and Lord Digory told him it was not. He always had hurt feelings when they insisted that such behavior was cruel to the servants. Winston insisted there was no such thing as being cruel to servants.

Ash caught whispers and heard chair legs scraping on flagstones as she finished her first round of the table with the fruited porridge. She nearly dropped the tray of baked apples when she came around the table and discovered the change in seating. Lathia had moved her chair from the far end of the long table to sit next to Camwell. She fluttered her lashes at Ash as she stepped up to serve her and the Justiciar. Standing this close, Ash had a disquieting view of Lathia's bosom development. Or rather, lack of it. She muffled a chuckle into a snort when she caught a glimpse of what had to be rolls of hosen filling Lathia's bodice. Life was so unfair. Why did the girls who didn't want bosoms get them, and the girls who did want them were forced to employ badly done masquerades?

Nimble fingers pinched her backside. Ash held onto the tray of apples and her voice and retreated. She would have enjoyed seeing the apples soak into Lathia's padding, but then everyone would be deprived of the treat of the leftovers, after the nobles had finished.

Thanks to Lathia, Ash didn't hear clearly when Camwell asked her a question. She stammered, scrambling for an answer, and the portly justiciar was not impressed when she got it right. That wasn't quite fair, because how many others in that hall, including Lord Digory, Lord Dunstan, and Lady Charlotte could have worked those calculations in their heads and come up with the right answer? Without using their fingers or making marks with a charcoal stick on the tablecloth? She was irritated enough she nearly gave in to the urge to anticipate his questions and answer some before he finished saying them. Lady Charlotte wouldn't approve, even if Lord Digory and Lord Dunstan found it amusing. She had been kind enough to take Ash aside, the first time she gave in to her temper and played that trick, and explained to her what kind of trouble she could make for herself by displaying a lack of respect. Even if the person she mocked didn't deserve her respect, his office and rank did demand it from her.

Ash had taken away a lesson from that talk, and her admiration for and loyalty to Lady Charlotte had tripled. She realized that staying invisible whenever possible was the safest path for someone like her, with no family, not even a surname, until she reached her maturity and could make choices for her life. And perhaps not even then, if she wasn't wise and cautious all the preceding years.

Finally, Friar Ipswich pronounced the morning blessing and the family and their guests rose and departed. Ash and Petroc led the race to bring all the leftovers into the kitchen. Thanks to Camwell's presence, which the kitchen staff obviously hadn't been warned about, pickings were lean. Ash split an apple with Wynn and chewed slowly, savoring the spices and juice as they got to work. She headed out into the dining room to clear away the trenchers and pull the cloths off the tables to haul to the laundry.

Cheers rose from the kitchen. She hurtled down the hall back to the kitchen to discover that Myrtle, the headwoman, had flirted outrageously with Seneschal Gilbert to get him to open the larder and dole out a smoked sausage for everyone. Lady Charlotte never served sausages when the justiciar came to visit, after the man had gone into raptures over them. She feared one day, he would demand to add Fern, the woman in charge of the smokehouse, to his staff. Then Fairhold would be deprived of her skills.

Ash licked her fingers clean before hauling the tablecloths and napkins to the laundry. She didn't want to waste a drop of the spiced fat. After dropping her burden in the laundry, her next stop was at Lady Charlotte's study, for the morning list of errands.

A kitten mewed from behind the heavy oak door of the library. Ash stopped short in horror, instantly envisioning the vicious little creature shredding a precious book into bedding and wetting it. Yes, cats were useful in hunting vermin, but as far as Ash was concerned, they should stay in the shadows and middens with the vermin they hunted. She stomped up to the library door to push it open. The sooner she got the nasty little furball out of the library, the better.

"I win!" Lathia leaped from the shadows, arms spread and glee twisting her pudgy, spotty face. Her head hit Ash just under the juncture of her ribs, tearing the yelp of dismay from her lungs.

They went tumbling sideways, knocking over the lectern precariously piled with psalters. Lathia squealed as a rain of dust and ragged bits of papyrus and wooden covers pelted them. One cover splintered and cut her cheek and she wailed. It sounded far worse than the banshee howling that old Pegleg Rufus, the blacksmith, produced when he told ghost tales by the bonfires at solstice and equinox.

Chapter Two

"What did you do that for, you pox of a ninny?" Ash coughed and spat to get the dust out of her mouth.

She scowled at Lathia and crawled out of the girl's reach. Friar Ipswich was going to burst into tears when he saw the destruction of the psalters. Ash might, too. She had hoped to spend a few more hours in the scriptorium, helping to copy the psalters onto new parchment and preserve the old songs. Ipswich had agreed if Ash's handwriting were clear and steady enough, he would arrange for her to learn some basic illumination skills, to decorate the manuscripts. Scribes earned quite good money and were given private quarters.

That possibility had now gone up in dust. With it went another avenue of escape from a life of drudgery and hard labor and the inevitable humiliation of unmasking. Which seemed to draw closer every time Ash checked her body's changes.

"I wanted—all I wanted—I won!" Lathia wailed. "You have to give me a kiss!"

"I'd rather kiss the sow that just farrowed." Ash thought she might just lose that luscious sausage.

"But—but—but—" Lathia rolled onto her back and inhaled deeply enough to make her lacing creak, then let out a shrieking wail that rose a good two octaves. She kicked her feet and slapped her hands on the flagstone floor, raising more dust and further shredding the psalters.

Lord Digory and Lord Winston hurtled through the library doors, knocking each other aside and stumbling over the two girls. Ash rolled out of the way and scrambled to her feet. Lord Winston gasped and waved his hands in dismay and dropped to his fat knees next to his daughter. Lord Digory stuck his forefingers in his ears and carefully picked his way through the carnage of the destroyed psalters to a library chair. He beckoned for Ash, wincing when he had to take a finger out of his ears.

Amazingly, Lord Winston got Lathia to sit up and lower her volume. She clung to him, whimpering and rubbing her wet face and snotty nose against the front of his shirt.

"What happened?" Lord Digory asked, when he could speak without having to shout.

Ash knew better than to tell the entire truth. She had seen Lathia before when the silly girl hatched one of her ridiculous schemes and it failed miserably.

"Sir, I heard a cat and I came in to remove it before it damaged any books." That was the truth, at least. Lady Charlotte had always advised the servant children to tell the truth whenever possible, because they wouldn't have to work so hard to remember what they had said when questioned later. "When I stepped through the door, I collided with Lady Lathia. Perhaps she was trying to find the cat. We fell and knocked the lectern over. Friar Ipswich will be very upset, sir, to see what happened."

"Hmm, yes." Lord Digory studied the debris strewn across the floor in the doorway. "I, however, shall not consider myself deprived of that promised chorale." He winked at Ash.

"Yes, my lord." She fought not to smile. While she admired Friar Ipswich's scholarly ambitions, the entire countryside lived in terror of his singing voice. It had been compared to a drunken pig tumbling inside a giant barrel studded with nails.

"Liar!" Lathia shrieked. "Papa, he dragged me in here! He touched my bosoms. He showed me his manhood!"

Ash nearly choked with the effort not to laugh. Very obviously, Lady Charlotte had never given Lathia the lecture on telling the truth.

"Shameful!" Justiciar Camwell bellowed. The force of his voice made the other library door swing open. He braced his bulk in the doorway. Leena was right behind him, although she had to lean far to the right to see around him. "Such filthy, lewd actions are unworthy of the noble reputation of Castle Fairhold."

"I did no such thing," Ash said.

Lathia insisted, yes, Ash had done those things, and far worse. While her father led her away, she babbled, sometimes incoherently, adding to the lewd and anatomically impossible things Ash had supposedly tried to do to her, all in the space of less than a minute since Lathia attacked.

"My lord, I do swear on my soul, I did no such thing," Ash said, and clasped her hands behind her back to keep from clutching at Lord Digory. From the corner of her eye, she watched Justiciar Camwell. The man had a reputation for reaching down from the high seat when he was presiding in court and taking hard swings at the accused. Some had never faced punishment for their crimes because the blows had knocked their brains loose permanently.

"Oh, I believe you," Leena said. "She's quite unladylike, and quite spoiled. Forgive me, Uncle Digory, but she has done this three times since winter solstice. She attacks the servant boys who don't have the muscle to resist her. The boys run in terror for their lives, and she trips over her own feet trying to chase them and insists they attacked her. Did she claim you showed her your manhood?"

"Yes, mi'lady." Ash felt sick when she wished she could laugh.

Justiciar Camwell looked back and forth between the two of them, his expression somberly thoughtful. She couldn't tell if he believed Leena. She had the awful feeling he was one of those court officials who operated on the belief that nobility were always right, no matter what horrendous, unfair actions they had taken, and servants and peasants were always wrong. Simply because of their lower rank. Lady Charlotte and Lord Digory had both said, multiple times, that such thinking was wrong and damaging to the good of the kingdom. It didn't matter that King Ebrosion himself supported their way of thinking. Too many of the nobility held to the belief that their higher rank meant they were infallible, therefore always right, even when they outright lied.

Ash was relieved to be sent away with a pat on her shoulder by Lord Digory and his promise that he would deal with the matter. That relief died under Justiciar Camwell's glare. Her spirits dropped even further when Lord Digory told her to report to Lady Charlotte. When Ash faced the lady in her study, she trembled with the very real fear of her patroness's disappointment in her. What if the lady she admired greatly believed the lies being told about her?

By the time Ash reached the noblewoman's study, Lady Charlotte had heard of the events in the library and Lathia's claims. Ivy, her ladies maid, passed Ash on the stairs going up to the tower room, rolled her eyes expressively, and gave her a sympathetic pat on her shoulder as she headed down and Ash climbed up. Lady Charlotte had Ash tell her side of the events. Her quiet sympathy had just started to ease Ash's trembling when Lord Winston burst into the room.

"See here, you filthy little drudge," he began, his face quite flushed and sweaty.

"Winston, none of my servants are filthy. We take very good care of them," Charlotte said, stopping him with a gentle gesture of one upraised finger.

"Be that as it may." He wiped his face and took several deep breaths. "The outrage."

"I didn't do anything, mi'lord," Ash insisted when the man paused for another breath. She was amazed he hadn't had a cataleptic fit, racing up the stairs to Lady Charlotte's study as quickly as he had. The study had deliberately been placed in the top room of the north tower to discourage unwanted visitors. "I certainly didn't try to kiss her."

"Why not, may I ask? What's wrong with my daughter that a healthy young man wouldn't want to take advantage of her?"

"Oh, I wouldn't have any idea," Lady Charlotte said. "Perhaps the fact that every male in this castle over the age of ten is terrified of her? She pinches every servant she can reach, both male and female, and if they don't laugh when she thinks they should, she even bites."

Winston gasped, clutching at his heart. He landed so heavily in the chair facing Lady Charlotte, it creaked and wobbled and threatened to break. "I find that impossible to believe."

"Ash, she bit you four years ago, did she not?"

"Yes, mi'lady." At a nod from Lady Charlotte, Ash rolled up her sleeves, to show the scar. Several of Lathia's teeth had torn the flesh. The wound had burned for a day after being inflicted, so that Ash had feared there was venom in the bite.

Lord Dunstan made sure he was there to see and hear it all when Winston repeated the conversation to his daughters. He reported to Ash later that Lathia shrieked insult and defamation and demanded a trial by battle. Leena shut her sister up for nearly twenty minutes, when she informed her that such a trial meant Lathia would have to take up arms against Ash.

"I'm deathly tired to the point of illness, at having to defend you against the justified claims of your victims, little sister," Leena had said, in a tone of voice so calm and bored, Dunstan didn't know whether to laugh or fall asleep, as he later told Ash and several of the serving boys who were his constant companions. "You're fourteen now. Time for you to behave like a lady, think before you act, or pay for your behavior if you can't stop making unjustified claims and demands."

Lathia had wailed so loudly, her voice high and off-key, it made the rare glass goblets in the display niche in the Grand Hall chime and wobble. Then she had fled. She tottered up and down hallways and stairways, bouncing off the walls, until it occurred to her that she had outrun her father. No one else was chasing her, begging her to calm down and promising dire punishment for Ash. She stopped wailing and went to her room and promptly ate herself sick on honeycakes and dried plums.

Ash believed the entire ugly mess would have faded away by the end of the day, simply because as Leena had said, this had happened multiple times before. Lathia and Lord Winston were too proud to pursue a complaint that would embarrass them both yet again. Especially since Lord Digory and Lady Beatrice both declared they wouldn't punish Ash because Lathia's record spoke for itself.

However, Justiciar Camwell chose to get involved. He convened an inquiry, and if justified, to be followed by a trial. Ash considered implementing her most desperate escape option: put on a dress, sneak out of the castle, and stow away in a merchant's wagon that would take her out of Alfordia altogether. She had no hope of a fair trial. Lathia was nobility, no matter how ridiculously and foolishly she had acted, and Ash was a servant with no family and no surname and no claim on anyone with power and influence.

"Never you fear, dear lad," Lady Charlotte said, when Ash reported to her study the next morning to discuss the process of the inquiry.

Ash had spent quite a restless, sleepless night. Mostly because every servant in the castle and three-quarters of the soldiers had come to find her and sit with her for ten or fifteen minutes to speak encouragement and disparage Lathia. How could she sneak out of the castle when nobody would leave her alone to melt into the shadows and vanish?

"Mi'lady, why does he feel an inquiry is necessary? You and Lord Digory believe me, don't you?"

"Oh, absolutely. Camwell is a pompous fool who thinks to make a name for himself by setting new precedents. The king is quite enamored of all sorts of new philosophies coming over the borders. Camwell, as an official of the courts, is required by law to support and teach them. The one that I fear has given impetus to his interference in this matter is the theory that people earn worth and power, rather than being born into it." Lady Charlotte reached out and caught hold of Ash's hand and gently squeezed it. "I quite approve, and high time. Far too many idiots sit in seats of power, using authority they don't know how to handle and making ridiculous decisions, just because they were born in the right bed. While this will very likely turn out well for you, in the decision ..." She sighed and the mischief fled from her face, and she looked her sixty-plus years.

"It won't matter to the fools who depend on bloodlines to justify their positions. When you are exonerated and that vicious little tart proven to be a liar once again, the bullies and power-seekers will assemble to punish you. Quite a few will be lined up to earn her father's approval, in hopes of marrying her and inheriting the family titles. What use are titles without land, I ask you? At last count, nearly two hundred people would have to die before Winston has a chance to hold land once again. Yet too many fools think inherited titles are more valuable than property. I can't imagine why. The king hands out a dozen new titles every year, with no land to provide income to support the newly made noble. Ridiculous. And yet that vicious Lathia will have a dozen suitors, willing to risk their sanity for the chance to have 'Lord' in front of their names."

She sniffed. "What is the world coming to?" Then she looked at Ash, who stood quietly in front of the table piled high with books and papers, and she sighed. "I'm sorry, my dear lad. I shouldn't be meandering in my thoughts when we need to put together your defense for this ridiculous inquiry."

"I don't suppose I could ask Lady Leena to be my champion?" Ash said.

"Oh, now there's an idea." She patted her shoulder. "Wouldn't that be beyond their scheming minds? Leena is quite annoyed with her sister. She'd do it, in a heartbeat. Hmm, maybe we should disguise you as a girl, on top of it?"

Ash stumbled backward, feeling as if she had been clubbed between the eyes. Hadn't she been a regular idiot, panicking and silently shrieking against the cruelty of her situation?

"Lad? Are you ill?" Lady Charlotte beckoned Ash closer. She felt her forehead, then the pulse points at the base of her jaw. "You are quite pale, and trembling. That is an idea, too. You could faint and perhaps we could fake your death. Sneak you out of the castle .... No, Camwell would demand your body be examined. For all his clinging to all sorts of backward practices and unjust beliefs, he wants to be considered a man of science. Whatever that is. I just know it is highly inconvenient, and involves taking things apart."

"Science is a new philosophy that denies magic. Scientists believe everything can be explained by physical reactions and interactions and events, if enough investigation is done," Ash explained.

"Idiocy! What is the world without magic?" The elderly lady shook her head. "I have a good mind to ask Hazel to set some sort of pox on him, just to teach him a lesson. No, Camwell considers himself a man of science, and that means all sorts of newfangled, messy foolishness, instead of using dignified magic to find the answers. Things like autopsies. Ah, I can see from your white face you know what that means."

The thought of someone examining her body, whether dead or merely faking death, crystalized a thought that had been swirling through Ash's mind for several minutes now.

"Mi'lady, I must ask your forgiveness." Ash tugged on the top buttons of her jacket.

"What are you doing?" Lady Charlotte blinked.

"I have deceived you for years now. Ever since I came into service at Fairhold."

"Lad, that isn't the way to prove your innocence."

She sat back in her deep chair, holding up one hand as a shield between her and Ash, who had dropped her jacket. She yanked hard on the simple pin holding the neck of her shirt closed. Two seconds, and she had her shirt open enough to expose her chest to her navel.

"We'll think of—" Lady Charlotte stopped short, and for several seconds didn't move, didn't blink, didn't breathe.

Then a delighted smile crept across her wrinkled face, widening far enough to reveal most of her unusually white, strong teeth. She tipped her head back and let out low, rippling laughter that shook her whole body for several moments. Her face was flushed as she struggled to catch her breath, to shout for Lady Leena to join them.

The maiden warrior must have been waiting only a few steps down the stairs of the tower room, because she dashed through the curtained doorway before any servant could respond. She frowned at the sight of Ash standing there, holding her shirt open in front of Lady Charlotte. Then she laughed, before the girl could turn around, presenting her bare chest and the proof of her body's betrayal.

"Why didn't I think of that?" Leena dropped into a chair facing Lady Charlotte. "Rather ironic, I was trying to consider how to take you aside and offer advice on hiding ..." She gestured at Ash's chest.

"You knew?" Ash pulled her shirt closed. She stared at Leena as she went to one knee and reached blindly for the pin that had fallen to the floor.

"We spend quite a lot of time learning how to disguise ourselves as boys and young men, when we go about the king's business in parts of the kingdom where they're rather dogmatic against sensible things, like letting women wear trousers and use swords and read." Leena shrugged, then she thumped her chest with her fist and extended her arm in a warrior's salute. "I was worried for you when ..." Again, she gestured at Ash's now covered, budding bosoms.

Ash still hadn't found the pin. She gave up trying, and tugged the shirt closed as best she could, leaving a long, narrow strip of exposed flesh. The touch of air against her bare flesh woke that particularly itchy spot between the buds, a silvery patch as large as her thumb, that she refused to look at too closely. She feared it was taking on the shape of a star.

"You could have done me the courtesy of warning me," Lady Charlotte murmured. Her eyes twinkled and her mouth pursed as she fought a grin. "Oh, my dear Ash ... you prove your cleverness once again. And make me more determined than ever to keep you with me."

"This should shred Lathia's idiotic story quite beautifully. She'll have another temper tantrum and claim it's a lie and we're all being cruel to her. The justiciar is just the thick-headed sort of idiot to side with her, and we certainly can't have Ash open her shirt in front of him. He'd have her horsewhipped and put in the pillory for public vulgarity."

"You're right. We need to think of the best way to present this proof," Charlotte said. "Camwell is a moron and your father doubly so, but it won't do us any good to humiliate them as they so richly deserve."

"What are our chances of sending Lathia into a cataleptic fit, if we hit her with this in just the right way? Then we can slap an enlightenment spell on her, or make her sleep until she gains some courtesy and common sense." Leena frowned and leaned in closer. "Is that a star glowing right there?" She pointed at the increasingly itchy spot between Ash's buds.

"Yes. I'm in dread of finding out what that means." Ash considered, for half a second, confessing about the glowing star on her buttocks. No, there were too many complications in her life right now as it was. Better to clear herself of the seduction and assault and insult charges, then move on from there.

"Well, you need to consult some higher-level magic specialists than we have available, that's a given," Lady Charlotte said. "I dare say you have some magical destiny lying ahead of you." She shrugged. "Well, what do you expect? Clever child, surviving on your own with no family or surname, and carrying off that deception and disguise very well the entire time you've been here. You must tell us how you did it."

"Yes, you must." Leena gestured at the bench Ash had yet to use. "I wish I could have done that. I would have run away to join a questing company the first chance I got, if I could have convinced people I was Father's son and heir. Girls have too many restrictions. What's wrong?" She reached out to grip Ash's arm.

"Lord Dunstan. I wanted to go on his quest next year. He won't let me come if he knows I'm a girl!" Ash burst into tears for the first time that she could remember. Tears were, after all, such a girlish thing.

"I'm sorry, my dear, but I fear your questing activities will be curtailed for the foreseeable future." Lady Charlotte made a sympathetic murmur and drew Ash into her arms. That dried her tears immediately, in utter shock. Ash knew she should pull back, but it was so utterly nice to be held, to have her back patted, and to know that the lady she nigh on worshipped liked her and wanted to help her. She stayed there and enjoyed the comfort, because she knew it wouldn't last.

Chapter Three

Two hours later, Justiciar Camwell glowered at Ash, who stood in front of him on his left hand. The first session of the inquiry had been convened in the chapel, where Friar Ipswich had been busy setting up wards to prevent any magic being used either for against the two parties in the proceedings. When Ash stepped over the threshold, she felt a brief sting, as if a spark had landed on each star embedded in her buttocks and breastbone. Should she be worried or hopeful, at this sign of magic of some sort residing in her? Would that work against her?

Did the justiciar glower at her because he sensed the magic, and suspected her of trying to cheat? Before she finished that thought, Camwell turned to glower at Lathia, who stood on his right in front of him. From the corner of her eye, Ash saw the younger girl offer the justiciar a sweet smile. His glower rippled slightly, hinting at nausea. Ash started to smile, but he turned his head to her again, and his glower returned to full strength. She stood as still as she could and tried not to tremble.

"I find this entire situation highly disturbing," he began, addressing the witnesses still entering the chapel, then focused on Ash as he finished the statement. "First, that so many of your fellow servants wished to avoid testifying at all in this matter."

Lathia snickered. He turned to face her so swiftly, droplets of sweat flew off his hair, hitting her face with tiny pinging sounds.

"I found it necessary to put them under a truthfulness compulsion," he partially hissed. "And what did I discover? You paid some of them to lie and say that this boy," he flicked his fingers at Ash, "had pressed his attentions on you multiple times in the past. The others, you threatened into silence, if they refused to lie for you." He snorted. "I find it only slightly humorous that when you offered your questionable favors to them, your words were received as threats. The young men in question were terrified, and some were nauseated."

"That's a lie!" Lathia shrieked. "They insisted that I had to pay them, or they would lie to defend Ash!"

"Shall I put you under a truthfulness compulsion? It's quite painful for those who resist it. Or those who are unable to speak the truth in the ordinary course of the day."

"Sir, that is an insult to my household," Winston brayed, rising to his feet at the right side of the room.

Lord Digory caught him by his shoulder and pulled him back down onto the bench beside him. Whatever he muttered to his cousin caused the other man to turn bright red, then go very pale, and shudder. His gaze fastened, wide-eyed with horror, on Ash.

"I don't know why you're making me stand up here like I'm on trial," Lathia mumbled through a full-lipped pout. "I'm the one who was hurt."

"As a matter of testimony, the healer says that the boy Ash has bruises and you have none, meaning you landed on him." Justiciar Camwell sniffed when he said 'boy' and 'him.'

Ash wished she could find this amusing. Lathia's shriek of fury would be deafening when the truth was revealed and her extensive lies were slapped hard across her face.

"The healer is a liar!"

"Scribe, make this note," Camwell said, turning to Malchus, who sat at a small table placed at right angles to the long table where the justiciar sat. "Quote me directly: the silly flitterhead is unable to speak the truth. Or act with proper decorum," he added, ending on a loud sigh.

"Father, did you hear what he called me?"

"Lathia ..." Winston closed his eyes and thudded his head once against the wall behind him. "Shut up."

"But Father—"

"Now!"

She yipped, flushed bright red, and started to open her mouth, but Camwell's glower darkened. She paled, nodded and hunched her shoulders.

"He should have said that years ago," Leena whispered to Lady Charlotte. Chuckles and whispered comments rippled through that side of the room.

Leena, Lady Charlotte, most of the kitchen staff, Friar Ipswich, Pegleg Rufus, Petroc and nearly half the servant boys had crammed onto the benches or stood against the wall or sat on the floor on the right side of the room, indicating their support for Ash. She would have felt quite flattered, if she didn't have awful visions of their reactions when the truth finally came out.

"Quiet!" Camwell roared, twice as loud as Winston, with enough force to bring down quite a few curdles of dust from the ceiling beams and decorative tapestries.

Ash wondered if she would be employed with the other, smaller members of the servants to climb up there and do the long-delayed cleaning. Or maybe forced to do it alone?

"As I was saying," he said, after a few loud huffs to catch his breath. "I find it highly disturbing, and rather strongly indicative of just who is the victim and who the attacker in this ugly little scenario, when I tally up who was bribed and who was threatened to lie. Who wanted to tell the truth despite the bribes and threats. Who accepted the bribes and who didn't need the threats. You have a number of folk who are jealous of your skills, boy," he added, glancing at Ash. He flinched away, as if looking at her hurt his eyes.

"Be that as it may, the testimony, both false and true by its very silence, cannot compare to the massive deception that has been carried off lo these many years by ..." He fluttered his fingers at Ash. "What is your true name?"

"True name?" Lathia squeaked.

"Ashlyn, Lord Justiciar." Ash fought not to look at Lathia. "Just Ashlyn."

"What kind of a name is—"

Camwell pointed one pudgy finger at Lathia and a single spark of dark green magic rolled along the edge of his broken, dirty fingernail. She squeaked into silence.

"And how long have you carried off this deceptive masquerade?"

"Sir, if you mean pretending to be a boy so I could read the truly interesting books in the library and get to wear trousers and ..." Ash shrugged. "For as long as I can remember."

"Your lady says you are quite intelligent." Camwell nodded to Lady Charlotte. "Just how far back can you remember?"

"Sir ... I remember being caught up in a net with other children when that enormous wave wiped out all the towns between Tippessee and the shore. We were all muddy and cold and the people taking care of us put us all in trousers and long shirts. I found out then boys had much warmer clothes, so I decided to keep the boy clothes. It just made sense."

From the corner of her eye, she saw Lathia's mouth drop open, and a little thread of drool slip from one corner.

"It just made sense. How old were you when you decided what made sense and what didn't? The flood that made Tippessee a coastal town was nearly twelve years ago this fall. You don't look much older than that."

"Granny Phlox, whom I assigned to tend the children," Lady Charlotte said, "estimated she was perhaps two or three at the time."

"I find it hard to believe a child of three years can remember much of anything," he muttered. "Just how did you come all this way to Fairhold?" He turned back to facing Ash. His frown seemed to soften a little. She wasn't sure if that was a good sign or bad. "That is a three-day journey by horse."

"You can lay the blame at my door," a new voice said from the doorway. It was raspy, like a bundle of hazel switches rubbing together.

Ash turned, shivering a little, to see Hazel standing on the threshold, holding her moss-colored shawl tight around her. Her face was quiet and pale, her eyes large and dark and unreadable in the shadows. And her hair stood out in all directions like a hedge hid inside it. Ash sometimes wondered if that was where hedge witches got their names.

She nodded salute to Lord Digory and Lady Beatrice, and her gaze slid over Winston as if he weren't there. Her gaze swept the room and she curtsied when she made eye contact with Lady Charlotte.

"And who might you be?" Camwell said.

"This is Hazel, our local hedge witch," Lady Charlotte said. "She saw the wave coming a full week before it hit the coast and swept all those villages to Tippessee. My son can testify that we both sent warnings to the king and to the Collegium of Enchanters. On Hazel's urging, I went to Tippessee to look for the newly made orphans she also saw in her vision."

"It's a pity you didn't see the deception this one played on all of you," Camwell said, flicking his fingers in Ash's direction.

"Who says I didn't?" Hazel grinned brightly and stepped over the threshold, setting off a shower of sparks as the wards reacted to the magic in her blood.

Camwell blanched for a moment, others gasped. Lady Charlotte and Lady Beatrice exchanged demure smiles. Wynn hurried to get up and offer Hazel the edge of the bench he had been perched on. She winked at him, making his face flush bright red.

"Was anyone else party to this? Shocking. I find it highly shocking that any servants in this upstanding household would scheme against their lord and lady."

"No one else that I'm aware of knew that Ash was a girl," Hazel said.

"You didn't employ any magic to blind eyes to what they should have seen, did you?"

"Me, sir? My magic isn't that strong, to maintain a disguise or illusion spell, day in and day out. That would be exhausting and wouldn't leave me any magic to perform my duties that I owe to my lord and lady." She nodded to Lady Charlotte, then to Lord Digory and Lady Beatrice on the other side of the room.

"Hmm, at least some people know what is right and proper," Camwell muttered. He looked down at the papers spread across the table in front of them, shuffled several, and made noises like he was talking to himself. None of the words made sense to Ash. Then he raised his head and looked at her again. "So very sad," he said, his voice softening to a pensive rumble. "Either you are a skilled liar and cheat, or the inhabitants of Castle Fairhold are utter nincompoops and utterly oblivious. Which is it?"

"Sir?" Ash blurted.

Lathia snickered. Camwell's head snapped around again and he skewered her with a glare that came close to setting her on fire. Ash felt the heat of it.

"Sir, I am small and thin and plain, so it was easy to carry off the deception. And my outdoor chores made me rather dirty all the time. I think that makes it easy to convince people that I was just what they had been told I was. A boy."

"Indeed? So you don't consider yourself a liar and cheat and fraud?"

Ash trembled. It took all her willpower not to turn pleading looks to Lady Charlotte and Lady Leena. They had told her to keep her gaze fastened on Camwell throughout the inquiry. She had to impress on him that she wasn't going to burst into tears or faint or display other signs of mental or emotional weakness.

She wanted to crawl between the cracks in the stone pavement and vanish.

Lathia snickered.

"Both of these *maidens*," Camwell paused to emphasize the word, "are at fault here. No one is innocent. This creates an interesting situation, ripe for experimentation and a lesson to be learned for both sides. Yes, lessons must be taught. I decree a trial period, a quest. Success or failure will determine which one is the victim and which one is merely a selfish little snot that lies as naturally as breathing." He focused his gaze and the force of his voice on Lathia as he spoke.

"What sort of quest?" Lord Digory asked.

"Hmm, that requires some thinking, and some preparation." He sat back in his chair, making it creak and groan in protest, and crossed his arms. "We will return here in two days. That will be sufficient time to come up with the trial and the means and the method."

~~~~~

Leena escorted Ash out of the castle. Lady Charlotte asked her to do it to protect her from Winston's few manservants who were loyal enough to try to harm her. Ash glimpsed one of them and wondered if the wrinkly, sour-faced man had some kind of magic that he would try to use against her. She couldn't imagine any other way he could best her.

"Hmm, they're all like that," Leena said, when she caught Ash watching the man as they crossed the main courtyard of the castle. "Only the desperate are willing to put up with the pitiful wages my father offers, and they're the only ones Lathia doesn't terrify."

Ash didn't feel any tingling or stinging in her two stars, but she suspected using her two birthmarks to detect the presence of magic might be a dangerous kind of mistake. When she asked if the manservants had any magic, Leena laughed under her breath.

"If they ever had any, they foreswore it or stifled it, working for my father. He's the sort who won't allow anyone around him to be more
~~~~~

powerful. People say my mother's family has magic in their blood, but what fledgling magic she had faded away after she married him." She didn't continue until they had crossed the dancing meadow that lay between the castle's outer walls and the first of the pastures for horses and cattle. "My patron fears that the leach potion still exists, and my father or perhaps his father obtained a large supply of it, and they erased what magic my mother had, and I might have had."

"Leach potion, mi'lady?" Ash asked. She looked up at Leena and caught her breath at the brief expression of hurt and anger that touched her face, gone as quickly as it appeared.

"A tonic originally created, they say, to ease the suffering of those awakening to their inborn magic but having a hard time of it." She rested a hand on Ash's shoulder, guiding her to walk a little faster as they cut a corner across the horse meadow and came to the low, raw stone wall separating it from the cow pasture. "Magic doesn't always arise easily for those chosen to bear the weight. Sometimes the power hurts. Sometimes it steals the mind. Sometimes it crushes the body with a heavy burden that the bearer never recovers from. Why do you think seers are usually blind? Why do you think so many healers are twisted and broken in some way? The magic needs a power source, and when the channels for power to feed that magic are blocked or are thin and twisted, the magic draws its strength from the flesh of the possessor, who is then possessed. The master becomes the servant." She inhaled slowly, deeply, with thin lines forming around her eyes and mouth, just for a moment. "Watch your feet."

Ash flushed and caught herself before she tripped over a stone partially hidden in the tall grass. She had been so fascinated by the subtle play of emotions on Leena's face, she had ignored the land around them. A snort escaped her when she saw the brown deposits dotting the field. This was not a good place to be distracted. Best to watch where she put her feet for the time being.

"The leach potion wasn't a tonic after all?" she asked, after they had walked for several minutes and were nearly to the other side of the cow pasture. "Tonic implies something good for you."

"Exactly. The leach potion wasn't called the leach potion until the demand for it spread beyond the kingdom where it originated, and a small battle erupted, to force the alchemist who created it to share the recipe, so others could make it in their countries. Several wizards joined forces and took apart the falsely labeled tonic to discern the ingredients and process. That was when they realized it had been designed to kill magic before it could finish blooming into life, not help ease the process."

"You think your father made your mother drink it?" Ash asked, her voice dropping nearly to a whisper.

"Oh, he wouldn't have been that open. He put it in her food for maybe years. Killing her magic weakened her body and mind." Leena's mouth twisted, as if she fought not to say something. They climbed over the stone wall of the cow pasture, and ahead of them was the thatched cottage where Ash had lived when she first came to Castle Fairhold. "Just see the difference between Lathia and me, from prolonged dosing with the foul stuff. Mother's family couldn't do anything to help her, by the time they realized something was wrong, but they were able to do something for me. My patron had me cleansed, and I wear several defensive charms. Every once in a while, my father tries to slip some potion into my food, but he's essentially given up on me as a lost cause. He couldn't interfere when mother's relatives helped me petition to join the warrior maidens, and he's such a hide-bound fool, he thinks he can't marry me off to better his fortunes. Everything rests on Lathia now, which is why he'll do everything dirty and dishonorable anyone could imagine, to punish you and exonerate her."

"He wouldn't try to destroy my magic, would he?"

"If he finds out you have any. I'd suggest pretending to be far less than you are, until this whole ridiculous inquiry is over."

"Could you take me as your servant? Take me to the warrior maidens?" Ash sighed and spread her arms. "I'm not exactly built to be a warrior, but ... isn't there something I could do to be useful?"

"I will confer with Aunt Charlotte. Right now, Granny Phlox wants to see you. She might have some words of wisdom to help you through this. And it's only common sense to get you away from the castle, from the curious and those who are angry you fooled them so easily."

Leena squeezed Ash's shoulder, then gave her a gentle shove forward. She stumbled a few steps and looked back once. The older girl nodded to her and stepped back, clearly not going the rest of the way with her. This reluctance to return to the only childhood home she remembered was ridiculous, Ash knew, but she couldn't help it. Her legs wobbled for a few steps before she silently scolded herself to stop being a ninny. Granny Phlox was stern, but she was never cruel, and more than once she had turned into a whirling fury to defend the children given into her charge. If they were her pups, then she was a she-wolf, unhindered by her blindness.

Ash took several deep breaths and focused on the muffled thud of her heart in her ears as she approached the door of the cottage. She wished now she had come back more often to visit Granny Phlox, especially after nearly all the boys who had been brought here with her had gone away, either adopted or apprenticed. Three boys who had been infants when Lady Charlotte brought them here still lived in the cottage and spent their days tending the cows and chickens and pigs in the nearby fields and byres. That was no excuse for neglecting the old woman who was the only mother she could remember.

"Is this judgment?" Ash whispered, pausing in raising her hand to knock. She grinned, knowing how Granny Phlox would react if she posed that question to her. Granny had a wry, commonsense view of A'theosius and what the creator expected of people. She shook her head and thumped three times on the frame of the door.

Silence.

Ash held her breath. Granny should have called out. Had she grown deaf since the last visit? Or was she ill?

The latch rattled. The door slid open. Lantern light spilled out, over the shoulder of Hazel.

"Ashlyn. Good." She chuckled when Ash gaped at her. "Did you think you could keep your secret from me?"

"My name—" Ash shook her head. She was going to say her name wasn't Ashlyn, but a sensation like a warm breeze swirled around her, and she heard echoes of a woman calling to her, laughing, calling her Ashlyn. Tears warmed and blurred her eyes at the sudden certainty she heard her mother's voice. "I haven't used my name for … years."

"Yes, well, change is being forced upon us." Hazel stepped back, pulling the door wide open. "We don't have as much time as I would like. You are blessed with powerful friends. Whether they are powerful enough … well, only A'theosius knows."

"Is that my pup?" Granny Phlox's creaky voice emerged from the shadows, twined with a warm chuckle that always hinted she was ready for mischief, and could outdo her twelve charges in any sort of trouble they might try to make.

Ash stepped inside and inhaled deeply, testing the air, using the scents of the long main room of the cottage to tell her if anything had changed, for good or ill. For a few steps, nothing smelled familiar. Had she been gone that long? Then she wondered if the change was in her. Hadn't Lady Charlotte said something just this last winter, how prolonged exposure to anything dulled the senses, and only the new or changed gained any real notice? Inhaling slowly, she continued forward, to the corner where Granny Phlox had always perched with her knitting or mending or her seemingly never-ending task of mixing dried herbs into dose-sized bundles for seasoning and healing.

Chapter Four

Now she caught the aroma of tangy and bitter and pungent, swirled throughout with the unmistakable pong of boys who feared the touch of water unless they could swim in it. Ash blinked away a sudden burning in her eyes. Tears, not discomfort. What was wrong with her that she had this ridiculous tendency for weeping? If this was another change accompanying the blossoming of her bosoms, she needed to find a charm to stop it before any more damage was done. Was there such magic?

"So, you've come running back to Granny. Are you seeking answers, or just a hiding hole?" the old woman murmured, reaching out a skeletal hand.

She took hold of Ash's hand across the table before the girl could look around for one of the stools tucked under the table. One of her fondest memories was of long talks with Granny, helping her with her never-ending work, perched on a stool, learning to do her work by feel and smell, because the room was always in shadows. The old woman held on until Ash sat down, then patted her hand and reached into a basket to resume her task.

"I don't know," Ash said after thinking for several moments.

"Wise answer." Hazel caught a stool with the side of her foot and shoved it out where Ash could find it, then tugged another out for herself.

"Give them time," Granny said, her words punctuated by the crackle of a dried seed pod opening. "The question is if we have much time at all."

"I felt the wards snapping into place around the chapel from outside the castle," Hazel said. "That much magic at work … I'm worried."

"Why?" Ash wriggled once, remembering the feeling like a spark on her two stars. "Do I have magic?"

"Of course you do." Granny cackled softly.

"And that's the problem," Hazel added. "I've always disliked Camwell. Working to impress the powerful people and indebt everyone he can to himself. Flaunting what power he does have. Acting as if he is everyone's friend, and when he takes something by his authority it's actually a gift given of their own free will. I've lived in terror for all you children, from the moment he was assigned to this side of the kingdom."

"Why terror?" Granny said, before Ash could frame the question. "You survived the flood. Why did you survive, and your parents didn't? There's magic destiny of one kind or another wrapped around each of you twelve, and far too many wrong-minded folk running around, using magic they don't understand, awakening magic before its proper time, causing ripples in the stream of magic underneath the land ... attracting the wrong kind of attention."

"It's exhausting keeping my eye on all twelve of you, but the farther apart you all are from each other, the safer you are. Less chance for magic to build up to the point of making noise. Like the noise from those warding spells." Hazel gripped Ash's wrist. "Did you feel or hear anything, when you stepped into the chapel?"

Ash nodded.

"Loud, or soft? A bird's chirp is easily hidden among all the other notes of magic, but a loud clanging bell ... that's hard to disguise or mistake for something else."

"No sound. A stinging, just for a moment." Reluctantly, Ash touched the spot on her breastbone. She certainly wasn't going to gesture at her buttocks. What if Hazel wanted to see the stars? Bad enough she had opened her shirt for Lady Charlotte, to prove she was a girl.

"All right. All right. That's good for you. For all of us." Hazel jolted up from the stool and paced down the length of the room. "No sounds, that means your magic is still sleeping." She reached the end of the room and turned around, pivoting on one heel, and came back toward them. "I should have come up with an excuse to get you out of the castle. The warning signs were all there. But I didn't foresee the attack. I should have. Sleeping magic attracts trouble, to force it awake. But it's too soon."

"Could someone be manipulating events?" Granny continued placidly working on opening the seed pods, dropping the dried contents into one basket, the empty pods into another, her hands and voice steady. Calming.

"What am I?" Ash clamped her mouth shut to keep from spilling the flood of questions she felt burning on her tongue. Was she a lost princess, perhaps? The stolen child of some centuries-old prophecy? Did the flood take place to kill her and prevent some prophecy of doom? Was she the child of a powerful enchanter, maybe an entire family of powerful enchanters, taken from her family to steal her magical heritage?

A snort escaped her and her face warmed as she wrapped reins tightly around her imagination. She was very glad she had held back from speaking. What ridiculous speculations.

"There's no knowing, pup," Granny said. "And that's the problem. Hazel can't tell, and she's been studying you and the other pups since you came to live here. All that hazy potential is dangerous. It means you're open to being snagged and forced onto a path, your magic stolen or warped into something evil, instead of the great good and wonder A'theosius intended when you were conceived. What we understand of magic led us to believe that because of how you were gathered in one lump after the flood, you need to be together to fulfill that potential and destiny. We hoped that separating you, once you were old enough for the magic to awaken, you'd be safe."

"The problem is that the justiciar is asking his questions and stirring up memories better left sleeping. He now knows you came from Tippessee. He could be asking questions about all the boys, not just you," Hazel said. "The more questions he asks, the more people remember and start talking, and the greater the chances that someone who's been hunting all of you for the last twelve years follows that trail of talk right back here." She plunked down on the stool, letting out an exhausted sigh. "This is beyond my strength and the limits of my sight."

For several long moments, the only movement and sound came from Granny's fingers smoothly, patiently working the seed pods and separating useful from waste.

"Could we just ... run away?" Ash asked.

"Running will tell everyone you've got something to hide," Hazel said. "Something to fear. If anyone comes looking, asking questions, you're more likely to be dismissed if you sit still and act like you've nothing to fear." She snorted. "The time for running away and creating false assumptions was this morning, before breakfast. Too late now."

A rapping on the door startled Ash and Hazel. Granny didn't flinch in her steady movements. The door creaked open and Leena peered in.

"The hue and cry is starting. Father is accusing you of running away. And stealing all the castle's silver." She held out her hand, beckoning. "I'm sorry, but we'd better go back before they decide to clap you in chains or decide that you've just confessed."

"There's far too much I still need to tell you," Hazel muttered, as Ash got up. "Later. I need to work on dampening whatever magic the justiciar tries to use on you, so it doesn't set off any alarms and draw the wrong kind of attention." She patted Ash's shoulder as the girl stepped around the table to hug Granny Phlox.

"I'm sorry," Ash said. "I should have come to visit more often."

"Never you worry, my dear." Granny smiled, her blind gaze aimed over Ash's right shoulder. "Just you remember what I taught you. Wash regularly, say your prayers, and keep your eyes open. You'll do just fine."

"May A'theosius make it so," Hazel murmured, as Ash hurried to the door.

Dunstan met them halfway back to the castle and led them around several outbuildings, through gaps in two walls and four hedges, so they came in through the back way and up an outside stairway hidden in a tangle of old ivy and grape vines. No one saw them coming in, and Ash thought that was a rather dangerous tactic. Wouldn't that give more weight to Winston's accusation that she was trying to run away and avoid her just punishment?

She knew the hidden pathway they followed. She and Dunstan and several older boys had found it and built up portions of it to be easier and swifter to follow, and harder to detect. They ended up in the tower one floor down from Lady Charlotte's study. In moments, Dunstan saluted them and hurried down the stairs, while Leena and Ash went up. Ash never got a chance to ask why he hid her from the searchers. Lady Charlotte put her to work copying the pages of the psalters that had been salvaged. Leena took refuge behind a screen painted with a pastoral scene seconds before Gilbert the seneschal came huffing and puffing and sweating through the door.

"My lady, I'm sorry to report—" He stopped short. Or rather, his feet stopped short and the rest of his tall, gawky body tried to keep moving forward. His eyes bulged as they focused on Ash. "Excuse me, my lady … but has the boy been here the whole time?"

"What whole time is that?" Lady Charlotte nodded to Ash. "Very good. Your handwriting is fine enough to make me fear Malchus will demand you be assigned to help him from now on."

"Never mind, my lady." Gilbert wiped his sweaty face and nodded to them both. A lopsided, weary smile brightened his face as he turned and left.

Leena waited until the slapping sounds of his big feet on the stone steps faded to nothing, then she chuckled and came out from hiding. "The king's advisors could learn something from you, Aunt Charlotte. You didn't speak a word of falsehood, but by now Gilbert is insisting Ash has been up here working with you the entire time."

"Thank you, mi'lady." Ash raised her hand just in time to keep from depositing a large blotch of ink, thanks to the trembling she couldn't calm.

"Hmm, yes, but how long will such tricks work before we're caught? We need to spend extra time in prayer until this whole ridiculous inquiry has ended. I truly hope Winston is so offended that he vows never to grace us with his presence ever again." Lady Charlotte's tone hinted at boredom, not irritation or concern. One corner of her mouth twitched up before she bowed her head over her own copying work.

~~~~~

That night, Ash was barred from the long room where the younger servants slept. Justiciar Camwell, no doubt urged by Winston, had decreed that to avoid further accusations of flight, she should sleep with a guard nearby. Since Lord Digory refused to put her in one of the dungeon cells, a storage room by the castle kitchens was emptied for her. Winston sulked but agreed, because the door had a lock. The guard who led Ash there winked at her and neglected to turn the key.
~~~~~

The room had no window to climb out, and she would have to go past the kitchens and two hallways where guards walked the night watches, before she could reach a door or window out of the castle. Ash told herself to be grateful. The room smelled pleasantly of spices and beeswax and vinegar that had been stored there and spilled on the flagstones of the floor over the years. Myrtle left three honeycakes under her pillow, despite loud grumbles over having to empty out the room.

The next day, Ash was excused from serving breakfast, and worked in the kitchens until Lady Charlotte was ready to begin her day's work. She worked in the tower room until long past the dinner hour, when Captain Reginald himself came to escort her to her lonely room. He said nothing to her, but his hand resting on her shoulder was gentle.

Ash reflected that while she found great encouragement from this proof that many of Castle Fairhold's inhabitants were her friends, that encouragement wasn't great enough. Her fate still rested entirely in Justiciar Camwell's hands. From all the remarks others had made, his sense of justice was strongly tainted by his personal inclinations.

~~~~~

Early in the morning on the second day, Ash walked into the chapel by herself. Lady Charlotte, Lord Digory, Lady Beatrice and Lord Dunstan waited in the back of the room. Winston and his daughters hadn't entered. Ash let herself hope, just for a moment, that the family had fled the castle during the night, to avoid the humiliation of whatever quest Justiciar Camwell would inflict on Lathia.

Camwell hadn't arrived either. What were her chances he had decided this was no longer entertaining, and had left as well?

As instructed, she said nothing. She bowed to her lord and ladies and the heir and went to kneel on the right-hand bench facing the long table. No one else was allowed in the room. She knew where all the spyholes were, and imagined she heard whispering and shuffling among the servants crowded together in the narrow passageways through the stone walls. Ash had thought long on what the justiciar had said about the people who wanted to testify against her as well as for her. She had never really thought anyone would resent her book-learning or other skills. She had always tried to offer her abilities to help others, simply because common sense, impressed on her by Granny Phlox and Lady Charlotte, said to make friends and not enemies. What good did it do anyone to refuse to help when she was able?

The door creaked open. By the heavy footsteps, the dragging of heavy cloth on the flagstones, she knew Justiciar Camwell had entered. Did she dare hope Lathia would be in trouble for not arriving on the hour as instructed?

"Well, that is telling," Camwell huffed as he paused between the two
~~~~~

benches and looked at the empty one, then at Ash. "Are you ready to hear your tasks ... what do you prefer to be called?"

"Ash, sir. It's what I know."

"No, I meant, are you a maiden or a lad?"

"Sir? I'm clearly a maiden. I'm starting to ..." Ash shrugged. "I've already been trying to figure out how to either hide it or ... I'm sorry, sir, but could I think about this once I know what the task is?"

"Well, at least you do have some common sense. I expect you to do quite well."

"In what task, exactly?" Lady Charlotte rose and crossed to the bench and put her hand on Ash's shoulder. "You said a quest?"

"Indeed." Camwell turned with a furl of his robes and strode to the judgment table. He sat down and held out his right hand, which clutched a small drawstring bag of moon-blue cloth netted with silver threads.

A chill wrapped around Ash's throat and crawled up her scalp. Her two stars warmed. No stinging this time. Could she interpret that as a good sign? A promise, rather than a warning? She inhaled and blinked in surprise at a flicker of silvery-blue light across the cloth.

"Ah, interesting," Camwell said. "You feel the presence of magic, do you? And how long have you hidden that interesting gift?"

"Sir? This is the first time this has ever happened," Ash said after a moment of thought. "Other than feeling ... something from the wards." She wasn't going to admit where in her anatomy she had felt the stinging. After all, she had no idea how prudish Camwell might be, if he would be offended hearing her say *bosoms* or *buttocks*. Better to be even more prudish herself.

"We don't expose the younger servants to use of magic, or defensive restraints," Lady Charlotte added, nodding at the bag. "Not until they've gone through the first examinations, to determine if they have any special skills or potential. Friar Ipswich tests the older children with the three-part cords at solstice. We go from there."

"Indeed." Camwell's eyes narrowed as his gaze flicked back and forth between Lady Charlotte and Ash, several times. "I applaud your care for the commoners under your care, Lady and Lord. Now, let us see..."

He put the bag down on the table in front of him and tugged on the drawstrings. Light flashed across the bag again as it fell open and revealed two rings that looked like a braid of silver, gold, and onyx.

"Ah, spirit rings?" Friar Ipswich leaned in through the doorway only far enough for his head to be visible.

"And more." Camwell's gaze shifted from Ipswich to the shadows in the corridor behind him. His lip curled in momentary disdain, then he sat back and gestured with his free hand. "Come in. At long last."

Winston and his daughters came in. Leena held her younger sister by her collar. There was a dark palm mark across Lathia's left cheek, and scratch marks on Leena's neck, and a tear in the deep collar of her dress. Ash guessed Leena had had to forcibly bring her sister to face Camwell. Winston didn't look at either of his daughters. Lathia dragged her feet and resisted for a moment when Leena guided her to kneel on the bench.

"You. This is all your fault," Lathia whispered, somehow managing to spit even though there was only one sibilant in her words.

"Silence!" Camwell stood, bracing his arms on the table. He glowered at Lathia. "Both of you are in the wrong, but you, Lady Lathia, make a mockery of the full meaning of the word 'lady.' You shame your father, and quite sadly, you destroy your chances of ever making a decent marriage, because every castle where you terrorize the servants has little reason to protect your reputation."

"Terrorize? Truly? How can you justify such a word?" Winston blurted. "It's just an innocent girl having some fun with her inferiors. They should feel flattered she includes them in her fun."

Ash felt Lady Charlotte stiffen, standing taller, and the hand gripping her shoulder tightened.

"Such attitudes are a relic that should have been left in the dark ages," Lord Digory said. The temperature in the room dropped so quickly, Ash expected to see breath fog coming from everyone's mouths. "I am highly disappointed in you, Winston. Did you learn nothing from the Outbreak? From the enchantment invasions? As King Ebrosion has declared, and the kings of ten surrounding kingdoms have agreed, along with the most powerful enchanters across the continent, if *anyone* can manipulate magic, then *everyone* is equal in potential and ability. People's worth is determined by their actions and what they do with what A'theosius has given them."

"Religious fanatic," Winston spat. "Even worse, deluded by newfangled philosophies. When we were boys, no one would have doubted my daughter's word for a moment, and that boy would have been whipped for laying a hand on her."

"When in point of fact no hand was laid on your daughter at all?" Camwell said.

"It is the word of a lady against a nameless servant boy that isn't worth the dirt required to cover his grave!"

"Ash is a girl," Dunstan said. "Why can't you remember that?" He would have said more, but Camwell silenced him with a shake of his head.

"Wrong on so very many counts," the justiciar sighed. "Point of fact, there was no seduction. The only attacking was done by your daughter, not aimed at her."

"And this filthy servant gets by with no punishment at all?" he wailed.

"Of course not. Both of them, when you take the charges down to the basics, are liars." Camwell gestured at the rings. "Each of you, take a ring and put it on the heartline finger of your right hands."

Ash waited until Lathia got up, pouting, stomped to the table, and dithered over choosing her ring. They were identical, as far as Ash could tell, so why did it matter which one she chose?

"It's too big," Lathia whined as she stomped back to the bench. She held up her hand, showing the ring hanging loose on her finger.

The ring shimmered and visibly shrank in a matter of moments, drawing a squeak from her.

Ash stepped up and scooped up the second ring and slid it in place. Whatever her punishment, delay would just prolong the misery.

"The rings will not come off until each of you has fulfilled your quest," Camwell said. "They will record and reveal to me your progress and your actions. You will be required to answer questions from time to time, and you must answer them truthfully. In a sense, this quest is to teach you both to be truthful. Do you understand?"

"Sir. Yes, sir," Ash whispered.

Lathia dropped onto the bench, hiding her face in her hands, and burst into wailing tears.

"See here," Winston said, rousing from his slump, "how is this fair? How can you justify punishing my daughter's harmless little ... " He hunched his shoulders as if he felt the glare Lord Digory aimed at him. "Yes, I must admit, she was rather thoughtless. But she meant no harm! She's an innocent child."

"She's a vicious little snot who believes everyone has a duty to adore her," Leena said. "She's convinced herself she's beautiful and desirable, and no one can resist her. She's an embarrassment, Father."

"And how would you know, spending most of the year training or whatever it is you silly girls do when you pretend to be warriors?"

"Pretend?" Leena drew herself up tall and straight and her father shrank, going pale under the force of the icy fury in her expression. "She's the reason I stay away so long. She's the reason the last four suitors didn't stay beyond introductions."

Lathia's wail rose in pitch and volume.

Chapter Five

"Enough!" Camwell slammed his hand down on the table. "I will give the list of conditions that must be fulfilled, the requirements of the quest, and then I will leave this place. I recommend, Lord Winston, you show discretion and consideration, and you leave this place even more quickly. And you wait until Lady Charlotte invites you before you inflict your presence on her household again." He nodded to Lady Charlotte, who nodded to him, without a flicker of emotion in her expression.

Camwell extended his thick, gnarled hand, and Ash saw a much larger version of their rings on his thumb. It glimmered, a faint greenish haze traveling along the silver band. "Cease your false whimpering. Say nothing until I give you leave."

A spark of green hit Lathia's throat. Suddenly silent, she sat up, eyes wide and astonished and, not surprisingly, dry, despite all the wails and sobs she had been emitting just seconds before.

Who's the worse liar? Ash wondered.

There are degrees of lies, and you have very few on your conscience, a whispery sort of wind-through-grain voice replied. Her ring throbbed slightly, and Ash thought she heard the voice in the back of her head, between her ears. *However, yes, you must learn to be more truthful. If it is any comfort, I think this will be more an effort of being conscious of telling truths and falsehoods, rather than needing punishment and discipline and constantly being lectured.*

Hello. Ash knew it paid to always try to be polite. *Are you the ring? Well, of course — is that what 'spirit ring' means? Are you a disembodied spirit? A ghost?*

We can discuss my origins and limitations and philosophical underpinnings later. The justiciar is ready to speak and you really should listen, even though I am perfectly capable of reminding you of this day when necessary.

Ash sat up and tried to ignore Lathia, who clutched at her throat and kept moving her mouth and making gasping sounds, as if by force of will she could regain her voice.

"You will search for magic. You will infiltrate four caverns. You will find reclusive magic users. You will learn and codify the proper rankings of power and their names. And this is most important." Camwell paused and looked back and forth between both girls. "You will cross five borders in your travels, before your sentence is fulfilled, but you will not cheat and try to cross the same border five times."

"Sir?" Ash hunched her shoulders, expecting to be scolded. "What do you mean by caverns?"

"I leave that up to you. The terms are vague to give you flexibility and grant you the pleasure of adventuring." He chuckled, for a moment seeming to be somewhat jolly. Ash couldn't convince herself for a moment that he was being friendly and helpful with the "flexible" conditions. "You have the means of understanding, and more important, learning. I leave the rest up to you."

Learning? She caught her breath at a flash of what she thought, hoped could be understanding. *Ring? Are you supposed to teach me, along with keeping watch on how I fulfill the quest?*

Exactly. The voice chuckled softly. *And here's something to keep in mind. Camwell will be watching. That's the whole purpose of these quests, to entertain him. He was quite the world traveler in his youth. He's got a false leg hidden under those robes, so his travels are limited now. He sees the world through sending people on quests. So, do keep that in mind, when you're talking to people and reacting to anything that happens to you along the way.*

He can't actually see me, can he? Such as when I'm bathing or … or other things?

No. At least, not all the time. I'll warn you if he does activate a vision spell. He can't do it very often, because the magic is draining, and the farther away you are, the more energy he has to use up to find and watch you.

Is that why the conditions of the quest are so vague? So we wander, and he sees more of the world?

Exactly. I do think I got the better part of the task this time around. We're going to have fun, I think.

~~~~~

Ash returned to her storage room quarters. Any time she was not working in the kitchen, under the watch of a guard, she had to stay in her room. She supposed it was meant to be a punishment, at Winston's insistence, but she was quite enjoying the solitude and quiet. The kitchen room was more privacy than Ash had ever enjoyed, other than when bathing. She had been content with her pallet of blankets on a high shelf in the sleeping room, refused by the other boys because everyone banged their heads on the ceiling when they sat up. Now, she had a cot with a straw tick mattress, a blanket and pillow, and a pack for clothes and any sundry items she might bring with her.

She hadn't considered needing to pack. Ash had planned to simply wear her few clothes that weren't Fairhold livery. She hadn't thought she would need the pack that Myrtle handed her when she returned to her room from hearing the conditions of the quest. It was almost too large for her, a castoff from the gear the Fairhold soldiers used. Then Fern stepped
~~~~~

into the room with a good four pounds of smoked and dried scraps of meat. Followed by Sylva, from the castle sewing rooms, with a clever little drawstring pouch fitted out with needles and threads and patches for her clothes, including leather patches for her boots. Other servants followed in quick order, coming one at a time, with helpful little gifts such as a spare copper or three, a packet of sweets, extra socks, tiny waxed packets of salt and other seasonings, a flask of healing tonic, other bits and pieces, and most important of all, wishes of good luck. The pack was three-quarters filled when Dunstan stepped into the room.

"You might need this," the castle's heir said. He held out a pouch on a long strap. "It's got a secret compartment to put coins, so they don't jingle and give you away. And any thieves you run into won't think you have anything to steal. And there's a journal and those enchanted carbon sticks that won't even need sharpening."

"Thank you." Ash wondered if he would be offended or embarrassed if she hugged him. Now that she was revealed as a girl, would he mind? Then she remembered something, a much better response to the princely gift. She dug under the cot for the shallow chest that held her few possessions other than clothes and brought out a roll of papyrus. "I've been making this for you. It's only about two-thirds done. It was for your birthday, but I probably won't be back by then."

"I wish I could go with you."

"We would have great fun, wouldn't we?" She blinked away moist heat and partially unrolled the papyrus, to show him the drawings and notations she had made across the surface. "It's something of a map. I was researching all the places you might like to go to on your journey, and some notes of trouble people have run into, so you could avoid them."

"Now I really wish we could go together!" He unrolled the sheet more and grinned, his eyes scanning the contents. "This is amazing. Thank you. Please promise me you'll return in time to travel with me?"

"You still want me, knowing I'm a girl?"

"We don't have to tell anyone, do we?" He gestured at her, still dressed as a boy. At least Justiciar Camwell hadn't ordered her to put on a dress or change her appearance to let the world know she was a girl.

"Who knows what I'll look like by then?"

"We had such fun when we were little, didn't we?" He leaned back against the wall next to the door and rolled up the papyrus. "Why did we have to grow up?"

Ash refrained from pointing out that she had only been able to be the young lord's playmate for a few years, before his schooling and her servant duties split them apart. She had thought for a while she had been chosen because for her first few years at Fairhold, she was roughly the same size and coloring as the heir to the castle, to act as a duplicate to draw danger away. While she had been taught to read alongside him, the glory days of playing and lessons hadn't lasted long. She supposed she had been a fool, hoping to regain that friendship and fun on Dunstan's adventure.

"You, Ash," a gruff voice called. "No use hiding in there. You're to come with me. Lady Lathia wants to talk to you."

"Well Ash doesn't want to talk to her." Dunstan stepped into the doorway and turned to face the man before he could fill the doorway.

"Who are you to tell me—" The servant, in Winston's pea green livery, blanched when he saw the heir of the castle blocking his way. "Your pardon, Lord Dunstan, but my mistress wants to talk to—" He gestured at Ash. "Be honest, are you really a girl, or are you just pretending to be one to get out of trouble?"

"You're just as rude and stupid as Lathia," Dunstan said. "Get out, and tell her I said no. And remind her that Justiciar Camwell said she's not to have any contact with Ash for the rest of her stay here at the castle." He waited a few seconds, but the man just looked at him, his mouth starting to drop open. "Go!"

"Thank you. Again," Ash said, once the man's retreating, stomping footsteps had faded away.

"You know, that's something I didn't think of. She's supposed to leave you alone here, but what's to stop that snot from pestering you once you're both out on the quest?" Dunstan shuddered. "Every time they show up, I expect Cousin Winston to try once again to match me with one of his girls. Leena is all right but she's five years older than me. And Lathia ..." He looked a little green around his eyes and down his throat. "We need to get you out of here tonight."

"We?" She grinned at him, and for a few moments she did indeed feel as if they had returned to being playmates and good friends.

Dunstan was three months younger than her, and now he stood a good head taller, two hands wider in the shoulders. He was only middling good with sword and spear, and didn't care for racing on horseback, or handling the obstacle course, but he was a wonder with bow and arrow, and reading maps and deciphering all sorts of word puzzles. Ash had quite looked forward to adventuring with him and seeing how his cleverness could compensate for his lack of muscle and speed. She suspected sometimes that she enjoyed time in the library so much because Dunstan usually showed up there, if she studied long enough. They rarely talked, but there was something incredibly comfortable about sitting and reading together in blissful silence. Almost as lovely as their childhood games of adventures together, pretending they could fly, or breathe underwater or walk through stone.

"I have some ideas." He rolled up the papyrus a little tighter. "Promise me you'll be back before I have to head out?"

"I—" She flinched, as that dratted star on her buttocks flared to icy life. "I'll try. My very best, I'll try. Who knows what I'll run into, or how long it will take to find the justiciar's caverns?"

"True." He nodded, his expression solemn, giving a good picture of the solid, thoughtful man he would be in a few more years. "Well, I'll be back later with a plan. I hope."

He gave her a nodding salute, as if they were equals, which quite took her breath away, and then he was gone.

More servants came, with advice or warnings, things they had heard Lathia and her father plotting, a few more copper coins, a nearly new shirt, an oilskin pouch of healing herbs, a second knife, longer than the one she carried for eating. Ash was quite overwhelmed.

She worked in the kitchens for the midday meal and dinner, which interfered with Lathia's attempts to waylay her. Myrtle sent away three servants who came looking for Ash, demanding she report to Lathia, despite the justiciar's orders. What did Lathia want to say? The odds of her apologizing for the attack and lying about it were miniscule.

Unless she thought apologizing would remove the ring?

No, more likely Lathia thought if she could badger Ash into confessing everything was her fault, that would remove the rings.

Ash had an enjoyable time in the kitchen with Myrtle and the other kitchen workers. It was hot and loud and she came away with an aching back and shriveled, wrinkled hands because most of her time was spent scrubbing pots. That was more than made up for by laughter and getting first tastes of everything being sent to the dining room. And other servants from different parts of the castle peered in to wish her good luck and offer more bits of advice.

Malchus's apprentice, Damian warned her not to try to find the enchanted castle to free herself of the ring. Then other people gave her advice about the enchanted castle, or the enchanted forest that surrounded and hid it. Mostly along the lines of, "If the enchanted castle is nearby, or you hear it's heading your way, run." Just how could an enchanted castle be *heading* her way? Which castle? In which kingdom? Which kingdom should she avoid? The people giving the advice always hurried away on tasks before they finished telling her.

"The enchanted castle? You don't know about the enchanted castle?" Codswall, the fletcher, stared bug-eyed at Ash when she asked him. She asked because he didn't run off right away. He finished settling down at the table where Myrtle waited with a trencher piled high with all the odd bits carved off the roasts and vegetables and loaves of bread that weren't pretty enough to be served to the nobility.

"Why would the lad—" Myrtle sighed. "Sorry, this will take some getting used to. Why would the lass here know about that wretched place?

It's been far too quiet nigh these last twenty-some years. We all thought it had finally come to rest somewhere. Far away in another kingdom, if A'theosius is kind."

"How can a castle settle anywhere?" Ash asked, fighting very hard to keep her voice calm and even. Something trembled to excited life inside her. She had thought up until now she had been hearing wrong when people mentioned the enchanted castle. Here was something that sounded interesting, just because it defied common sense.

"That's the thing. It's roaming the enchanted forest, and the enchanted forest, well ..." Codswall waggled his bushy eyebrows. "Makes you think it can be everywhere at once, when really, maybe it's nowhere at once. Just little bits and pieces of it that connect to real places. What you need to be careful of, lad—sorry, lass—what you need to be careful of is that most of the time, them what goes in never come back out again."

"The forest or the castle?" Ash asked.

"Maybe both," Myrtle said.

"But what is its name?"

"That *is* its name. The enchanted castle is the only one, so why does it need a name?" Codswall nodded, grinning, and reached for the enormous cooking fork that Myrtle gave him to eat with. "Don't make much sense, you're thinking? And you'd be right."

"There are many castles all around the world that are enchanted. According to legends and lore," Ash pointed out. "Why does this one get to be the only one?"

"Because," he said, swallowing his first mouthful hastily, so she thought he might choke. Had he chewed more than once? "Because this castle is full of enchantments. Full of magic that's broken, or magic that's been chained up to keep it from roaming the world and causing all sorts of havoc and insanity. Full of magic things, cursed things, and I wouldn't be surprised if every prince who's gone missing on a quest and every kidnapped princess under a magic spell or curse is there, held prisoner. It's said to have thousands of statues, all people turned to stone for their crimes, or because some enchantress with a headache decided to be nasty. And it's full of magic books. Not just books recording magic spells, but books that *are* magic." He chuckled and took the opportunity of the pause to stuff a whole roasted onion in his mouth. He waved the fork at Ash, silencing her until he finished chewing and swallowing. "Thought that would catch your attention. But don't you go in there. Run for your life. All the magic that's wrong in this world is stored there, or held prisoner there, or it might just be the source of all the magic that's gone insane and renegade."

"How will I know when I'm getting close to it?" she asked.

"It's not you getting close to it that matters." Myrtle picked up a chicken leg and waved it at Ash for emphasis as she spoke. "It's when the castle starts getting close to you that you need to be careful."

"How can it get close to me? How does it move?"

"No one knows how, or why, they just know that it moves. It was anchored, they say. Maybe chained down would be closer to the truth. The castle is a live thing, thanks to all that magic filling it. Live things, wild things, dangerous wild things, need to be chained up, locked up. Anchored, you see? And they also say that greed and arrogance snapped the anchor. The castle started moving around the enchanted forest, and then one day there was so much momentum, like a pendulum, you see?" Codswell demonstrated with his free hand swishing back and forth across the table, nearly knocking the trencher onto the floor. "One fine day it knocked the enchanted forest loose of its moorings, too."

"Why haven't I heard about this before?" Ash asked.

"You ain't read all the books in his lordship's library yet, have you?" Codswall said, giving her a look that Ash hated to see. The one that adults used far too often, and variations on, "You should know better," or "You should have thought of that before."

"Like we said," Myrtle patted Ash's hand, "it's been quiet the last twenty-odd years. No princes going missing, no princesses swallowed up by magical creatures that come darting through one of the portals and vanish through them again, faster than thought. It's like you don't tell stories about the boggies at the dark of the moon, because that just summons them. You don't talk about things you don't want to wake up and hear you say their names, because they'll decide you want to see them, and they show up and cause all kinds of trouble." She nodded for emphasis. "Just like that."

"Where does the enchanted forest go, then, if it's been knocked loose, too?" Ash asked after considering that information.

"That's harder to say." Codswall filled his mouth and chewed slowly, eyes half-closed as he made a visible effort at thinking. "Most of the stories I've heard say that the enchanted forest was anchored to the portals. Those are the only ways in and out of the enchanted forest," he hurried to say, pointing the fork at Ash and nearly touching her nose, when she opened her mouth to ask what portals were.

She knew what portals were, but she had the feeling, as with many things soaked in magic, they weren't the way they should be. Or at least, the way they were in the non-magical parts of the world.

"Each kingdom, when there were a lot fewer and larger kingdoms, had a portal into the enchanted forest, and it used to be a simple enough matter getting in and out. Just find the portal, walk through, mark the place where you stepped out, and go back the way you came in when you want to leave." Codswall shrugged. "When it got knocked loose of its moorings, the portals got ... fuzzy, blurry, I suppose you could say. They didn't always let you in, because from what people say, on the enchanted forest side the portals could go to more than one kingdom, and you can't open a door to two rooms at the same time, can you? No, you cannot. The trick is, even if you can get into the enchanted forest, doesn't mean when you find the way you came in that it'll let you get out again that way. I've heard tell of stories where a man went into the enchanted forest, and when he left a few hours later he thought he came out the same way. But he came out halfway around the world. And even worse, it was years for them what he left behind." He nodded, eyes somber, eyebrows waggling for punctuation, as if he thought Ash wouldn't believe him.

She believed him. She thought Codswall was one of the most commonsense people in Castle Fairhold. If he believed a story, he had good reason, and even better instincts about things and people.

"Is there a book about the enchanted forest or the enchanted castle in the library here?" she asked.

Codswall didn't know. Myrtle didn't know. Ash hurried to finish washing and drying the dishes and scrubbing the pots and pans from dinner, so she could visit the library. Walking carefully in the shadows to avoid Lathia, of course. The guard assigned to her had slipped away to visit his sweetheart. She promised herself she would return quickly enough he wouldn't get into trouble.

Chapter Six

"The enchanted forest?" Friar Ipswich echoed, when Ash asked him, more than an hour later. "Ah, that would be a useful tome indeed." He shook his head and leaned closer, lowering his voice. "Understand, I don't hold you responsible for the damage to the psalters, but it would heal my wounded soul greatly if you could manage to procure a book about the enchanted forest while you are on the quest. Could you try?"

"I will try," Ash said, despite the brief flare of resentment and knowing Ipswich did blame her, a little. "So we don't have a book?"

"We did, or so the previous keeper of the library believed. There is a notation that King Ruprick perpetrated what can certainly be called raids of every library he could reach, looking for information on the enchanted forest, and especially the enchanted castle, trying to tame them." Ipswich pursed his lips and gazed off into the distance for several moments. "Yes, Ruprick VII, of Rathelshiffer."

"A king of another kingdom stole our books?"

"For being so well-read ..." He shook his head. "Ash, kings never steal. Even when they take what belongs to another king, they do not believe it is stealing. No matter what damage and injustice follows in the wake of their actions. Wars have been born from one king pursuing what he considers his rights granted by A'theosius, and another disagrees with him. Like nasty little boys, arguing over who is their mother's favorite."

"Are all nobles that way?" Ash blurted, despite knowing otherwise. Hadn't Lady Charlotte and Lord Digory defended her far more than she had expected or hoped? She had known for years, from the comments of other noble visitors, that Lady Charlotte and her family acted toward the servants and commoners under their care with far more generosity and respect than most nobles. Even King Ebrosion didn't live up to the high standards of conduct and egalitarianism before A'theosius promoted by the seers and holy folk, and he supported such teachings.

"The old ways fade slowly. The new ways are embraced only when they are just as beneficial to those in power as those under their dominion. If you're thinking of trying to find those missing books ... well, it might be safer for you to go into the enchanted castle itself and face the wrath of the magical library, than to enter Rathelshiffer. Every Ruprick since the first of the name has been odious, arrogant, and self-righteous. Supposedly there is a family heirloom that causes each Ruprick to be a copy of his predecessor. Like a butter mold, I suppose."

"Can you tell me anything about the enchanted forest?"

"Run away. If you hear a portal has opened, if you hear the enchanted castle is approaching, run away," Ipswich finished, his voice turning hollow with portent.

Each partial answer or non-answer just birthed more questions. Ash had the awful feeling that no matter how long she stayed talking with Ipswich, she wouldn't learn anything useful. Or rather, answers that didn't require hours of thinking and untangling words of doom from the useful bits. She thanked the friar and headed back through the castle to her room. If she was lucky, she would get a few hours of sleep before Dunstan came to help her slip away in the night.

Hazel was waiting, sitting in the doorway of the darkened, cavernous kitchen, when Ash returned to that wing of the castle. At least the guard hadn't returned.

"Got you a friend for your journey," the woman said. She tipped her head toward the door of Ash's room.

"Thank you. That is very kind," Ash added, as she had seen Lady Charlotte and Lady Beatrice do when faced with awkward situations. Hazel could be a good friend and a bad enemy to have.

"Everything needs boundaries," Hazel said, her voice losing its rasp and going hollow. A sure sign that her prophetic gift had taken over. She reached out and clutched Ash's shoulder.

Ash tried to focus and listen and remember. She would save thinking about the meaning for later. Although she dearly wished that visions and prophecies would be polite enough to simply leave her alone.

"It was knocked loose of its moorings by arrogance and greed. When the sword falls, make sure it doesn't fall on you, and you on it."

"Thank you." Ash couldn't quite breathe until Hazel let go of her.

"The castle. The enchanted castle." Her voice cracked and she closed her eyes and slumped forward a little. "Don't look for it. But when you find it, take it."

"Which one?" The shiver up her back into her scalp told Ash exactly which castle Hazel was talking about, but common sense said to be absolutely sure. This was the wrong time and place to make mistakes and assumptions.

"Many castles hold enchantments." Hazel sniffed. With a quirk of her lips she was back to the Hazel Ash knew, and preferred. "Fortunately, more enchantments are free, roaming the world, taking up residence in woods and streams and ponds and mills. There is only one castle that's built of enchantment, a place where broken and twisted and rogue magic is sent to keep it from wreaking havoc on the rest of the world."

"But Friar Ipswich just warned me to stay away from it."

"Smart man, despite all his book learning." Hazel winked.

"Why do I need to find it?"

"That little trinket will need removing, and a safe place to hide it. And set it free. Set you free. Not now. Not for a long time. It's a friend, aren't you?" She caught up Ash's hand and stroked the spirit ring with her thumb.

I promise you, good woman, I will protect the maiden and guide her in discovering this intriguing magic simmering in her blood, the ring responded.

"Yes, but the one who holds the strings will not loose the knot at the proper time. He's a greedy old thing, using others for his adventures and entertainment because he's too fat and too enamored of his pleasures to stir far afield. He won't let her go. Which means she eventually has to cut loose of you."

"Justiciar Camwell?" Ash reflected that she didn't need to guess, it was a given.

"Wouldn't you like to settle in one place, no longer sent off on missions, surrounded by your own kind, sharing stories and keeping watch on the nasty bits that would like to hurt anyone and anything they can touch?" Hazel said.

Settled? The ring sounded surprised.

"The castle will have the right spell to cut the knot. When the proper time comes. It's a storage place, an enormous, expanding, aware, roaming treasure chest of magic. Think how much fun you'll have in the company of a thousand trinkets of power, just like yourself."

Yes, that does sound rather attractive. And I wouldn't put it past the justiciar to break his word to you. I'm sorry, Lady Ashlyn. It never occurred to me that he would use me to imprison and hurt someone.

"That's quite all right," Ash murmured. She wasn't sure she liked being addressed by her full name, although being called "Lady" did give her a funny little thrill in the pit of her stomach.

"Then we're all agreed? You'll protect her from the justiciar's spying eyes and guide her when faced by the castle, when the time comes?"

I do vow. May I shatter into useless dust, if I do not fulfill this final duty, the ring responded after only a few seconds.

"Thank you. It's refreshing to run across some magic thingamabobs that have a sense of honor and fair play." Hazel nodded twice. "Now, on to my reason for lying in wait for you." She gestured at the door of Ash's little room. "Your companion."

Ash pushed the door open and raised her candle to better illuminate the room. A glowing ball of faerie light bobbed against the ceiling. She glanced around the room, wondering which of the servants Hazel had chosen to accompany her. Would she be allowed companions? She had already heard Lathia's wailing from several rooms away when Justiciar

Camwell refused her request for all her father's servants to accompany her. Lathia was allowed two servants. Total. A bodyguard, and someone to tend to the baggage and horses. Ash hadn't asked, because she hadn't even dared hope, but could she ask borrow a donkey for the quest? Not that she had had any baggage to speak of, until the generosity of her fellow servants surprised her. Until she heard Lathia complaining that she wasn't allowed to have two changes of horses, Ash had assumed they would both be on foot. She also hadn't thought to ask for companions.

Who had Hazel asked or persuaded, maybe threatened to accompany Ash on this quest?

Petroc's face filled her mind, then Wynn's. Both would be wonderful companions. Brave and strong and loyal, and definitely the most clever of all the servants near her age.

Her face warmed as she realized that she hadn't immediately hoped for Dunstan, who had even said he wished he could go with her. As kind as he was, clever and well-intentioned, Dunstan had a sense of helplessness about him.

Movement among the blankets on her bed. Then a fuzzy, grayish-yellowish bundle slid out, and two enormous, slightly ragged ears popped upward.

"It's a rabbit," she said.

No, that's a bunny. There's an enormous gulf of difference, the ring said.

There is? Ash thought back, catching herself just in time to avoid saying it aloud.

Common sense said there was something special about that bundle of fuzz and big, liquid eyes and enormous teeth if Hazel chose it as her companion. Intelligent. And likely with feelings that could be hurt. Insulting something that might save her life or at least keep her out of trouble was not a wise way to start her quest.

"I'm sorry. Bunny?" She bowed to it. Now that she was a few steps closer, she saw the bunny was twice the size of any rabbit she had ever seen.

"This is Fang." Hazel gestured and the bunny hopped down off the cot and sat up on his hind legs. His ears twisted and bent, pointing in different directions, bobbing up and down. They reminded Ash of the castle's soldiers practicing flag signals.

"Is he ... talking with his ears?" she ventured.

Fang sat up taller and grinned, nodding vigorously. His front teeth were three times wider and longer than any front teeth she had ever seen, with a rather large gap between them. Ash thought she could perhaps fit her thumb and forefinger in the gap.

Did his teeth have a ... reddish stain?

"He likes you," Hazel said. "I knew he would. I think you two will get along famously. Maybe you've noticed his teeth?"

"Ah … yes."

"Wonderful things, his teeth. He can cut through wood like it was flax, and scratch escape holes through stone like men would saw through wood. And those hind legs of his are quite clever at pummeling and punching. And when he's all hunched up and giving big-eyed, melting looks, nobody would expect to be ambushed. As for understanding what he's saying …" She sighed. "Well, we don't have time to teach you, so the two of you will have to work out how to understand him as you travel along. Time is of the essence. You need to get out of the castle and away from Fairhold Downs before dawn."

"Why? What did you hear? Lathia is going to try to sabotage me, isn't she?"

"Lathia? That nasty piece of fancy rubbish? I've been too busy dealing with more pressing problems." Hazel gestured with a nod at Fang. "He's the one who needs to get out of the Downs, and out of Alfordia, as quickly as possible. I keep telling him, if he insists on only eating red, and being the messy eater he is, sooner or later he'll be accused of murder."

"Oh." Ash supposed that made sense, with the red stains on the bunny's chest fur and teeth and being named Fang. "Who's after him?"

"Who isn't? I've had him four days now, and he's rather helpful around the cottage, but word is that the bunny council has collected their individual magics and they've got a tracking spell at work. And yes, before you ask, that's one of the big differences between bunnies and rabbits, or coneys, or hares, or the dozen other odd names for all the varieties of the breed. *Bunny* means magic in the blood, larger size, bigger teeth, and an inconvenient inability to control their tempers."

Ash swallowed down the urge to remark that she always thought bunnies were baby rabbits. Certainly not an entirely different, temperamental, magical breed.

Perhaps she wasn't quite as well-read and educated as Lady Charlotte and Friar Ipswich thought.

Her mind snapped over to all the things she had learned about the enchanted castle already today. It was filled with books, wasn't it? How much could she learn from those books? Useful things, of course.

"All right, so Fang and I shall leave under cover of darkness. Where do you advise we go first? Ring?"

Fang made a definite snickering sound and bounded across the room in two leaps, which revealed just how long and muscular his hind legs were. His feet when they touched the flagstone floor flattened out to twice the width of Ash's hands. Yes, she could see how handy those feet would be, slapping and pummeling and punching adversaries.

On Fang's second bound, he had more than crossed the room, and would have slammed into the door, except Hazel reached over and flung it open just in the nick of time. He flew out the door with a muffled thud, the sound of bunny fur and bunny muscle against a stone wall.

He says down always works quite well, the spirit ring said.

"Down?"

"Oh, yes. A tunnel. They won't expect you to vanish down a bunny hole, when everyone expects to give the two of you a ceremonial send-off at the castle gates in the morning." Hazel beckoned, and they followed Fang by the sound of thumps moving down the darkened hallway.

"Ceremonial?" That sounded rather nice.

Until she thought about the ominous words: the two of you. Meaning Lathia would be there. And her father. And their disgusting, arrogant, loyal servants. Just what were Ash's chances she could get beyond their reach before they tried something nasty? If something happened to Ash, would the quest be canceled, since Lathia by default would be declared the winner?

"The only people who like ceremony are historians. Those who have to stand through ceremonies don't care for them, and you don't want to be the one at the center of the ceremony," Hazel said. "That's a sure-fire way to ask destiny to take a long, hard look at you and decide to make life painfully interesting, so you earn all sorts of inconvenient fame."

"That sounds uncomfortable."

"Indeed. Hedge witches have ceremonies, but we make them as short and simple and practical as possible, and then we make up for it with long, comfortable, lazy parties. I'll get you invited to one when you come back." She caught her breath, and for a moment her gaze went distant. Her eyes took on a greenish glow. She blinked, and they were ordinary hazel again. "If you come back."

Ash chose not to respond to that.

They came out of the castle by the yard where the laundry dried and Fern prepared the many herbs she used for the smokehouse. Fang had crouched down and was sniffing at a spot at the base of the high stone wall surrounding the courtyard. His ears bobbed forward three times, then he dove headfirst and a spray of dirt erupted.

"That's the spot. It should lead straight under the moat at the shallowest point, if I don't miss my guess," Hazel said. "You'll have maybe fifteen, twenty minutes to gather up your things and hurry back out here. Say your goodbyes, but only to the people you trust not to make a fuss and betray you. We don't want them knowing you're gone until morning."

Who did she need to say goodbye to? Who really mattered to her?

Ash thought back to all the people who had surprised her throughout the day, coming to her with advice and little bits of useful things. She was surprised because she had striven to be as invisible as possible. She had obeyed every order as swiftly as she could manage, to avoid reprimands. She had kept herself neat and clean and quiet, and avoided anyone in a temper, or with reputations as bullies. How had she not managed to be unremarkable, and easy to ignore and even forget?

The only ones who really mattered were Lady Charlotte, Dunstan, and Granny Phlox. She supposed that odd talk the other day counted as her goodbyes with the old woman.

That left Lady Charlotte. Who, of course, was waiting in her study, rather than having retired for the night already. She put down the scroll she had been studying and smiled when Ash peered through the gap between door and frame.

"Come in, my dear. Ready to fly away?" She held out her hand.

"I'm not staying for the ceremony in the morning."

"Wise decision. I overheard that odious child insisting that her father make you travel with her, to do all the work for both of you." She sniffed delicately. "She actually said that was all you were good for. So you must prove how drastically, terribly wrong she is. Won't you?"

"I'll do my best, mi'lady. Would you—is it rude of me to ask you to say goodbye to everyone for me?"

"My dear girl." Charlotte held out both her hands, and Ash put hers into them. "I am honored that you would trust me to protect your flight. Do you know where you're going first?"

"Over the border, as quickly as possible. I've been given so much advice, there's no way anyone could guess where I would go, or should go…"

Charlotte squeezed her hands once more, then released them. "I fear I must apologize."

"For what?" Ash couldn't comprehend Lady Charlotte ever doing something bad enough to require admitting she had been wrong.

"I should have tried harder to find your parents, or at least some kin. It was simply easier to assume everyone had perished when the sea swept so far inland. It was too easy to simply snatch up all the homeless, parentless children who had no one to speak for them, and convince myself I was doing a good thing to give them homes and training and work. When actually, I was merely looking ahead to the needs of Fairhold."

"Oh, no, mi'lady, I would rather be here than anywhere else in the world! I will always be grateful that you brought me to Fairhold."

"Truthfully, child? How can you say that when you have never been anywhere but Fairhold?" The elderly woman shook her head, smiling with just a touch of teary brightness in her eyes. "When you have had your adventure, then come and tell me where you would rather be. I suspect you will find some grand and glorious new home, the place that has always called to your heart. The place, I think, you have been seeking, all unknowing, when you devour books about far off lands."

Ash thought about those words many times during the long night that followed. She crept down the corridors of the castle, extra cautious because this was when danger and disaster always struck in the books she had read: right before the hero escaped brutal enemies and treachery. Now would be the time one of Winston's servants would find her, capture her, and drag her to face Lathia.

She darted into dark corners and doorways, and one time crawled under a heavy piece of furniture when she heard voices or footsteps approaching. Most of the time, she recognized the voices of fellow servants, but three times the gait of the lone walker or the voices in conversation didn't sound familiar. Those were the ones to avoid. When she reached her room, her sense of time's passage told her the twenty minutes Hazel had given her to make her goodbyes had run out.

Fortunately, she had packed and repacked her new satchel and the pack and laid out the new jacket and hooded cape Lady Beatrice had given her. She was already wearing the new boots Lord Digory had told Fitzcairn the cobbler to adjust to her size. All she had to do was snatch up baggage, arrange pillow and old clothes and boots under her blankets to appear as if someone was sleeping there, and then she was hurrying down that narrow, dark corridor again. The guard still hadn't returned. Was that by his choice, or had Hazel temporarily hazed him, to delay his return?

That didn't really matter, did it?

Chapter Seven

Hazel was no longer by the wall when Ash reached it. The spot where Fang had been digging was lost under a pile of dirt. She couldn't see the hole, and certainly not the bunny. What if there wasn't room for her few possessions to travel that hole? Yes, Fang was much larger than any rabbit she had ever seen, but could he dig a hole, a tunnel, large enough for her? She didn't want to get stuck. That was an inglorious, rather frightening way to die.

"Fang?" She stepped up to the edge of the pile of loose dirt and tried to look down into the hole. The moon was at just the wrong angle so the wall cast a huge shadow across the hole. Ash knew no one could see her, but she couldn't see into the hole. "How am I supposed to go down there? How do I know the hole is finished? Fang?" She wished she knew how to whisper and yell at the same time.

Perhaps I may be of assistance, the ring said.

"Oh. I'm sorry. I completely forgot—" Ash thought her face was hot enough to cast its own glow.

No apology necessary. You certainly aren't used to having me around, or any magical assistance whatsoever. Am I correct?

Yes, very. And I should be conversing with you in my thoughts, so no one knows we're here.

The ring glowed, a pale bluish cast that generated no shadows. She thrust her hand down into the deeper darkness and found the hole Fang had dug. It certainly looked wide enough for her to go down on her hands and knees, and not scrape her back against the top of the tunnel. A moment of thought, and she had a few answers to some of her questions. She put on her new jacket, with the satchel slung across her chest underneath it. Then she threaded her new cloak through the straps of her pack, tied the ends in a loop she hung from her shoulder, and set it up to drag behind her as she crawled.

Are you able to call ahead to Fang and ask if he's done, and I should come ahead?

He's out and waiting, the ring responded after several moments of silence, when she quite expected the hue and cry to arise from the castle.

Ash looked back once, and shivered, as she studied the outline of Fairhold against the starry sky. Half the walls shone with a silver glow from the moonlight, while the rest were lost in darkness and shadow.

Then she turned and went down headfirst, on hands and knees, into the hole and under the wall.

The ring's light comforted her, though at times the close proximity of the sides of the tunnel made breathing difficult. Ash knew her imagination might just run away with her if she couldn't see where she was going. The tunnel sloped down just steeply enough the pack slid and pressed against her feet and rump, as if silently urging her to move faster. She nearly panicked once when she imagined the tunnel going down at this angle forever, taking her deep underground, never to come up again.

Please, Ring, is Fang out and above ground?

Yes, and growing impatient. I wonder if perhaps it would be wise not to teach you to understand the signs he makes with his ears. You're far too young for such language.

She sputtered laughter, and that somehow pushed the sides of the tunnel out enough to make the air not quite so thick in her lungs. Soon after that, the tunnel flattened. She counted then, every time her ring hand moved forward. When she got to ninety, it angled up again. Silently begging A'theosius for a gift, she tipped her head back so it touched the ceiling of the tunnel ... and saw moonlight.

It was an almost terrifyingly small dot, but it was indeed moonlight. Ash crawled faster, and now the pack dragged behind her. Several times it seemed to catch on something, probably a root that she hadn't noticed because she didn't scrape against it when she passed. Each time, her heart seemed to stutter, then she took another deep breath, leaned forward, tugged the pack free, and moved on.

The dot of moonlight didn't expand quickly enough. She developed a cramp in her neck from looking upward. Ash took to bowing her head to focus on the ground in front of her, and after twenty crawling paces, reaching forward with her right hand, she let herself look up again. Finally, the moonlight grew larger, and closer, and breathing became a little easier.

The scent of apple blossoms tickled her nose, and she lunged forward, doubling her pace. With a gasp, she fell out. Her pack anchored her so she twisted sideways instead of falling down the sudden drop. Ash lay still, turned halfway on her side, staring up at the tangle of white-robed branches.

She was in an orchard. Where was the closest apple orchard outside of Castle Fairhold? Her mind jammed with dozens of questions. The most important being where she should go now that she was out and away. But she couldn't know which way to go, until she knew where she was.

Fang landed by her head, close enough the fur from his toes brushed her forehead. He bounced up and down, ears bending at impossible angles, twisting and jerking upright.

"What is he saying?" she asked the ring. Her voice cracked. Her mouth was dry and tasted of dirt.

He wants you to get up and move before the guard dogs come.

An apple orchard with guard dogs. Old Clispes the silver merchant was the only one who had guard dogs on his orchard, and everyone mocked him for it. Lord Digory had an orchard three times the size, and the apples were twenty times better than the sour things Clispes grew. Anyone who wanted apples could come in and enjoy them but could only carry away what they could hold in their hands. That was fair, and followed the king's example of generosity. Clispes disdained that practice. He had a wall around his orchard and guard dogs, and people stole from him just because the man was such a miser. Certainly not to eat the apples.

"How am I going to get over the wall?" she muttered as she got to her feet and untangled her cloak from the straps of the pack.

You're outside the wall. Just follow Fang.

The bunny bounced three more times, then darted forward, hopping with huge bounds that didn't rise far but covered enormous distances with each leap. Baying started up somewhere to the right. Now that Ash was on her feet, she saw the branches of the apple trees stretching over the walls, like prisoners begging for rescue. She hauled her pack up onto her shoulder and set off, trying to keep Fang in sight. They followed the line of the wall for five of his hops, then he darted to the left, out into the open.

Why are we worried about the dogs if we're outside the walls?

Someone went inside and left the gates open, the ring responded after several moments.

Ash would have laughed if she had the breath. Her legs and back ached from the long crawl, and now she ran lopsided, with the weight of her pack pulling her sideways with every other step. Perhaps someday in the future, she might find this memory amusing. She hoped she would be able to tell it to Dunstan and Hazel and Lady Charlotte. First, she would have to vanish into the darkness and evade the hunting dogs.

Who had left the gates open, where were the gates, and who had decided to irritate old Clispes when he had no apples?

The surrounding countryside was full of idiots, and it was a very good thing she had to head out on Justiciar Camwell's quest.

She heard voices behind her. Male voices. Were those the escaping intruders? Or Clispe's servants?

Ash glanced back once, even though she knew, and the older boys had warned her, looking back slowed her. And she might trip or knock herself off balance. Three shapes ran through the moonlight. They had no torches. Probably the intruders. Servants or guards, if Clispe actually paid for guards, would have torches or lanterns.

Ahead, Fang darted to the left again, vanishing around a wide expanse of something that turned out to be a boulder maybe twice as tall as her, and five arm spans wide. As soon as she passed it, Ash saw more enormous chunks of rock. Now she knew where she was. The Giants' Graveyard.

Now was not the time to learn if the ghost tales the boys told in the servants' quarters on stormy nights were true. Depending on who was telling the story, and how bloodthirsty he was, the Giants' Graveyard really did have giants under those massive boulders, and they were restless and vengeful. People really did vanish when going through the graveyard at night. According to Cadswall, the ground was riddled with enormous pits, and the unwary plunged into them.

Ash slowed down, trying to remember what Cadswall had said about surviving a visit to the Giants' Graveyard at night. Had he said anything? Other than "Don't go into the graveyard at night"?

Fang leaped out of the darkness, giving her shoulder a glancing blow, knocking her sideways and spinning to the right. Ash shrieked. The sound echoed off the rock faces all around her. The dogs in the distance went silent for a moment. Ash flung her arms upward, just in time to keep from slamming her face into a rock. She gasped for breath, as the ground under her right foot shifted.

It fell away from under her. She scrabbled at the rock face, trying to find a knob, a crevice, something to dig her fingers into and hold on. Fang leaped at her again, his hind legs and forepaws and claws digging into her new jacket. The weight of him pulled her to the left. She fell, choking on a shriek, and rolled halfway, until her pack stopped her.

Fang jumped up and down, slapping her face with his ears.

He says get up, the ring said.

"I figured that." Ash groaned, her hands scraped and sore, her knee throbbing, and rolled back the way she had come.

The ground shifted under her hands. It was about to collapse. Terror shot cold heat through her blood and suddenly she was on her feet, darting away, all aches and stiffness and breathlessness driven out of her body. Behind her, a massive crackling and groaning echoed through the Giants' Graveyard. She darted past a pillar of rock that expanded as it rose skyward, like an enormous mushroom. When she looked back, she saw the boulder she had slammed into slowly sinking downward.

"Please, Fang, get us out of here."

Voices shouted and dogs barked, muffled by the scraping and groaning of falling rock and the hissing of sand gushing upward. Ash winced at the thudding of her feet pounding on the rock, and imagined it was as thin as paper under her. Any moment, that rock would crack and crumble and she would fall. Clenching her jaw, she hurtled through the darkness and shadow and thin streaks of moonlight, following the bouncing, faintly glowing shape of Fang as he led her, weaving through the pillars and hills of rock.

Then they were out in the open. She staggered and almost fell when the ground dropped out from under her. But it was only a double step height. She caught herself, going to one knee, and pushed upright. Behind her came the echoes of other feet banging on the thin rock, echoing in the caverns underground. Ash braced for the sound of rock shattering and boulders falling.

Ahead of her, Fang came to a stop. Meaning he bounced up and down, not forward. His ears flapped forward rapidly enough to blur in the moonlight. She slid to a stop several paces away from him and bent forward, gasping, bracing her hands on her knees.

Now that she wasn't running, she could spare some concentration to try to determine where she was in relation to where she wanted or needed to go, the route to take from here. The Giants' Graveyard was close to the southern border of Castle Fairhold's territory, and the southern border of the kingdom. Did that count as two borders?

Likely not, the ring responded, when she asked.

She thought that was rather unfair, but she knew better than to think it too loudly. If Justiciar Camwell could check on her progress in the quest through the ring, maybe he could hear her thoughts, and might count that against her. He already despised her for being a liar.

"Does the justiciar know where I am all the time?"

Only when he activates the spells attached to the collection of rings.

"Collection?" Ash shook her head, as if that would help straighten out several thoughts that had been bouncing around in her head, much like Fang had bounced around and among and even off the boulders on their mad dash through the graveyard. "What happened to him being a man of science, if he has such a dependence on magic?"

He believes in science as a new kind of magic, and wants to prove the two bolster each other rather than cancel each other out.

"That doesn't seem right." She gasped for a few more breaths. "I just don't have the wind or the energy to figure out why."

Fang bounced two steps toward her, then three steps backward, and gestured with his ears, half-bent and pointing forward. She supposed she was starting to understand his signs.

"We need to keep moving?"

Of course.

There were no sounds of crashing and shattering rock, behind her, coming through the graveyard. No voices, and no dogs. She took that as a good sign. Tugging on the straps of the pack, she adjusted it on her shoulders, and gestured for Fang to lead the way.

Thirty steps for her, ten hops for him, brought them to the edge of the woods. If Ash remembered correctly, according to maps of the kingdom, she was one village away from the border between Alfordia and Cammerlang. If she could find the River Ebony before it plunged underground, it would point her in the right direction, like an arrow shot, and the shortest distance to the border.

The woods turned out to be a thin line of trees, maybe four thick. They were in and out again almost before Ash saw the moonlight on the ground on the other side. She caught her breath at the sight of the Ebony, so named because the water descended into a black hole. Right now it was a silver stream in the moonlight, so calm it looked like a flat ribbon. Ash turned sideways, orienting herself to the line of trees, then the water. She needed to go left to get to the border. According to the few soldiers who had availed themselves of the library at Fairhold, it was a two-hour ride by horseback, and a day's walk on foot, to reach the border.

Fang went right. Ash nearly called out to him, but that wasn't wise. Just because she couldn't hear pursuit didn't mean it wasn't there. It simply meant anyone out here in the moonlight and approaching the border had the skills to stay silent and unseen. She wouldn't be friendly toward someone approaching the border at night, if she were on patrol duty here. Ash wasn't about to take the risk of wearing an arrow.

She followed Fang. He raced along the bank, bouncing from one chunk of gray, faintly glowing rock to another in the moonlight. He leaped higher, seemed to hang in the air for two heartbeats, then went down. And vanished. With a splash.

Ash nearly dropped her pack as she raced up to the rock Fang had launched from and looked down. He waved his ears at her, standing in a pool of water that looked black in the shadows and moonlight, and barely covered his feet. The water went under an overhang of rock, vanishing into darkness. He bent one ear and pointed down with it. That was easy enough to understand.

Sighing, she looked around for an easier, more gradual way down. She didn't feel like jumping, and discovering that everywhere but where Fang had landed, the water was over her head. She found several rough-looking steps, like someone had hacked them out of the stone and then wind and rain had smoothed out the edges. She stepped down. Fang pointed with his left ear, then splashing softly, hopped into the darkness.

Ring, could we have some light?

The glow this time was stronger than in the tunnel, reflecting off the water.

Thank you.

My pleasure.

The sound of splashing came to her, and soon she saw where the pool ended, with overflow going down a series of steps. Fang paused at the top, watching her. When she caught up with him, he slid down to the next step with soft splats from his wet fur on the rock. Ash followed because there was no other choice. She was relieved to see that only the center of the steps, perhaps as wide as the spread of her arms, was wet. She stepped carefully on the dry right side, easily envisioning the wet soles of her boots making the rock slick, and her feet flying out from underneath her.

Fang, she suspected, was having far too much fun, considering the circumstances. Should a rabbit or any other variant of the species, even the magical variant of bunnies, enjoy all this mucking around in the dark and wet and hurtling into unexplored, unfamiliar places? Unless this underground place wasn't unfamiliar to him? Maybe he had brought her down here because he did know the way? That should have been comforting, but all those wretched considerations kept rising to the front of her thoughts. He was supposedly fleeing for his life from unjust murder charges. How or why a rabbit or bunny warren would press such charges was just a little too much for her mind to grapple with right now. Plus thinking too long on what Hazel had said would eventually force her to contemplate whether those charges were just after all. Yes, he had a taste for red food, but surely bunnies, if they were indeed magical, could tell the difference between red juice or pulp, and actual blood? Ash supposed that someone might have taken advantage of his strange tastes and committed murder, and made it look as if he were guilty. She was quite familiar with unjust accusations by the actual guilty party.

They reached the bottom of the steps. The pool of light from the ring didn't extend far enough to see what lay ahead of them, other than more darkness above and before and to the right. The trickle of water that had come down the steps formed another pool to her left.

Fang bounced several times, splatting and shaking out his wet fur. Then he hurtled forward again, with several flicks of his ears, clearly indicating she should follow. How else could she interpret those unnatural bends in his ears, except for the crooking of two rather large fingers, beckoning her closer?

"Where are we going?"

Her voice echoed back in chimes. Something nearby was made of glass or maybe crystal. The lack of anything close enough to reflect the light indicated some vast, open space. Should that be comforting, or frightening?

"Are we in a cavern? Have I fulfilled one of the items in the quest?" A chuckle escaped her. "Well, maybe Lathia helped me, in trying to interfere with my quest. I hope that doesn't mean I owe her something. Does it, ring?"

Indeed, I should think not. Especially since her intention is to capture you and force you to do all the work. More specifically, all the thinking. And I'm afraid that her two assigned servants are already plotting how to foist her care entirely on you, so they can abandon her as soon as they cross a border and are legally free of her father's authority.

"How do you know all this?"

The echo-chimes sounded a little closer. She envisioned massive crystalline growths hanging from the ceiling. Either the ceiling was getting closer, or the growths were longer and larger. Ash shuddered and pushed away an image of gigantic crystalline teeth, blocking her way. Perhaps she was in the mouth of some gigantic rock creature that ate its way through stone and earth?

Oh, her ring and I are in contact. Often on these quests, we're the only company each other has. It takes quite a while for our wearers to figure out that we're there, and some of them never think deeply enough to ask for help. They think we're just there to keep watch on them. My friend is a little jealous of my luck in being with you. She's thoroughly disgusted with Lathia already, and they haven't even set out on the road yet. She's more than happy to pass on everything the selfish little twitterhead thinks and says, to warn us. We're not exactly forbidden to offer help or speak until spoken to, but she's taking her cue from Camwell's thoughts and feelings. He rather hopes Lathia is miserable and learns a valuable lesson. He's quite looking forward to her being revolted and terrified when she realizes she has had a companion looking into her selfish, whiny thoughts all during the quest.

"When will you and the other ring be free of us?" Ash asked after several moments considering all the things he had revealed, said and implied. She had been about to ask when she and Lathia would be free of the rings, but it occurred to her that no matter how onerous it was to be a servant, it had to be ten times worse for the spirit rings.

The ring chuckled, vibrating on her finger, tickling a little, rather than making a sound she heard with her ears.

Bless you, child. How did you grow to be so polite? It has been my experience that those who are forced into proper manners have a tendency to be the opposite when they aren't being watched by their superiors.

"Oh, Lady Charlotte spends time with all of us, talking with us, teaching us how to think and consider. It only makes sense that we should act the same way toward everyone, just like we should always try to tell the truth. It's just easier. We don't have to keep remembering how we acted or what we said, and try to support it and be consistent, if we tell the truth all the time and we're polite all the time."

And does that sort of training actually work?

Chapter Eight

"I suppose so. Most of the time anyway."

Fascinating. Your Lord Digory and Lady Charlotte are unique people. The sort of people King Ebrosion would like all his nobles to be. As it is in the palace, so it is in the castles, so it is in the villages, and gradually the entire kingdom. Or at least, in theory. Nasty examples and brutality are so much easier to spread than proper manners and kindness.

Ash caught her breath as she realized that Fang had vanished, from hearing as well as sight. No splatting hops, or soft thuds.

Now, as to your question. We will be loosed from your fingers and summoned back to our master by magic when the quest is complete. Supposedly, only one of you needs to complete the quest, but Camwell has the ability to adjust the terms of the magic to adapt to the needs of those being punished. And sadly, to adjust to his own curiosity and tolerance.

"Tolerance?"

He may grow so disgusted with Lathia that he sets her free early, so he doesn't have to endure any more of her pettiness and whining, or anything embarrassing she does. You ... well, he seemed particularly interested in how you would fare. He looks forward to being quite entertained as you figure out riddles and escape tight situations.

"Meaning he will keep you with me longer than necessary? For entertainment?"

I fear so. Try not to be too clever?

Ash laughed, despite the concern for Fang that was already tightening the cords in her throat and prompting her to walk softer and slower.

"Do you see Fang anywhere?"

Hmm ... odd. He seems to have stepped through a temporary doorway in realms.

"Doorway? Realms?"

Oh, you do have quite a lot to learn about magic. Despite the wealth of books in your castle library, obviously you didn't have access to the right ones. There are multiple layers or perhaps the right word should be echoes, vibrations, copies of the physical realm you inhabit. Like a musical scale, I suppose, where each half-note is another world, just a sideways step away. Multiple people can occupy the same space, but you and the other someones standing in your shoes are not aware of each other. And thank A'theosius, not affecting each other.

"Ring, what do I do? I can't leave Fang behind. I have the feeling Hazel made me as responsible for him as he is for me."

"Well, that's a refreshing attitude," a scratchy tenor voice said. The sound came from the source of the crystalline echoes overhead.

"Hello? Who are you? Where are you?" Ash shook her head. "Please, if you've taken Fang, could you give him back?" She remembered all the warnings, all the mistakes made by adventurers in a dozen stories with situations exactly like this. "I'm very sorry if we've gone where we shouldn't be, and if we've broken anything. We're rather distracted, fleeing from trouble."

"Yes, I know," the voice said. "Your friend is rather excitable, isn't he? He's something of a rare find, even for a bunny. Do come in and sit for a while, won't you? It will be much easier for me to examine you if we're in the same place and time."

A line of light appeared in the air only three steps away. Ash held perfectly still when every instinct shouted for her to run. The line extended down to the cavern floor, and rose to just higher than her head, at which point it turned a sharp angle, running parallel to the floor. Then it pivoted, showing an edge as thick as her hand. She fought a moment of dizziness as her perceptions slid sideways, and suddenly there was a door of darkness hanging in the air. Through the opening, she saw a massive room, with couches scattered here and there, bins full of scrolls, lanterns hanging from nothing in mid-air, shelves full of books, other shelves full of dishes and goblets, and enormous tapestries covering the walls, hanging from a ceiling at least three stories overhead. Ash took a step forward, then stopped, feeling a little queasy, when she realized the tapestry directly in front of her was moving. As if the unicorn and lion and gryphon woven into it were alive.

The gryphon turned its head, looked directly at her, and winked.

"Come in, do come in, keep out the draft, please," the tenor voice said, coming through the doorway now instead of overhead.

It's all right, the ring said. *I've been granted access to the knowledge in this sideways dimension. This is Blaz, the border guard. And you haven't done anything wrong.*

"The border between kingdoms?" Ash had to consciously tell her foot to move, and the other one to follow. She stepped into the vast, well-lit place, and felt the door out of the darkness swing closed, felt the reverberation as it thudded into place. She turned quickly, in time to see the line of light vanish from mid-air.

Then her eyes adjusted, and she looked all around, her mouth dropping open as she took in bookshelves rising as high as the ceiling three stories overhead. It was made entirely of softly glowing crystals that shimmered through the spectrum as she gazed at it. Ash thought of the glory of having so many books to read, then wondered how anyone could get to those books, because she didn't see any ladders.

Then she saw Blaz, or rather the man she assumed to be Blaz. He looked rather shabby-comfortable, a bony face and long neck and bony hands sticking out of oversized, saggy trousers and shirt, with a long robe over them, and a multicolored sweep of knitting wrapping in loops several times around his neck. His curly ebony hair looked tangled, his nose was long and pointed, and his scraggly beard hung down in a waterfall of fuzz nearly to his belt.

More important, he floated down from a point in the bookshelves two-thirds of the way up to the ceiling. So that answered the question of accessing all those glorious books.

"Sir Blaz?" Ash bowed, because after all she was wearing trousers, not a skirt.

She wondered if she would have to start curtseying, once she had to start wearing a dress at least part of the time. After all, her secret was out. Warrior maidens could get away with wearing trousers, but she wasn't a warrior maiden. Women farmers wore trousers, and those in crafts where skirts would get in the way. Maidservants in castles, especially prosperous castles like Fairhold, had to wear skirts.

"Or is it Lord Blaz?" she hurried to add, and mentally gave herself a slap on the wrist for meandering in her thoughts. "What is the proper title for a magic-user, sir?"

Blaz tipped his head back and laughed, just as his feet touched the carpeted floor. He had an amazingly deep, rolling laugh for someone so thin, and in contrast to his tenor speaking voice.

"Just Blaz will do. Judging by your coronas, you and I might just be equals in the ranking of magic users."

"Coronas?"

Please don't overload her with new words and concepts, the ring said. Somehow, the voice came from all around them, instead of whispering through Ash's mind now.

"Ah. Sorry. To be brief, this is an in-between place, touching many reverberations of reality." Blaz gestured upward, spreading his arms to take in the entire amazing room. "As such, all magics go slightly out of tune. Not enough to be irritating. Goodness, now, how would I do my job if I was constantly getting headaches or itching? But enough to set up shimmers of light, as different kinds and levels and intensities of magic brush up against each other. Like the sparks you get from rubbing a silver wand with a piece of silk. You, you fascinating young creature, have several colors of magic, or at least the possibility of magic. You're still rather young for any potential to have progressed past the blooming stage."

"I have—I do?" Ash held out her arms but saw nothing.

"It takes training to see." He gestured down the length of the room, where she could just see a long table that seemed to be more neatly organized than all the other tables and shelves and clusters of chairs. "Please, let me get my assigned duty over with, and then we can relax and talk, for however long you are comfortable here. I suspect you will grow uncomfortable and need to leave sooner rather than later." He beckoned and set off down the long carpet that certainly looked like a river spilling across a grassy meadow.

Ash hesitated to step onto the blue. What if it really was water? Or what if this magic he said was in her woke up and she fell into the river? She stayed on the side, keeping her boots on the green and brown of grass and dirt and stone. After she thought she saw several fish swimming through the blue threads of water, she kept her gaze off the river altogether.

At the table, Blaz gestured her into a deep chair with high arms, piled with pillows and several fleeces. When she had put down her pack and peeled out of her coat and unslung the satchel, and was about to sit down, a smacking and swallowing sound coming from the next chair stopped her. Ash leaned over enough to look over the high arms and found Fang, chomping his way through an enormous bowl of strawberries, raspberries, tomatoes, and scarlet grapes. Juice liberally splashed his fur from above his eyebrows and down his chest. He gave her a sleepy grin, twitched his ears at her, then went face-down into the bowl again.

"Sir—"

"Oh, please, no formalities. I'm a very low-level magic user, and very young for my prestigious position." Blaz gestured around the cavern again.

Ash had the feeling he wasn't being sarcastic, but rather very proud.

"The ring said—I'm sorry, ring, but do you have a name?"

It's somewhat hard for flesh-and-blood mouths to pronounce. Ring is fine, especially since you did make the effort to be considerate. That makes all the difference in more worlds than you can count.

"All right." Ash finished settling into the chair. Weariness slammed into her, so she thought she could close her eyes and fall asleep in it in a matter of minutes. This had all the trappings of being called to judgment in front of the lord of the castle, but none of the terror and rapid searching of memory, trying to determine what she had done wrong that she had forgotten. "Blaz, the ring said you were the border guard. What border? And what do you guard against?"

"Oh, a magical border, of course, entirely braided into the physical border." He gave a grunt of satisfaction and pulled a large bound book out of the middle of a stack of equally large books. Ash estimated there was no book shorter than arm's length, or thinner than Blaz's long, bony arm. The books above it hovered for several seconds before settling down onto the others below. "Some magical creatures are forbidden to cross into other kingdoms. Either their presence in their assigned kingdoms is essential for maintaining certain magical rhythms and flows, such as ensuring that magical springs don't get stopped up. Or, they aren't allowed into other kingdoms because they'll throw off the balance of magic there. Most of the time, the magical wards maintained by each kingdom's council are enough to prevent unadvised travel. However, sometimes there are naturally occurring tunnels beneath the physical borders, and magical tunnels naturally adhere to the physical ones. Don't ask. I didn't do very well in those particular lectures and exams." He winked at her.

"The wards upheld by the mortal magic user councils allied with each kingdom, unfortunately, only extend a nautical league or so underground. Most of the effort to maintain those magical shields is expended reaching upward, to prevent flight over the border. Thus, lower-level magic users like myself are assigned to maintain the underground barriers. It's fascinating, really, how many ordinary mortals find these passageways and consider it necessary to evade the notice of the mortal border guards. Granted, there are instances where the tolls are ridiculous, so I can understand trying to save a handful of coppers or even a few silvers, but ..."

Ash held perfectly still. While she hadn't run afoul of the word, she had witnessed enough situations where the frown, coupled with saying, "but," and then a long pause usually equated trouble, or special circumstances. Usually not very pleasant, and usually inconvenient for someone. Since she was technically the only other someone in the room with Blaz, that "but" was about to fall on her.

Blaz glanced down at the open book, which seemed to have something that sparkled intermittently on the open pages. "Well, nine times out of ten, I ignore the underground travelers and let them stumble their way under the border and find their way above ground. Eight times out of ten, they don't need any help. Which is rather convenient for me, because as you can see," he gestured around the room, at the shelves and bins of books, "I have a great deal of studying to do. And I regularly receive requests for research from higher ranking magic users, which is quite gratifying ... ahem, that is neither here nor there. Although I must admit, yes, I do get a little lonely ..." He shrugged and offered a crooked little smile.

What does that have to do with Lady Ashlyn? the ring asked.

Ash flinched a little. Why had it called her Lady, and used her full name? The last time someone had addressed her as Lady Ashlyn, she had been twelve. She had accompanied Dunstan and Lord Digory and most of the servant boys between the ages of ten and eighteen on an overnight trip to deliver wagons of wheat and potatoes and a dozen protective and healing charms to Lady Millifloria's domain. A regularly recurring curse levied against her late, unlamented father had sprung up, damaging the harvest that year. Everyone had assumed that with his death the entirely justified, well-deserved curse had expired. He had been punished. The defensive charms had been allowed to lapse.

The servants had been busy hauling sacks from the wagons to the storage huts and bins with the freshly renewed protective charms, when an old blind woman came racing up the path from the laundry courtyard. At least, everyone assumed she was blind, with the cloth wrapped around her eyes and the crooked cane whacking at the stone path in front of her. A hot stab in Ash's hindquarters, like someone had caught up a coal with fire tongs and slapped it against her, startled a yelp out of her. She turned around twice, like a dog chasing its tail, and stopped to see the old woman staring at her. Which actually made no sense, because she still wore the blindfold, yet Ash felt like she was being stared at. With angry eyes. Burning eyes. The woman swung her cane around and pointed it at Ash.

"You."

Ash ran, catching up with Petroc and several other boys who hadn't noticed when she yelped and stopped. She put several slower boys between her and the blind woman. It took all her force of will not to press a hand against the burning spot on her backside.

The same spot, she realized later, where that ridiculous, bothersome blue star softly glowed at night.

The blind woman barreled through the knot of boys just as they stepped through the gate into the courtyard, for another load of sacks of wheat and potatoes. She snagged hold of Ash's left arm and turned her around, so fast she nearly fell off her feet.

"Well, well, well … found you, didn't I? Want to be a great lady, do you? Want to be queen? Would you like that? Take my advice and never let a crown rest on that pretty little head. That's a sure way to lose it. Lady Ashlyn," she finished on a gust of foul breath

The other boys noticed, while Ash froze and her breath caught in her throat. She couldn't punch or kick, despite the desperate shrieking inside her head to fight her way free. The other boys pushed the old woman away. She cackled and let go of Ash, so she fell backwards and hit her head on the courtyard paving stones. Then the woman was gone. Ash gasped for breath a few times, and it seemed like the lowering clouds of an incoming storm just evaporated, allowing bright sunlight to spill over everything. Petroc teased her about tripping over her own feet, grabbed Ash's collar and hauled her upright. Nobody had said anything about the old woman as they hurried to the wagons and got back to work.

"It's the rules," Blaz said now, glancing down at the book. "The alarms went off. I need to test her, examine her, look backward and forward, if I can."

"You said I have magic?" Ash said, desperate for something to drive that disturbing memory back into the dark corners of her mind. "Will my leaving Alfordia unbalance things?"

"Bless you, no." He chuckled. "You're several levels higher and several species different from the type that have to stay in their assigned territories. That's part of the problem: you're an unknown, unassigned, and untrained. And I'll wager unaware, too. That's a dangerous combination. And full of potential."

"What kind of potential?"

"Amazing and terrifying. All depends on the choices you've made already, and the ones you are yet to make." He sighed and smiled wearily and rested his elbows on the book, his chin in his cupped hands. "I don't know about you, but I am heartily tired of all those prophets and seers and visionaries who speak in such vague, cryptic words that can mean a dozen different things, and you only understand them after the event has come to pass and the utterly stupid decision has been made, seems like more than half the time. Am I right? Well, I'll tell you a secret. They speak that way because they can't make heads nor tails nor any sense whatsoever out of the visions or dreams that have slammed into their brains. Yet they have to say something, give warning to whoever it's aimed at before their heads explode. It's a painful, frustrating thing, being burdened with warnings in a language you can't understand, except for a few useless words here and there. And I'm frightening you, aren't I?"

"A little," Ash admitted.

She decided she rather liked Blaz. He seemed nice enough, kind enough, if frustrated.

When he got up from the table and beckoned, she followed. One of the many tapestries bundled itself up, sliding up the wall, to reveal a door. The last thing she expected was to find a cozy bedroom, complete with a bathing tub of hot water and a set of clean clothes. Even better was a small table with a tray holding a large bowl of stew, fresh, steaming bread, stewed apples, and an enormous mug of milk. Blaz told her to wash and eat and sleep as long as she needed. He had preparations to make for her testing.

"I don't suppose I can just try to slip away, while he's busy?" she asked the ring, once the door closed.

You can try all you like, but until you have enough control of whatever magic you possess to open the doorway, you'll just wander. Or more likely keep coming back to the same place you started from.

"Will the testing hurt?"

Oh, I shouldn't think so. But while you're sleeping, I think I'll do some examining of my own, try to engage some of those books and other magical objects in conversation. See if I can do some preliminary work and shorten the whole process. How does that sound?

"That sounds ..." Ash sank down on the bed and muffled a moan at how thick and soft the mattress was. It didn't rustle like a straw tick or creak like a rope bed or send up clouds of dust. "That sounds wonderful. Thank you. For all your help."

Oh, no, I believe I shall be thanking you. This is proving to be the kind of adventure spirit rings long for.

~~~~~

The room cleaned itself up while Ash slept. Her dirty, wet clothes were cleaned and dried and neatly folded, and her pack and other belongings had joined her in the room, as she discovered when she woke. Or rather, when Fang jumped on the bed and nearly bounced her out onto the floor.

His ears flapped and pointed rapidly enough to generate a breeze. She didn't have to think very long to understand he wanted her to go out. Blaz was probably ready to do her testing. The door opened when she was two steps away, and Fang bounced out into the long, fascinating room.

This time, Ash walked down the middle of the long carpet, daring the water to turn real and try to drown her. She didn't feel wet against her boots, but she swore she felt the ripples in the current, and several fish bounced against the soles of her boots.

"Well, how are you feeling now? Rested? Refreshed?" Blaz greeted her, from high overhead. He came floating down, carrying a silver oval disk large enough to cover his chest.

"Much better, thank you. Do you have servants who take care of everything?"

"Oh, no, that's one of the benefits of sitting in a pocket between dimensions. It's an expanded bag of accommodation, linked to the flow of time by the frame of the doorway. Whatever is needed, it provides, and it is aware enough to know what you needed at that time. Specifically, a comfortable bed, a bath, clean clothes, and food."

"Bag of accommodation." She tested the words with mouth and mind and didn't notice that she had sat down in front of the table where he indicated.
~~~~~

Chapter Nine

Blaz put the silver oval disk down in front of her. He picked up a white, partially transparent goblet. Ash assumed this was alabaster, though she had never seen so much in one place. Lady Beatrice had an alabaster pendant she wore on special occasions. When Blaz handed it to her, she took it and waited, sniffing at the pale silver liquid inside.

"Take a mouthful, please, and spill the rest across the visionary plate," he said.

"Swallow?" she asked. "Or just hold it in my mouth?"

He nodded, a pleased smile brightening his eyes. "Passed the first test. I thought I sensed several defensive mentoring spells wrapped around you. They have been a part of you for so long, they are somewhat difficult to detect. I'll wager if you think back, you'll find many instances where you took a slightly different path from your fellows, because it just made more sense, though you couldn't explain why. Many instances of feeling like you had been advised to do something, go against what others wanted to do? A nudge at the right time to help you regain your balance or your footing?"

"Yes," she whispered, and shivered twice.

"Such spells should fade over time. *Unless.* Unless there is magic inherent in your blood, providing a place for the defensive spells to take root and grow, and become part of you. I do wonder who took such precautions, when you were so young. Perhaps you are a princess stolen from your cradle at your christening? Child of an enchantress with powerful enemies, sent away into hiding? No, how could you know?" he said when Ash could only shake her head. "I took the liberty of asking the spirit ring what it knew about you. No need to question you about your past. Your conscious past, that is. We shall look into the past further back than what you remember. That should answer many of our questions and fulfill my duties to examine you." He gestured at the alabaster goblet. "A comfortable mouthful and hold it. Spill the rest on the plate, and then choose, will yourself, to trust me as I search."

Ash hesitated, knowing if she asked the spirit ring for confirmation, somehow Blaz would know. She didn't want to insult him. She didn't want to look like a timid little twit. She thought about what Lathia would do, if faced with the same situation.

A snort of laughter escaped her. Lathia, with inherent magic that needed to be examined? A'theosius, protect them all from that selfish little trollop having magic at her disposal. At least, more magic than nobles could obtain by hiring mages or wizards or magicians or seers or whatever levels of strength and skill were available for hire.

A'theosius, help me? Show me the truth? Guide me? This is more than I ever dared dream of.

"Ah, interesting," Blaz whispered.

"What?" She paused with the goblet touching her bottom lip.

"What did you do just now?"

"I ... I asked A'theosius for help."

"Very wise. Admitting we need help is an act of wisdom far too many magic users neglect." He gestured as if to touch the bottom of the goblet, likely to tip it up so she had to take the mouthful or spill it on herself.

Ash closed her eyes as she opened her mouth. She tasted the liquid before she felt it, as light as air, hesitating on the tip of her tongue before rushing to fill her mouth. It tasted of nothing she had ever experienced before. That was no surprise. Even if other nobles criticized the family of Castle Fairhold for "indulging" or "pampering" their servants, there were many fine things she had seen but never tasted or touched. Ash supposed this was what silver tasted like. Light and cool and somehow ... an aroma that equated to the feeling she got when she watched lightning scratch tears in the sky.

Lathia would swallow some of this liquid silver, just because she had been told not to. Ash consciously closed up her throat and breathed through her nose. She leaned forward, bowing her head a little to keep the liquid away from the back of her mouth, opened her eyes, and carefully spilled the remainder in swirls and loops across the silver plate.

Please, Blaz, see the truth. My past. Help me understand.

Mist rose up from the liquid as it spread out into a thin layer, entirely coating the silver disk. Ash trembled and nearly swallowed a few drops as shapes formed in the mist and took on color. It was an entire village, set back from the shore, with a large hill like a wall between the village and the water. Was that a dune? People stood on that hill, hands clasped, tendrils of light in blue and green and silver wreathing them, entwining them. On another hill, with the village lying in the valley between them, children played or sat and watched the people on the first hill. The same tendrils of light wreathed each child and formed a shimmering, transparent wall between them and the village.

The sea turned white and black and curled upward, reaching to the sky, rising to three times the height of the hill that protected the village. The streamers of light shot forward from the people, hitting the wall of water that churned and foamed.

"Look away," Blaz whispered. "Find yourself."

Find herself? Ash trembled, and the silver liquid in her mouth seemed to twist and thicken and push at the opening to her throat. She would choke in another moment. She turned her head and looked at the children on the second hill.

The streamers of blue and green and silver faded, then strengthened, pulsing. Until suddenly they vanished. Gray and sickly yellow light streaked down from the sky and wrapped around the children, yanking them up like weeds and tossing them forward, through the sky, over the village.

They would drown, like their parents were about to drown, crushed by the water about to slam down on them.

Ash choked, wanting to cry out warning.

A single streamer of blue-green light shot out of the staggering people, who fell to their knees under the weight of the oncoming water. The light wrapped around a handful of children, yanking them free of the yellow and gray. The opposing light shattered, like a flawed mirror, and the children flew backwards, past the hill where they had been playing moments ago. Inland, far from the water.

The wall of black and white crashed down on the people, sweeping them into and over the village, over the second hill.

"No!" Ash screamed, choking on the silver liquid, spitting it out, wiping away the mist and the images.

Fang squealed and leaped up into her lap, smashing her into the chair, clutching at her shirt with forepaws and hind paws, patting her with his ears. She choked and spat and got silver droplets on them both. She clutched at Fang and gasped for breath, and though the ache filled her eyes and lungs, she couldn't weep, she couldn't sob. Ash shuddered until the airy-silver taste faded from her tongue.

A hand on her shoulder wrung a shriek from her. She looked up, poised to rise from the chair. Blaz held out a cup to her, the fumes of strong, sweet wine filling her nose. She snatched at it and drank, nearly choking in her haste to wash the taste from her mouth. It was potent, so she felt the path of the heat that traveled down her throat, hitting her stomach, spreading out through her body with every heartbeat and breath.

"I'm sorry," he said, and stroked her hair as she swallowed the last mouthful.

"Did that really happen?" There were so many other questions to ask, but she trembled just thinking of them. She might shatter if she gave them voice. She handed him the goblet.

"Oh, yes. That was the devastation wrought by a great conflict between several confederacies of magic wielders. The sea claimed a large portion of land and wiped out entire villages before that band of enchanters and mages and apprentices stopped it at Tippessee."

"I was found at Tippessee, with other orphans, pulled out of the water and mud."

"Yes, that makes perfect sense now. How ... fascinating."

"In what way?" She shivered and was grateful for the warmth and weight of Fang, still clinging to her. She hadn't appreciated how large and furry the bunny was, until now. His solidness kept her from feeling as if she might wither up and float away as dust on the wind.

"No children with magic in their blood were found in the aftermath. It was generally believed that inimical forces swept in and snatched the children away, to either raise them as their own, to come back and finish the destruction they started, or drain them of their magic, and store it up for a future battle. That you escaped them ..." He shook his head. "Well, there is no telling how much damage has been done to them, until many years in the future, when we can look back and judge the results."

"Do you—can you tell who my parents were?" Ash gestured at the empty silver plate. Even the liquid was gone. "It was so strange. I could see individuals, even so tiny, so much detail."

"I'm sorry. Again. All I could determine was that your parents were there, perhaps a number of relatives, shared bloodlines. Magic is inherited by bloodlines, as well as learned and gained through dangerous deeds. Be comforted that your parents died heroes. If you ever go to Tippessee, you will see a memorial to them, with all their names carved into a great wall of black polished granite."

"How can they be heroes when they failed?" Her voice cracked.

Fang chittered and gripped harder, so she thought his claws would go through her sleeves and trouser legs.

"That wave was meant to wipe out several kingdoms, going across half the continent. It died, the energy behind it dissipated. That is the power of willing sacrifice. The defensive wall your kinfolk helped to weave before they died still stands. If you go to the shore ..." His eyes narrowed and he studied her long enough Ash needed to move, to get out from weight of his gaze.

Fang complied slowly when she pushed his legs down and let her slide out of the chair.

"What will I find if I go to the shore?" she asked, taking a couple steps away from the table. It took all her force of will to turn and face him.

"Don't go to the shore. The enemy keeps watch, waiting for the day that magic defense falters. Chances are good the enemy is still watching for any of the children who escaped. You were saved from likely a dire fate by Lady Charlotte carting all those orphans further inland, to Fairhold. I advise you to avoid the seashore, until you have some understanding of whatever magic you possess, and control of it."

The stars could be telltales, the spirit ring offered.

Ash startled. The ring had been silent so long, not even humming on her finger, so she forgot it was there.

"What stars?" Blaz asked.

Lady Ashlyn has a star on her bottom, and another growing between her bosoms.

"Really?" He frowned and he settled on the edge of the table, stroking his straggly beard, while his gaze went distant with thought.

Ash was grateful he didn't stare at her bosom, or worse, her backside. If he asked to see either star, she swore she would hit him so hard she would knock him out of this dimensional waiting place, into another world altogether.

"I'm sorry. Again." He sighed heavily and slumped a little. "I have no idea if the stars are warnings, if they are identification marks to help your kin find you, or ... they could be something the enemy inflicted on you, to help find you later, when you had grown into power." He shrugged. "Again, I urge you not to go to the seashore. Not until you have the means and the strength, and preferably allies, to help you withstand any attack that may come."

Ash supposed that made sense, but she didn't have to like it, or even appreciate the advice. In many of the adventures she had read, the hero always found out he was something more than what he thought he was. Royalty. Child of prophecy. Born to magic. Stolen to prevent some great good from happening. She thought that was entirely unfair. Especially for the innocent child who wanted an ordinary life and had to deal with magical powers or some heroic destiny. By what right did the Fates or other overshadowing powers inflict such destinies on people? She had read enough histories and adventures, she could guess just what was waiting to happen to her. Now, not only did she have to avoid Lathia trying to put all the work of the quest on her, but she had destiny throwing challenges and trials at her.

And there was the wretched quest to fulfill. It wasn't like she could simply take off and seek out the most boring kingdom to live in, settle down somewhere in a quiet corner of the forest and hide from the world for the rest of her life. The ring allowed Camwell to know what she was doing.

"Can the justiciar track me down?" she asked. Blaz startled, then frowned even more deeply. She had probably confused him with the question unrelated to their discussion. "Can he send people to drag me back into the quest, or is it possible to just settle somewhere and hide for the rest of my life? Hide from magic-users and quests and such?"

Yes, I'm afraid so, the ring responded after several long moments. *I'm sorry.*

"No, I should be sorry. You were hoping for an adventure. Can he punish you if you don't push me into doing exciting things for his entertainment?"

"The justiciar sounds like a rather disagreeable person," Blaz said. "I'm aware of the basic details, but not this … However, I could try to help you. Plot out a course of travel to fulfill the requirements, but in rather … hmm … boring ways."

He gave her a list of rankings by power and authority and strength of all magic-users, not to be confused with the various gifts they possessed. That took care of one requirement of the quest. When Ash emerged from the tunnels and Blaz's dimensional pocket, she would have crossed one border, as well as traveled through a cavern. Perhaps they could count as two. The physical cavern, and the magical one.

"Unless telling him about you, about this place, would put you in danger of unwanted visitors?" Ash said.

The spirit ring chuckled. *He has to get through the first hole in the ground, then travel some distance underground before he trips the first alarms at the first magical gate. Even if he had the magic to set off those alarms, his bulk will get in the way of the physical travel to get that far.*

Ash found some comfort in that. In the end, she decided to only report Blaz's cavern if she fell short on the count.

"But what if I can't hide anything from him?" she mused.

You can't, but there's nothing in the magic that says I can't, the ring responded.

"Yes, but if he's checking on me from time to time, especially since I missed the farewell ceremony … won't he check? How do we explain the gap of time when he can't see what I'm doing?"

"You're outside normal dimensions. That means time, as well," Blaz said. "When you leave here, I'll put you back at the same place and time that you entered. I can also put a temporary forgetting spell on you, so you don't think about here, or me, if the justiciar tries to dig too deeply into your mind. It's all rather basic … hmm, actually, not so basic. Fussing with time, reweaving the loops, that takes some skill and strength. Fortunately, I have to be skilled in that area, to keep my little domain safely anchored and yet free."

Ash agreed to the defensive measure, but only after he assured her that eventually she would remember her stay in the cavern. She might not have liked the revelation of what had happened to her family, but that didn't mean she wanted to forget. Someday, when she could defend herself and keep from being noticed by whatever watchful enemy magic might be lying in wait, she wanted to return to Tippessee and track down her kin.

~~~~~
~~~~~

Ash didn't mind the darkness of the cavern when the door to Blaz's domain closed behind her. There was something comforting about it, even if it was just an illusion of being able to hide from Camwell. By her judgment, it was still several hours until dawn. She could get across the tri-part border of Alfordia, Cammerlang and Nordwell, if she could be said to be "across" it when she went under it and be several hours of walking into Nordwell before anyone realized she was gone. She hoped Camwell found Lathia's fury and disappointment very entertaining, and he would be disappointed in the dark, seemingly boring cavern she was now traveling through, when he finally checked on her.

She had the map Blaz had put together for her, and a handy little misdirection spell woven around it, to be triggered by any magic strong enough to touch her thoughts. The ring was woven with several spells, of varying strengths of intensity and invasion. The lightest simply let Camwell watch what was going on around her, seeing through the ring itself. Then there was another spell to hear what was being said or happening around her. Then another to see through her eyes. Another to share her senses, such as heat and cold, the taste of food, smells, and even pain. And lastly, the strongest one, and the one she feared: to look into her mind, to share her thoughts. If Camwell saw the map she used and investigated, the misdirection spell would awaken, covering up her memory of the entirely enjoyable hours spent with Blaz. It would be replaced with a false memory of finding the map in a chest in the library of Castle Fairhold.

She and Blaz plotted the map to guide Ash and Fang from one cavern to another, with as short a distance as possible between them, and across several borders as quickly as possible. The goal was to fulfill the conditions of the quest as quickly as possible, with the least exposure to interfering, distrustful officials in each kingdom. Blaz had done as much research as he could, even asking advice of other magical border crossing guards to find the most boring caverns possible for Ash to investigate. At least, boring in terms of magical items or influences. They chose caverns with splendid rock formations and enchanting underground streams, and one place an entire city built in the cavern and abandoned generations ago, with no clues to the identities of the builders.

Camwell wanted a travel log, and he would get one. Just not a magical adventure.

After she walked perhaps an hour, with only the light of the ring extending before her maybe the distance of ten steps, the cavern narrowed into a tunnel that took her upward. After another fifteen minutes or so, the ring doused his light. Ash nearly cried out in protest, but her eyes adjusted enough to let her see a patch of stars among the darkness. That was the mouth of the tunnel, not that far ahead of her.

We are safely in Nordwell now, the ring announced.

That bit of good news put some life back into her legs. She was wise enough not to put on speed and waste that extra energy. She still had some climbing to do until she was out and above ground. Fang didn't have any reservations on that score. He chirped happily and bounced ahead, leaving her far behind in mere moments. She counted the dull thumps of his hops and calculated the distance between them, then estimated how many more steps she had to take. Ash laughed at herself when she emerged into the open air eighteen steps sooner than she had guessed. Fang must have taken longer leaps than she had estimated.

The ring helped her study the stars and calculate where they had come above ground. He pointed out a bright star, just a little larger than the others, sitting on the tops of the trees directly in front of her, and told her to head straight toward it until dawn erased it from sight.

Ash walked until the first grayish light of pre-dawn touched the horizon to her left. She breathed out a sigh of mixed weariness and relief. Navigating by the stars was another skill she hadn't been able to pursue but had hoped to learn when she went adventuring with Dunstan. She had feared when dawn came up, she would find the eastern horizon behind her, and she would be heading due west, toward the seashore and that possibly dangerous monument at Tippessee.

"Well, Fang, we're three hours into Nordwell. Should we find some place to rest for a little while? Maybe we should sleep during the day and travel at night?" Ash turned, walking backward a few steps, and looked back the way they had come.

There was nothing in the rolling landscape to indicate exactly where she had left Alfordia behind, and where the north-south border between Cammerlang and Nordwell lay. She hadn't felt anything unusual when she left the kingdom that had been her home most of her life. Maybe that was because she had been essentially forced to leave. Right this moment, the servant boys she had grown up with would be waking, washing, dressing, and hopefully grumbling over her absence and how it had come about. When would someone come to rouse her from her temporary prison, and discover she was gone? How long would her friends among the servants keep the news secret from Winston and Lathia? Had Hazel managed to speak with Dunstan, so he wouldn't come early in the morning to help her escape? She hoped Lord Digory and Lady Beatrice would laugh, when they realized she had fled in the night.

Chapter Ten

Fang bounded off the packed dirt path they had been following. It was a straighter path than the road of packed gravel indicated on Blaz's map, maybe a quarter mile to the east of her, and maintained by the kingdom of Nordwell. The official road had been formed to guide travelers to the various inns and marketplaces that had the crown's approval and support. It meandered and sometimes made wide, weaving curves. The dirt path used by the common people was as straight as possible, to make their travels direct and swift, since most of them traveled on foot. Hiding among the common people suited Ash perfectly. Taking winding roads might be all right for nobles who wanted to be seen, and who had the money to pay the tolls and the higher prices charged by the inns along the way. Ash planned to sleep in the shelter of bushes.

That was how travelers found shelter and safe, hidden beds according to the books she had read. The real world might be different from the stories. That bit of advice, phrased several different ways, came from Pegleg Rufus and Seneschal Gilbert, and Myrtle.

Fang bounced across a field that seemed to be mostly weeds. Ash could see nothing growing there that looked like a food plant, or perhaps flax or cotton. It certainly wasn't a vineyard. She eyed the ditch running between the road and the field, a sure sign that this land belonged to someone who wanted to keep it free of flooding and turning into one massive river of mud. She took a few steps backward, then hurtled herself forward, stretching her legs to leap the gap.

"Ring, do you recognize these plants?" she asked, as she headed across the field, following the diminishing white dot of Fang.

She had a better view of the plants now. They were a tangle of intersecting stems, with dark green, palm-shaped leaves edged in black, and tiny, heart-shaped, deep crimson flowers. They exuded a coppery odor, mixed with something spicy-sweet when she stepped on them. Ash couldn't avoid stepping on them. There was no place to step that wasn't covered with the long, pale green stems. Or were they vines? Tendrils?

I believe it is called bloodweed, the ring finally said.

"Never heard of it. Well, considering the library at Fairhold was limited, according to Blaz ... what is it for? Do they eat the roots? The stems? I don't see any kind of grain or fruit. Just the leaves and flowers. Or is it an herbal? Medicine?"

I don't know. Sorry. If you think the Fairhold library was limited, you should see the paucity of reading material at Camwell's estate. If it wasn't for the fact that he travels, and we rings get a chance to converse with other magic objects and try to scavenge information from the libraries of the estates and castles where he stays ... well, we're pretty much limited to whatever official paperwork comes through his hands, otherwise. Ah ha, and that's where I saw bloodweed mentioned and described. The ring paused.

Ash looked ahead, afraid for a moment when she didn't see Fang. No, there he was, hopping madly out of a small hillock ... no, that wasn't a hillock. Her perception adjusted as she hurried forward, decreasing the distance. That was a small house, covered in bloodweed. Behind it lay several larger hillocks. She assumed those were other houses or maybe barns and outbuildings for a farm. Also covered with bloodweed.

Sorry, the only reference to bloodweed in Camwell's correspondence is a request for advice on dealing with it. It seems to be trying to creep over the borders of Alfordia from Halvol. I guess Nordwell has an infestation of the stuff too, but it hasn't come near the border yet, so Alfordia's officials aren't aware of it.

"So it's just a weed?"

And rather pernicious. There were comments about burning not doing much good, that the smoke just seemed to make side effects of the weed itself twenty times worse. There were references to several academic studies on preparations for dealing with the side effects before the burning took place. What strikes me odd is advice to read the collected works of the Helsingvan family before doing anything else. Camwell had quite a long, critical response when he read that addendum to the communication.

"Helsingvan? What country are they from?" Ash kept her gaze fixed on the gaping doorway of what she assumed was the barn. Fang had gone in there, his bounds much shorter and slower. She felt rather chilled as she waited and silently counted her heartbeats until he came back out.

I'm not really sure. Camwell has little respect for them and is rather upset every time he sees some collected volumes of their work for sale. In multiple languages. They are somewhat migratory, going from country to country gathering up legends and then determining if the stories of various monstrous creatures and places and darkly magical objects are truth or wish-tales.

"Monstrous creatures? As in twisted, warped things created by spells gone wrong and evil enchanters and sorcerers and mages and such?"

And apprentices who don't pay attention, or decide they know everything and start experimenting before they learn half of what they should.

"Somehow, I don't think it's wise to mock people who investigate such things. Since monsters and broken magic are very real, and dangerous."

Hmm, yes.

"So ... is bloodweed broken magic gone wrong and dark?"

That would be the logical assumption. I recommend you find Fang and retrace your steps and find some other place to sleep away the daylight. Or travel by day and find some nice, solid, charm-protected inn to spend the night.

"That sounds lovely." She shuddered and stopped, maybe ten steps from the opening of the barn. "Fang! Where are you? We need to –"

Fang darted out of the barn, taking a long leap that brought him nearly to Ash. He bounced up and down, gesticulating wildly with his ears, his eyes wide and threatening to bulge from their sockets. His forepaws swiped down across his face, following the line of his massive front teeth, repeatedly.

"What's in there?"

I don't know, the ring said. *It's hard to look inside his mind. There are so many tangled images. I'm seeing bloodweed and … oh, dear, how distressing. Dried up, dead, looking rather frightened.*

"Is there anything alive in there?"

No. And I think that's the problem.

"How can anything dead be a … it's not the plague is it?"

I don't think so. The ring didn't sound nearly as certain as she would have wished.

"I'm going in." Ash put down her pack, took a couple deep breaths, and squared her shoulders. She drew her belt knife, just in case. Just in case of what, she wasn't sure, because the ring had said nothing was alive in there.

Fang had stopped bouncing in front of her and had darted away, back the way they both had come. Ash started forward, walking on her toes, just in case noise roused something that shouldn't have been able to rouse because it wasn't alive.

Right now, she had the awful feeling that despite all the reading she had done, she didn't know even a fraction of all the things she needed to know to survive and win this quest contest.

Fang screamed. A bunny's scream was ten times louder and harsher and shriller than the shriek of a rabbit or hare caught in a trap or doing battle over females or grazing space. Ash nearly dropped her knife. She turned sharply to glare at him, refusing to shout and scold him because, after all, she wanted to be quiet.

He came bounding at her and she darted to the right, then ducked, avoiding what was clearly an effort to hit her. Ash spun around on one heel and ran into the bloodweed-draped doorway of the barn. Thin shafts of light cut through the darkness yet made it harder to see where she was going. And what lay before her. She caught her foot on something that shifted slightly, so she stumbled more than tripped over it. Ash tried to leap over the obstruction, and her other foot came down on something else that gave way, with a crackling sound. She twisted, trying to get off it, turning to the doorway just in time for Fang to slam into her chest. They stumbled backward, tripping again over the crackling, snapping things.

Ash landed with an *oof* of breath knocked out of her in moldy hay. At least, she hoped it was hay and not something noxious. Bad enough dust surrounded her, filling her mouth and eyes. She coughed and spat and shoved Fang away. His claws dug into her shirt, tearing it slightly. He held on, thumping her with his hind feet and his ears.

"Ring! Some light, please? And can you calm him down?"

You need to get out of here, the ring responded. He didn't glow as she had hoped. The ring's voice in her mind had a quiet sadness that chilled her more than the fear she had tripped over something dangerous and cranky, and it was awakening. And hungry.

"Right." She pushed hard on Fang with one hand and caught hold of the scruff of his neck with the other, and somehow yanked him free. Ash struggled to her feet, holding the struggling bunny out at arm's length. Easier to do that than fling him away as she dearly longed to do. Picking up her feet carefully, putting them down slowly, she kept her gaze focused on the light on the other side of the doorway. It seemed hours of walking away.

Fang calmed a little with every step, so by the time she stepped into the spill of light, even though she wasn't out of the barn yet, he hung from her hand, making little bleating sounds, and tapping her arm with his ears, in what she took as a conciliatory fashion.

"All right," she said, when she was entirely out of the barn. She put down Fang, fighting the urge to fling him to the ground and hope he bounced a few times. She paused to brush more of that dust off her arms, her jacket, her pants, and raked her fingers through her hair. Dust with a faded golden sheen flew everywhere, which was a relief. It was simple hay dust, nothing more. "What was that?"

Fang found dead bodies. The farmer and his wife and two grown sons.

"Are you sure?"

Bunnies have incredible night vision. He says they were all dried up, like old leather, but there was enough left of their clothes to tell what they were.

"Does bloodweed do that?"

I have no idea. I'm very sorry.

She bit back a retort that he had been saying that quite often lately. It wasn't the ring's fault that he didn't have the information she needed. As he had inferred, the only way he could gather information was to be exposed to books and documents and listen to people talking.

Once she got back to the beaten dirt path, Ash took the time to make sketches of the bloodweed plant, its different parts, using one of the bound blank books Blaz had given her. He had encouraged her to record what she saw and did and thought and learned on this journey. Once it was written down, she didn't have to keep thinking about it to keep it in her memory, and that way she could keep much of her adventures private, safe from Justiciar Camwell's snooping.

"All right, now should we still try to find a place to sleep the rest of the day away? You'd think all that excitement would have me wide awake, but I'm more tired than ever."

Ash looked back down the way they had come, toward the border of Nordwell and Alfordia. Then she turned and looked the other direction, to the unknown things lying ahead. At the very least, she could walk until she got to fields not overrun with bloodweed, and then take her chances. The ring agreed with her. Fang woke with a snort and a yawn as soon as she nudged him, and they headed off down the path again.

The path joined up with a road after another hour of walking. Ash assumed it could be called a road since the surface was pebbles rather than hard-packed dirt. She felt rather discouraged that the bloodweed still crept up to the edge of the ditch. When she commented on it, the ring pointed out the plant didn't look as thick and healthy as when they first encountered it. Perhaps the people of Nordwell hadn't sent to other countries asking for help in dealing with the weed because they had found a cure, or at least something that was attacking the plant.

Ash thought that was rather selfish. Especially since the cure, if there was a cure, had come a little late for that family lying in the barn, all dried up. Perhaps when they encountered people, they could ask what exactly bloodweed did.

"Don't you find it odd that we haven't encountered any people yet?" she asked, after another twenty minutes of walking. The bloodweed was indeed dying away, and other weeds were visible, darker shades of green and stalks of brown, and thistles of all kinds.

This part of the country is useless for farming, dominated by bloodweed, the ring responded after a few moments. *Why would anyone come this way?*

"True."

The road intersected another, which was again just plain packed dirt. Ash turned down the new road, which had no signs of bloodweed in the plants along the ditch. The ground looked like it had been tilled a short while ago, with neat ridges topped by fresh leaves and stems. Still, no signs of people doing any work. When she spotted a small shelter in the middle of a field, she picked her way down the neat rows and crept inside to sleep before she staggered entirely off her feet and went face-first into the ditch. Fang sighed loudly and curled up next to her. She used her pack as a pillow and was asleep before she thought to ask the ring to wake her in three hours.

~~~~~

Sunset woke her, spearing through the low door of the shelter. Ash closed her eyes against the pain, then her stomach punished her into full
~~~~~

wakefulness. She dug in her pack for some dried apples Myrtle had given her, and the crispy, salty wafers of travel bread. Now she needed something to drink, but at least her stomach didn't hurt.

"Fang? Ring, where's Fang?" Her voice was a little sharp, mostly from a sense of guilt that she hadn't noticed the bunny's absence while she was waking and then eating. Then a little more guilt over her relief that she hadn't had to share her skimpy provisions with him. Fang had already proven to be something of a glutton.

Out finding something to eat. He was quite upset that you had nothing he liked in your pack, the ring responded. He sounded amused.

"I need to get back on the road. I don't need to be caught by the farmer and accused of stealing." She raked her fingers through her hair, rubbed her eyes one last time, and crept out of the little shelter, dragging the pack and her cloak and satchel behind her. "Can he find us, do you think?"

The question is if we're able to lose him at all. The ring sounded amused.

Ash took that as a good sign. She picked her way down the rows, looking left and right for signs of people. Had the farmer and his family or hired hands finished up their work for the day and already gone home? Where had they been when she crawled into the shelter hours ago?

She continued down the road, watching for signs of the farmer's home. She hoped no one would mind if she asked for water. She had a small water sack Blaz had given her that he told her would hold everything she wanted to put in it, but not get any heavier and not expand. He hadn't been able to fill it for her inside the cavern, though, because of rules of clashing magic. The jug where he obtained all his water for drinking and washing and cooking was also magic. Apparently it was against the rules of magic to take from one magical container to fill another. Ash wondered just how long someone had to study to understand all the picky, fiddly rules of magic that seemed to lack common sense at times. Certainly, the world didn't seem large enough to hold all the books that were needed to hold all the rules. No wonder most successful magic users, no matter their rank, seemed to be old. Or at least have many wrinkles and streaks of gray or silver or white hair. Probably from the strain of years of study.

There he is, ahead of us, the ring announced, just as Ash spotted something in the distance that she hoped would be the farmhouse.

The road was headed due south, with the sunset and lengthening shadows on their right. The hoped-for building was on the left, vanishing into the encroaching dusk.

The dull white blur of Fang bounding down the road glowed faintly. Ash wondered if that was just the effect of the day fading into twilight, or perhaps a touch of the magic inherent in bunnies. That was something she would have to deal with soon: learning all the little details that made bunnies magical creatures. She supposed that would take up several hours of talking with and learning from the ring.

Oh dear, has he gotten himself into trouble? the ring said.

Ash saw it. A blur sat on the horizon directly behind Fang, where the road met the sky. That blur was moving. Following Fang. And if she wasn't mistaken, catching up with him.

That blur resolved into a group of horsemen, generating quite a bit of dust as they rode.

"He's moving rather fast, isn't he?" she said, and stepped to the side of the road. Ash had a sudden vision of Fang running into her with enough force to knock her over even harder and more painfully than he had in the barn. And those horsemen would run them both over, blinded by dust and whatever had them tearing down the road so quickly.

Bunnies can move faster than horses, when they need to, the ring said. *What did that idiot do to have those soldiers chasing him?*

"Soldiers?" Ash looked at the distant house that had vanished into the twilight altogether. There was no way she could leap the ditch and race there and beg shelter before the horsemen caught up with her. "Fang, what did you do?"

Then Fang reached her and bounded past her at an angle, leaping over the ditch. Ash raised her arms to shield herself as the soldiers shouted and their horses shrieked and skidded to a stop amid a deafening clamor of stomping and curses and jangling tack and the shrill sound of swords coming out of sheaths. All suddenly pointed at her.

"Where's the vampire?" the big, bald man with a black patch over his left eye demanded.

"The what?" Ash's legs threatened to fold, as weak as her voice suddenly.

"There it is, Captain!" another soldier shouted, and leaped from the saddle, over Ash's head, clipping the side of her head with his boot heel.

Fang shrieked as Ash went to her knees. The world spun around her for a few seconds and she fought to catch her breath as the hot tang of her own blood filled her nose. Hands snatched at her and men shouted and Fang screamed and struggled. Ash blinked stars and darkness out of her eyes as the hands pulled her back to her feet. Fang fell at her feet, so thoroughly tangled in a net that he couldn't twist enough to get his teeth on the ropes. Though he certainly tried. His face and the fur of his chest were liberally splashed with something dark red, almost black in the deepening shadows. It certainly looked like blood, she had to admit, but how could anyone confuse a lunatic bunny for a vampire?

"What did you do, you idiot?" she cried.

"Is this menace with you?" the captain of the soldiers barked.

He didn't give her time to answer. A gesture to one of his men resulted in Ash, whose head still felt rather wobbly and achy, being pulled up into a rather uncomfortable perch on the front of the soldier's saddle. Someone else grabbed up her pack, and a third soldier took charge of Fang, wrapping straps around the ropes to bind and paralyze him even further. The soldiers turned their horses and raced back down the road the way they had come.

The jolting ride aggravated the ache in Ash's head and she vomited up the little bit she had eaten. The soldier holding her leaned her out from the saddle with a tight grip on the back of her collar. He called out and the company slowed to a walk. It was all she could do to hold onto the front of the saddle while her head swam.

"Huh," the soldier said, when she finished. "Think that's proof, Captain?"

"I'll admit the boy isn't one, but that doesn't mean he isn't a slave of the vile thing." The captain turned in his saddle to glance at Ash with a clearly suspicious gleam in his eyes and a sneer twisting his mouth under his full moustache.

"Fang isn't a vampire," Ash said, after she had spat twice, to get rid of the bile burning her mouth. "He's a bunny."

"He might look like one," the soldier holding her said. "Doesn't mean much. Vampires can become all sorts of things and take over all sorts of things. I've heard tell they can turn into mist and trick women into breathing them so they can breed with them, and when their bellies are big, out burst a hundred bats." He grunted. "Or was it rats?"

"That's not how it's done," the captain growled. "Leave the thinking and book learning to the magistrate." He glanced back again and scowled at Fang, who just struggled and twisted harder, trying to get his teeth around one of the straps. "Give it a good dose, enough to make it sleep."

Ash felt queasy enough, she decided to be quiet and wait until they stopped. Probably to hand her and Fang over to the magistrate. She watched a soldier ride up alongside the horse carrying Fang. He opened up a leather flask and poured a dark liquid all over the bunny. The now-familiar scent of copper and spices filled the air. Fang sputtered and kicked harder and blinked away the liquid but didn't stop struggling.

"I used it all, Captain, and it didn't do a bit of good," the soldier with the flask announced.

Chapter Eleven

"What's it supposed to do?" Ash asked. *Ring? Have you figured out anything?*

Indeed I have. The ring sounded relieved and a little eager. *It appears that bloodweed is supposed to have an intoxicating effect on vampires. The captain is carrying a booklet in his saddle bag with all sorts of instructions on using bloodweed and how to deal with vampires in various situations. The flask, I must to assume, has a potion of bloodweed, and they expected it to put Fang to sleep.*

"Fang isn't a vampire," Ash said. "Bloodweed won't do anything to him. He's just a crazy bunny that likes to eat red things."

"What about them huge teeth?" the soldier at the back of the group called out. "Sure looks like a vampire to me."

"Your sister has huge teeth," the soldier with the flask said. "Does that make her a vampire?"

Several soldiers chuckled. The captain sighed, loudly, and nudged his horse to a faster pace. The rest of the company followed suit, and soon Ash was swallowing hard and taking deep breaths, trying to fight the queasies again.

Interesting, the ring said. The sound of his voice in her head countered the spinning, rising and falling sensation. Ash was grateful. *There's an entire section in the booklet about how to help the farmers eradicate bloodweed without burning. It appears that the bloodweed ash attracts vampires from hundreds of miles away. The bloodweed was imported from some dark kingdom beyond the Dragonspine Mountains. That should have been warning enough not to have anything to do with the weed, but the rulers of several kingdoms imported it, believing it would help in the battle against several invading tribes of vampires. Bloodweed is rather like catnip for them. A strong enough concentration will intoxicate them, unable to defend themselves, and thus easy to capture and kill. However, no one warned the kings that bloodweed grew faster than tubegrass in the tropics. It's taking over acres of the best farmland every month, and is difficult to eradicate.*

Why don't I feel sorry for them? she responded, and nearly wept when the blur on the horizon ahead of them resolved into the outskirts of a town. Soon, the thudding of hooves on packed dirt and pebbles changed to the clatter of hooves on cobblestones.

The next half hour or so was a jumble of shouts and people gathering around and cries for the vampire to be burned and demands for more bloodweed juice, and the captain barking orders to several people at once. Then, mercifully, a woman with authority in her voice ordered that the prisoners be put where they couldn't escape, and to send for a healer. Ash gratefully stumbled across a shadowy room to huddle on a bench and try to will away the hot throbbing on the side of her head. She nearly cried aloud when a cloud of spices surrounded her and a gentle, cool hand touched her head and tipped it back. She opened her eyes to look into a pair of startling green eyes ringed with gold, surrounded by a frizzy halo of white hair.

"Hurt something awful, doesn't it?" The woman's voice was quiet and low, with a humming of power underneath it. "Captain Creiklan, since when do you resort to trying to break your prisoners' heads off their shoulders? Without a trial?" she added.

"Accident," the captain said. His voice was almost unrecognizable with gentleness. He stepped into Ash's field of vision. "Sorry about that, boy. But you really do need to choose your companions better."

"Fang isn't a vampire," Ash said.

"That remains to be proven. How's your head now?"

She opened her mouth to retort that nothing had changed, but then she realized it had. The heat and the throbbing were gone. The white-haired woman, obviously a healer, smiled and handed her a wet cloth.

"Wash the blood off, lad. It's never wise to have open wounds when vampires are about," she said.

"Fang isn't—"

"Not talking about the bunny." She patted Ash's hand. "Your accent says you're from north of us. What possessed you to go wandering straight into the center of the battle against vampires?"

"Didn't know there were any," Ash mumbled, and pressed the cloth against the spot that had finally stopped aching. Most of the blood she wiped away had dried. From the amount, she had to wonder just how deep the wound had been.

The healer, who didn't give her name, left instructions that "the lad" should be allowed to sleep. That was difficult, because regular squeals and thumps and angry, muffled soldier voices came through the wall. Judging by the sounds, Fang was undergoing tests or treatments meant to keep a vampire subdued. Ash gave up shouting that Fang wasn't a vampire after she realized that calling him Fang didn't help him. The soldiers would just have to learn the hard way. How many tests did they have for identifying a vampire? Was it possible Fang might fail one?

Dawn came, far too soon. Captain Creiklan stomped into the room where Ash had dozed off again and told her, more kindly than before, to get up. She knew better than to ask if she could have some water to wash with, or even a bit of bread, although she was even more hungry than before. So, she was surprised when a soldier brought in a tray with a pitcher of water and bowl and towel, and a steaming bowl of porridge. Ash thanked them, which seemed to surprise them. Obviously, Lady Charlotte's insistence that everyone learn good manners and use them wasn't a universal practice.

She washed, trying to be thorough while hurrying. The water had a faintly oily feel, and a hint of some aroma she couldn't identify. Maybe plants grew on the sides of the well and left a residue. It wasn't unpleasant, just different. All that mattered was being clean. It felt more glorious than she cared to admit.

Ash covered her face with her hands to pray before eating. She peeked through her fingers and nearly laughed when the soldier bowed his head, and Captain Creiklan shuffled his feet, looking somewhat uneasy. It was nice to know the big, gruff, scarred man feared someone and something. She tried to ignore them, just standing there, watching her, as she picked up the flat spoon and started eating. Common sense said to eat slowly, if the queasies hadn't gone entirely away. She took small mouthfuls and chewed thoroughly. Even though the porridge was fine in texture, she chewed, letting small bits slide down her throat so she wouldn't lose it again.

On her third mouthful, she caught a slight coppery aftertaste. Ash sniffed at the porridge when she took her fourth mouthful. There was a spicy hint in the steam that didn't come through in the taste. What was it?

The fifth mouthful went down her throat at the same moment she realized what it was.

Bloodweed in the porridge.

The next moment, she was on her knees, retching. Captain Creiklan held the washing bowl under her mouth, to catch what came up. The soldier handed her the towel, dampened from what remained of the water in the pitcher.

"You wanted me to get sick?" she blurted, as she settled back on the stool.

"Technically," a woman said, in that same authoritative voice she had heard last night, "yes, we hoped you would." She walked through the door, wearing a long, dark blue hooded cloak. Her thick blond hair was braided and wrapped around her head like a crown, and a large golden key-shaped pin held her cloak closed.

"I'm not a vampire," Ash insisted.

"No, of course not. We use bloodweed to make us safe from vampires. They can't stand the taste of our blood. But bloodweed is also useful in detecting those with magic in their blood."

"You could have just asked me."

"Yes, we could have." She stepped over and caught Ash's chin with two fingers, to tip her head back. "Why are you traveling with that demented bunny that thinks it's a vampire?"

"Fang doesn't think any such thing. He just likes red food, and he's a messy eater."

"Hmm, that remains to be seen. Well, boy ...your arrival is most timely."

They want something from you, the ring said.

Ash held back a sarcastic response in her thoughts.

"Timely for what?" she asked.

'Bloodweed, in sufficient quantities, will intoxicate vampires into slumber. I could say a death-like slumber, but they are already dead." She sighed. "We have cultivated the bloodweed so it entirely surrounds the cavern where the infestation of vampires have settled. They are trapped."

I don't think so, the ring said. *Caverns always have dozens of entrances that can't be detected until it's too late to stop someone from getting in or getting out. If they're dug out by water and wind, then it stands to reason new openings are constantly being formed.*

Hush and let me listen! Ash retorted. Her head throbbed once from the force of her thoughts, mixed with lingering queasiness.

"With enough exposure, the vampires should fall deeply enough asleep that they will never awaken," the woman said. "The simple solution is to keep cultivating the bloodweed around the cavern, but it has escaped our control and threatens to not only overrun Nordwell, but spread over the borders to other kingdoms. Wars have been fought over far less damaging circumstances. We need to start burning out and cutting back the bloodweed, but doing so will reduce its strength around the cavern. We need to send someone in to determine if the vampires have dried up and gone to dust."

Is that what happened to the farmer and his family that we found? she asked the ring.

I don't think so. I would assume they were drained dry by the vampires.

Why didn't they turn into vampires, then? Did the bloodweed prevent it?

That's one of the many ridiculously wrong myths about vampires. It takes an exchange of blood between vampire and victim for that to happen, and the victim needs to have magic in his blood to push him over the edge into the transformation. Even then, it takes quite a large amount of blood. Too little magic, and the transformation is only halfway. Or even less.

How can a transformation be only partial?

You could have fangs, but no taste for blood, the ring responded after a pause. *Or worse, a strong taste for blood, and no fangs to make it easy to harvest.*

Ash thought she might be sick again. She was heartily sick of being sick.

The woman looked expectantly at her. Clearly, she wanted Ash to ask the logical question, but Ash knew better. Asking could be taken as volunteering. Her education might be lacking important elements, but she wasn't stupid.

"Magistrate, the boy doesn't understand," Captain Creiklan said.

"No, the boy understands far too well." She shook her head, sighing loudly, but visibly fought a smile. "We need someone with enough magic in their blood to resist the soporific effects of the bloodweed. In high enough concentrations, it makes ordinary mortals sleepy, slows their minds. If the vampires are not entirely asleep, they could be rather defensive, excitable. The magic in your blood will defend you against their blandishments, and even make you somewhat distasteful to them. Or so the research says.

Ring? Is she right? Ash asked, and was grateful she could speak in her mind to the ring. She wasn't at all willing to trust these people, that they wouldn't take the ring from her, or anything else they thought was magical or valuable.

Hmm, just because something is written down doesn't mean it's true, the ring said. *Besides, common sense says if bloodweed acts like catnip for vampires, and the smoke from burning it out of the fields attracts them, then the trap they've set to capture vampires is likely drawing more, who could burn the bloodweed outside the cavern and set the others free.*

"You don't have anyone with magic in their blood?" Ash asked. "What about the healer?"

"We have precious few with magic in their blood, and we cannot risk losing any more of them," the magistrate said.

"More?"

"Vampires are skilled seducers." Captain Creiklan snorted. "We've lost two already, who went in and decided they liked it better with the vampires."

"A boy who doesn't belong to anyone, with magic in his blood and a strange, manic companion is the perfect tool for our purposes," the magistrate added.

Don't tell them, the ring snapped, his voice loud enough to hurt inside Ash's head.

She had barely begun to consider admitting she was a girl. Now, she had to agree. Revealing her secret wouldn't make a bit of difference. These people were willing to risk a stranger's life.

"Where is the cavern?" she asked on a sigh. *Ring, do you think if there are always openings that nobody knows about, we can work our way around the vampires and escape this wretched place before they realize?*

Anything is possible. But you might want to catch up on all your missed prayers.

Ash hoped it wasn't too late to follow the ring's advice. The first obstacle she ran into, before a soldier returned to the prison house with the map, was when the magistrate informed her they would hold Fang prisoner until she returned. Ash took no encouragement from the fact the magistrate said "when" rather than "if" she returned.

"I need Fang. He defends me. He's fast enough to outrun vampires."

At least, she hoped so. The ring had said, after all, that most of the stories and legends of vampires were false, so hopefully their speed was one of the misbeliefs.

"He can dig through stone with those teeth, and he bounces around and jumps on things and knocks people out with his enormous feet," Ash added.

"Hmm, I can believe that," the magistrate said. "Why are you traveling with the misbegotten creature?"

"I was falsely accused of attacking a nobleman's daughter, and I have to prove my innocence in a trial by quest."

That earned a chuckle from her. "A handsome young lad like you probably seduces maidens with just a glance, no need for force."

Ash thought she might be sick at the very blatant flattery. That mixed oddly with the need to laugh, and a sliver of fear at the thought of the magistrate's reaction if she ever learned how neatly she had been deceived. Definitely, she had to find her way to the other side of that cavern and get out as quickly as possible, and never look back.

But she couldn't do that if Fang was locked up here.

Maybe she hadn't neglected her prayers as much as she feared, because the magistrate thought a little more, then gave in. Fang could accompany her into the cavern. Captain Creiklan muttered something about, "If they fail, at least the vampires will eat the freakish creature."

The soldier finally returned with the map. Ash spread it out and pretended to study it, while she moved her hand with the ring across the map, letting her companion study it.

Good news, and bad news, and frustrating news, the ring announced just a few moments later. *The vampires' cavern is one of those Blaz marked as empty and boring and safe to explore, as long as you keep to the upper galleries and don't go lower than the water tables.*

Of course, Ash responded with a sigh. *I wouldn't have expected anything less.*

Well, it just proves Nordwell is so utterly ashamed by how they messed up the plan to rid themselves of vampires, they're keeping the news of the infestation from getting out to anyone.

The villagers escorted Ash and Fang, still bound up tight and unable to bite anything, to the edge of the rocky valley where the cavern lay. Numerous people along the way assured her that going into the cavern in the daylight would ensure the vampires would be sound asleep, even if the bloodweed hadn't entirely worked. She would have plenty of time to find them and ram stakes soaked in bloodweed oil through every one of their hearts, and none of them would wake up.

Are they really that stupid? she asked the ring when she was finally left alone long enough to think. *Just because it's daylight doesn't mean the vampires are asleep if they're underground and in the dark.*

Yes, I fear they really are that stupid. They're so dependent on the thousands of fables and wish-tales, they've given up thinking for themselves. A little common sense could have helped them avoid the whole bloodweed problem.

What about the belief that vampires can't cross running water?

Also false. And garlic only makes them sneeze and have watery eyes. Granted, if you have enough garlic you'll make them sick and drive them away, but it's not a good, long-term protection. Garlic is better used by eating it and strengthening the blood to fight diseases.

In between uncountable useless bits of helpful advice from the villagers, the ring regaled her with more utterly ludicrous beliefs and stories about vampires. Ash nearly laughed aloud when he mentioned the belief that if a vampire stepped out into sunlight and sparkled, that was a sign he was on the verge of regaining his soul and eradicating his vampirism.

No real vampire has ever sparkled. Just by the simple fact that strong enough sunlight will burn him to a crisp long before any sparkling can begin. The ring made a rude noise, again challenging Ash's self-control, to keep from laughing. *Vampires don't need to regain their souls because they never lost their souls. They're an entirely different race. They can't make ordinary mortals vampires simply by drinking their blood.*

Then where did the belief come from that —

The escort stopped. They stood at the top of a rocky slope. The gaping mouth of the cavern, like a yawning man, etched in red-streaked and gold-streaked stone, waited for them. Ash played with the idea of putting a metal tray down at the top of the slope and riding it downward and into the hole. But no. While the slope was certainly steep enough to slide all the way down, she saw cracks and bumps and chunks of rock strewn all across the landscape before her.

Still, it might have been fun. If there wasn't so much danger ahead of her. Besides, she didn't have a tray.

"Well, Fang? Are you ready?" she asked, once the soldiers dumped the bunny out of the net wrapped around him.

He's ready. And eager to punch some vampires in the face, the ring responded, translating the rapid bouncing in place and squeaks escaping the bunny.

Do you have an idea how we can get through this cavern without running into any vampires, and come out far enough away they won't be able to catch us?

Considering how little similarity there is between the maps and reality? Sorry.

Ash was certainly tired of hearing the ring say he was sorry.

She pulled her shoulders back and tugged her pack up more securely into place. As far as she could tell, everything was still in it, despite being searched several times by the soldiers. The bits and pieces everyone had given her before she fled the castle were ordinary and quite frankly pitiful enough, she hadn't needed to argue with the magistrate to let her leave everything in her pack when they loaded it with the bloodweed-soaked stakes to hopefully kill the vampires.

Either it never occurred to the magistrate or Captain Creiklan that letting her take her possessions meant she could try to run away, or they thought her only means of escape was out of this end of the cavern. With all those soldiers waiting at the top of the slope, her chances of escaping in this direction were very small. Maybe they didn't know about the other openings into and therefore out of the cavern? Or maybe the map Blaz provided her was even less accurate than the ring feared?

There was only one direction to go: down and in and through. As swiftly and silently as possible. Ash nodded farewell to the magistrate and soldiers and started walking. If they thought she was making a silent pledge of success, let them. She meant it as farewell. Politeness, as Lady Charlotte had said numerous times, was always the wisest course of action. Politeness, Ash had discovered too many times, meant not correcting the mistaken assumptions of her superiors. Or her captors.

Far too soon, she reached the bottom of the slope. Fang had bounded ahead of her, but now he waited just inside the gaping mouth, sitting still and leaning inward. Very visibly listening. His ears slowly twitched forward and back.

"Anything?" she asked him when she caught up with him. "Ring?"

I sense nothing moving.

"That doesn't mean much if there are vampires in there, does it?"

Chapter Twelve

On the contrary, vampires do breathe. They don't need to, except to speak, but it's hard for all but the oldest vampires to break themselves of the habit. And their hearts still pump blood, just not as swiftly as mortal hearts.

Ash decided to be encouraged by that information. She said a silent prayer, mostly consisting of, "A'theosius, please help me? Keep me alive?" and stepped into the shadowy mouth of the cavern. The ring stayed quiet and dark until she had taken perhaps twenty steps into the darkness. Then he lit up, a soft, greenish light that spilled downward and forward, but not upward. That was helpful. She had an image of those soldiers noticing the light and coming down to learn the source, and maybe taking the ring away from her.

The cavern was quiet, but not the pulsing quiet of intensely staring, unfriendly eyes or dark, slithering things waiting to pounce. This was the quiet of soft breathing. Ash realized she felt a gentle flow of air, going past her toward the entrance behind her.

"If we follow that breeze to the source, will it get us out?"

Likely. But I fear the breeze is strong enough that the opening is too close, and someone will be waiting. They are rather cowardly, these people, but that doesn't exactly mean they are stupid.

Another hundred steps, slowly angling downward, and the gentle touch of air proved to come from a hole high up in the roof of the cavern. Sunlight spilled down. Ash paused to look up and study the cavern walls, hoping to find a natural stairway, or at least ledges and holes in the rock face that would allow her to climb. A shadow moved across the hole, and she saw the lower half of a soldier walking past. It gave her a good idea of just how small the hole was. And it proved the ring was right.

"Fang, lead the way?"

He chirped several times and the glow of his fur in the ring light seemed to grow stronger.

Ring, is Fang glowing on his own?

I believe so. The oldest bunnies are able to do that.

How old is old for them?

Oh … perhaps two hundred years.

Ash decided to be impressed.

If they don't make silly mistakes, the ring continued in a thoughtful tone, *and get themselves caught and turned into stew, or jump too high and knock themselves lightless, or fall too far down to bounce. It's really sad, how careless some magical creatures get when they confuse longevity with immortality.*

Oh. She made a mental note to write that down, once she got out of this cavern.

Fang bounced quietly ahead of them, disappearing for several minutes at a time, then bouncing back and pointing the way. Ash appreciated him scouting ahead, and hoped he wasn't taking ridiculous risks. He could bounce out of trouble, couldn't he? Of course, if vampires could fly, his ability to bounce might not be very helpful.

"Ring, can vampires fly?"

Only if they're old enough to change shape.

"How old is that?"

It depends on who's telling the story. And if the vampires they interviewed were telling the truth. There are the vampires who claim to be much older than they really are, to impress people, and the ones who are vain enough to want to be considered much younger than they are.

"What does it matter if they're immortal? Are vampires immortal?"

There's no way to be truly certain. They're not exactly popular, so they have no reason to tell the truth, either way.

"Were they lying about being able to make mortals immortal by drinking their blood?"

Well … yes and no. Ordinary mortals, no. Mortals with magic in their blood, yes. But they also have to drink the vampire's blood.

Ash gagged quietly. Then she stopped short.

"I have magic in my blood, according to the magistrate. Could they have made me eat that porridge with bloodweed in it to … trick me?"

I sincerely hope not, because that makes them rather more despicable than they are already, sending an innocent girl into the darkness to find out if the vampires are sleeping. They are depending on the magic in your blood to protect you.

"Can the vampires tell the difference in me? Can they sense my magic? Even if I can't sense it?" She thought of those dratted glowing stars. If that wasn't proof, she didn't know what was, and that wasn't much comfort right now.

"Indeed we can and we do and we have," a low, purring sort of voice said, coming out of the darkness.

And oddly, directly overhead.

Fang bounced back toward Ash, letting out a little scream and making his claws scrape on the stone floor of the cavern. He bounced high, glowing brighter, and illuminated a man crouched upside down on the roof perhaps two full stories above Ash's head. He nodded politely to her, looking as comfortable as another man would be taking a rest on a rolling meadow after a long walk.

Ring?

Yes, the ring said, *that is a vampire.*

How can you tell?

Besides his ability to hang upside down from the ceiling?

Ash wasn't sure if she should laugh, blush, scream, or pray this was just a bad dream and she would wake up and find out she had been dreaming, a victim of the spring fevers, and was still at Castle Fairhold.

"Hello." She wished the sharpened, bloodweed-soaked stakes had been packed completely out of sight in her pack. "We're just passing through. Honest. Those people who made us come down here are rather adamant we can do something."

"Yes," the man said. His smile looked odd, upside down as it was. Ash kept wanting to see it as a frown of menace. "Everything is funneled down into the mouth of the cavern. Wind, snow, the stench of bloodweed, and sound. And the acoustics are wonderful in here. We have no need to post sentinels. We get warning of invasion from miles away."

"Excuse me? Acoustics?"

"It's the study of sound. Our tribe is very popular for our skills with musical instruments and singing."

"Oh." Ash shifted her feet. She had the awful feeling that running would do her no good. Rather, it would just make the vampire overhead sure that she was there for no good, and he would chase her. Just how skilled was Fang with his teeth? Could he defend her? And if the vampires could hear everything that went on within the cavern, how long would it take for other vampires to know this one was in a battle, and come help him?

"If you're collecting lore, you might find it interesting that emotions have odors. At least, among … well, I was going to say the lower orders, meaning you ordinary mortals. But you're not ordinary, are you?" Again that widening of his smile, which looked even more frightening upside down. "Be that as it may, mortals have physical reactions twenty times more potent than my kind. By the way, we don't refer to ourselves as vampires. We've come up with many names, the most commonly used being nightborn. The more poetic among us refer to us as the children of the night. Inferring that you mortals are children of the day."

"That doesn't sound so bad," she offered.

"No, it doesn't. It implies balance, and each staying in their own territory."

"Please, I really am just trying to pass through and get out as far away from those people as possible. Maybe in another country altogether."

"These caverns are quite extensive. We don't pay much attention to your mortal boundaries and politics and such, but yes … I think the waterfall doorway does open onto a different geo-political system.

Suppose I act as your guide? What would you give me in recompense?"

"She has nothing," the ring said. Audibly.

Ash stumbled backward and flung out her hand. As if that would do her any good? She was stunned first to hear the ring with her ears rather than in her mind. And frightened by the feel of tiny prickles of heat, in synchronization with the words.

"I didn't know — why didn't you tell me you could speak aloud?"

"You didn't ask. And quite frankly ... I wasn't exactly sure I could do it. However, while I know our friend up there can hear me in our normal mode of conversation, it takes some effort for him to hear, and it isn't wise to give a vampire a headache. Excuse me, it isn't wise to inflict pain on one of the nightborn," the ring amended.

"You are too kind. And a little amusing," the vampire added. He chuckled, a rumbly sort of sound. His feet detached from the roof of the cavern and he plummeted straight down, startling a yelp out of Ash. He slowed inexplicably two man-heights above the cavern floor and turned so he landed on his feet.

Now his smile looked more normal, but that really wasn't much comfort, since his face was bathed in the mixed glow from the ring and from Fang, who stayed pressed up against Ash's legs, vibrating with a silent growl. She didn't know bunnies — or hares or rabbits or coneys — could growl. Squeak and shriek and chirp, yes. Growl, no. Then again, Fang wasn't ordinary even for his own kind.

"Before you ask," the ring continued, "she can't remove me, so you can't in all fairness demand that I be given in payment for acting as our guide."

"Hmm, interesting. This sounds like a story I might enjoy. And that's something else my kind is passionate about, besides music and collecting all sorts of unusual aromas. Stories. One's tastes become rather refined, and in some ways limited, when you have the potential of living for centuries. If we're lucky, we manage to collect so many songs and so many stories, when we hear something we haven't heard in decades, it feels new." He made a low, liquid sort of bow. "That is the bargain, I think. I will guide you to the waterfall entrance of the cavern, and you shall tell me stories. Starting with how such an odd trio came together."

"I don't know that many stories," Ash said. "And I've been a servant all my life, so I don't know that you'd find anything I could tell you interesting."

"On the contrary, you're already quite fascinating. A polite, cautious, intelligent, well-spoken maiden disguised as a boy, accompanied by a bunny, wearing a spirit ring, and unwilling to wreak violence and become a hero?" He chuckled. Oddly, now that he was right side up, the vampire's laughter didn't strike her as quite so menacing. "I am Morris. And you are?"

"I'm Ash. And this is Fang. And the ring is just the ring. I can't pronounce his name."

"Can't? Or won't?" Morris tipped his head to one side, his smile going chilly for just a moment. "Is this one of those tricks, where the name of a magical object invokes a curse or does something ridiculous to anyone who's been giving you trouble?"

"No, she is entirely telling the truth," the ring said. "My name in the tongue of the spirit rings is entirely unpronounceable by mouths of flesh and blood. Even the very different flesh and blood of your kind." Instead of prickles of fire, now the ring vibrated, his voice tickling her finger.

"Well, she at least is telling the truth … So, do we have a bargain?" Morris held out his long, elegantly slender hand. Ash didn't let herself hesitate to clasp it. She managed to hold back her little yelp of surprise that his skin wasn't clammy or cold or stiff, like she expected one of the living dead to feel.

"I agree, if ring does. And Fang. What do you think, Fang?" She looked down at the bunny, who finally let go of her legs. Ash nearly gasped at the sensation of pins and needles immediately racing down her legs. Fang had been holding on tightly enough to cut off feeling.

Fang took two steps away from her and stood up on his hind legs, head tilted back, ears flattened down the back of his head, and studied Morris for several long seconds. Then he nodded and dropped down into his usual resting crouch, and his ears came up. They flexed and bent and pointed forward, flapping in what she had learned was his way of saying yes. She supposed he was essentially saying, "Yes, let's go."

"Very good." Morris gestured to the right. "It would be helpful, friend ring, if you doused your light and allowed the cave growths to light our way. They're rather colorful and pleasant to look at, and some combinations are soothing to the mind."

Fang chirped and went up on his hind legs, spreading his arms and bending his ears forward and down to tap his chest. Ash's ears ached in sympathy, as she tried to figure out how he did that without breaking his long ears off at the roots.

Morris laughed. "Forgive me, hoppy friend. Yes, please douse your light as well."

Fang nodded once and his glow faded out, just a little faster than the ring's greenish light. Ash closed her eyes, encouraging them to adjust to darkness faster. Then she realized she was afraid to open them and find that Morris had been either playing a trick on her or exaggerating. Her only choices, she knew, were to turn around and throw herself on the questionable mercy of Captain Creiklan and the magistrate, plunge into the darkness on her own, constantly fearing that every sound or breath of air would herald a vampire attack, or trust Morris was as friendly as he had presented himself. She opened her eyes and prayed she hadn't hesitated too long. It was not wise to insult the creature of the night who had offered to help her.

"Oh," she whispered, as streaks and swirls and pillars of luminous pink and purple and green and blue in multiple shades and variations grew into gentle life all around her. Now she could make out the dripping teeth of rock coming down from the ceiling, and the lumps and dips in the floor, and just where the walls bent in and out, wavering to show the force of wind and water through the years, all of it stretching far into the distance.

"Fascinating," the ring said. "I have heard of such things, but none of the questers who wore me ever went into caverns like this. I wonder if this is why Camwell made caverns part of the requirements this time. The man can be rather ridiculous, if the truth must be known."

"I grow more curious by the moment," Morris said. "This shall be quite an enjoyable walk, I can see." He bowed and gestured down a wing of the cavern where the roof angled gently downwards. "This way. It is not the shortest path, but it is the easiest for those who can't walk on the ceiling or stop breathing for half an hour or so."

"Why stop breathing?" Ash asked. Then she thought of something. "Wait." Her hands shook slightly as she put her pack down and pulled the bloodweed-soaked stakes out of it. Friar Ipswich and Lady Charlotte had both spoken to the castle children about how gestures of good faith and trust always generated more good faith and trust. "Where can I put these so they don't offend anyone?"

"You can leave them right here. There are several creeping creatures that enjoy the taste of bloodweed. They'll eat it all up in, oh, the space of a fortnight." Morris nodded as she put the stakes down. "Thank you. Now ... what are these requirements you mentioned?"

Ash let the ring carry the conversation for the first hour or so. She was delighted to discover he really was a talented storyteller. He started by introducing the various characters in the story that involved her. Then he explained Justiciar Camwell's passion for travel stories, and his intent to prove science and magic could work together and support each other. He had a growing disdain for those self-proclaimed scientists from other lands and enchanters and sorcerers and wizards who insisted the two canceled each other out. Quite viciously and passionately at times.

Morris was a good listener. He made all the appropriate sympathetic and disgusted and amused sounds in all the right places, as the story of Lathia's ambush and Ash's defense unfolded. Once he passed the point of the girls receiving their rings, the ring passed the story over to Ash. That irritated her a little, because she much preferred to listen to stories rather than tell stories, especially her own. Especially when the ring interrupted every few sentences. He either made her back up and give details she had left out, or he added in little actions of others that she hadn't witnessed, but he had thanks to Lathia's spirit ring and various magical items scattered throughout Castle Fairhold.

"Wait. That glass teardrop in Lady Charlotte's window is magical?" she blurted. "I thought it was just decoration."

"That glass teardrop is the tear of a phoenix, given to Lady Charlotte's great-great-grandmother as a gift and blessing," the ring said. "Such things don't ensure all-enveloping healing and defense against illness, because their powers are limited. Barring great crises and waves of plagues, a teardrop that size can protect a castle the size of Fairhold for … oh … two hundred years. It eventually runs out of healing magic. The greater the crisis it has to work against, the faster it shrinks and wears out. It lost half its size when it kept the yellow spot from devastating the entire castle and the surrounding three villages."

That gave Ash quite a bit to think about. She had to be prodded to continue her story. The ring continued to stop her to add details, and Morris asked questions, as she related how Friar Ipswich and Hazel had given her advice, and Fang had come to join her on the journey. Morris was gently amused by their escape from the castle.

Ash hesitated to talk about Blaz and his cavern home, hidden between layers of reality. She wasn't sure if she was betraying him, somehow. Still, it wasn't like she had opened any doors or stumbled through a passageway to his cavern. He had pulled her in.

"Ah, a bag of accommodation. I should like to see one of those, someday," Morris said, when she described the room she had slept in, that fed her and provided bathing and clean clothes. "You have had quite an adventure already. If only the purpose of bloodweed had turned out as the enchanters intended, I could go on adventures like that."

"Wait. Enchanters made bloodweed?"

"Oh, indeed. But finish your story, please. Relate how you got from the border guardian's cavern to this one."

Ash did so, again hesitating when she got to the farm overrun with bloodweed. She mentally slapped herself. Just when would she learn to think fast enough, to avoid awkward moments like this? Clearly, the farmer and his family had been drained by the vampires.

"I know what you're thinking," Morris said. "Dreadful sight, I imagine. No, the fate of Branly and his wife and sons is a sad one, but we did not kill them. In some sense, they killed themselves. Through greed."

"How?" Her voice cracked a little. Ash was surprised that she wanted to believe him.

"Well … the shameful truth is that my kind is quite able to breed with your kind. We have no control over which parent the children will take after. It can be quite painful when a mortal mother can't raise her children in the daylight, and the converse, when a nightborn father can only visit his children at night, when they're asleep, and their mortal relatives either raise those children to despise or fear their father, or to be ashamed of their mixed blood. And sadly, for several generations afterward, a child can be born on either side who has to leave their parents, because they took after a grandparent or great-grandparent they never met." Morris sighed. "Branley is great-great-grandson of my cousin Serena. And his wife is the granddaughter of ... let me see, I can't recall the name now. Both marriages were those passionate affairs that poets so foolishly celebrate, love snatched from the jaws of death and all that rot. Two young people choose each other to defy their parents, but when the going gets tough and they long for the lives they each had left behind, the marriage dissolves. Although how you could call it a marriage, when no priest of either faith would officiate ..." Morris shook his head. "What matters is that both Branley and his wife, Elorra, had mixed blood. They thought they could make a tidy profit growing bloodweed, refining and concentrating it—"

"To use against you? Like that soldier used it on Fang, when he thought he was a vampire?"

"Gracious, no!" Morris wrinkled up his nose. "Bloodweed is an intoxicant, and when the nauseating properties are refined out of the mixture, it can be quite ... addicting. Branley intended to grow rich pandering to the weaknesses and boredom of his nightborn relatives. However, his family's mixed blood made them susceptible to the bloodweed's other qualities. When their farm was overrun with the first blooming this spring, they were overcome. Several of us tried to warn them, but they wouldn't leave their farm and come take shelter with us. The ugly side of bloodweed is that it puts out thousands of tiny roots, finer than hairs, to spread across the land, and when it finds warm-blooded creatures that sit still for too long, those roots drain their blood away. I would wager what you saw ... well, the family has been dead for five days at the most. I talked to Branley six days ago, and he laughed at me and threatened to douse me in bloodweed elixir if I didn't stop being such a prophet of doom and gloom."

"Idiot," the ring said. "And greedy, which just compounds the stupidity."

Chapter Thirteen

Morris sighed and nodded. He honestly seemed saddened by what he had related. Ash wondered what it was like to have a relative, of any kind, even as distant as Branley was to him. Blaz had revealed what kind of people her parents were, but until she visited that monument in Tippessee, she didn't even have a hint at names or homes or relatives.

When Morris asked her to continue, she told how she had found the small shelter in the field and how Fang had gone searching for food and found something messy and red, so it convinced the soldiers he was a vampire. Morris chuckled when she described the chase and winced when she told how she had been kicked and knocked unconscious for a moment. He clucked his tongue a few times as she related the sequence of events, the questioning and being fed bloodweed in the porridge.

"Oh, how very wrong they are. Eating bloodweed doesn't make them distasteful to us. It makes resisting the urge to drain them dry even harder, because the euphoria of bloodweed remains in mortal blood, but the intoxicants are filtered out." He shook his head. "The true irony is that quite a few people in that wretched village are regular providers of blood. The bloodweed in their food makes them oblivious when we come to feed, and heals them quickly, so there are no marks. It's really rather ironic and a little amusing, but ..." He waved for her to continue.

The rest of the story was anti-climactic. Ash told how she and Fang had come down the slope into the cave.

"And then you met us. Or were you sitting there on the ceiling, waiting for us to come to you?"

"Oh, I was sitting there for some time, but I wasn't really waiting. I was deep in thought, so I didn't even know you were there until you were nearly underneath me." He chuckled. "I decided the next several years shall be devoted to writing poetry. I rather like the image of the lonely, isolated, melancholy poet, so I decided to wander in the portions of the cavern everyone avoids. It's entirely by chance I came this far from the inhabited areas. And I have to admit ... this is far more fun than sitting and dreaming up rhymes."

"Just how big is the cavern?" the ring said. "I get the inference your people live nowhere within reach of those villagers."

"Gracious, no. They would have to come in here and walk for two days straight just to get close to our residential caverns. You think these growths that light our way are lovely?" Morris gestured at a particularly fascinating swirling pattern of greens that darkened and lightened and darkened again. "They're rather plain, compared to the colors and brightness and patterns in the cultivated areas. No, we retreated far enough back that the fumes from bloodweed in all its growth cycles could never reach us. Nobody comes out this far at this time of the year because it's the blooming season, and the fumes are twice as potent."

"You mentioned enchanters made bloodweed?" Ash said.

"Oh, indeed. Some enchanters among the nightborn thought they were powerful enough and wise enough to manipulate the very seeds of life within living things. They wanted to combine several plants to create a general ... well, you can't really call it an antidote, can you, when being nightborn isn't a disease? But they wanted to alleviate some of the less appealing aspects of being nightborn. At least, less appealing from the mortal point of view. The goal was to help us stop drinking mortal blood, and just get by on strictly animal blood. And allow us to walk in the sunlight, to protect us from the fear you mortals feel toward us. And the brutal results." He sighed. "It didn't work out as they hoped. It wasn't really their fault. An alliance of enchanters and sorcerers decided they had no right to try such a thing and set out to punish them for their arrogance. It turned into a massive war of magic, and the newly born bloodweed plant was warped, turned into an intoxicant that would eventually build up in our bodies to poison us and kill us." He shrugged and spread his hands out, palms up, in a "What can you do?" gesture.

"That's awful," Ash said. "And so unfair."

"Thank you. We believe so." He sighed. "And yet, we do have hope. I have found it strangely fulfilling to sit in darkness and watch sunrises. Do not ask me why, because I cannot explain it even to myself. Except perhaps for the oldest prophecies ..." Morris shrugged. "But that is ... a story for another time. Ring, tell us a story from your many travels?"

The ring complied, and told many stories of brave people and cowards, thieves and falsely accused criminals, desperate folk and those who made foolish decisions or were tricked by schemers. Ash wondered if the ring picked some of those stories to teach her, and perhaps to warn her. They reminded her of many stories she had read in the Fairhold library. She had devoured every story and adventure where magic had some part to play in the outcome. Ash thought she had a glimmer of the pattern that seemed to influence actions and outcomes throughout the world. There was a sense of current, of purpose, of some greater power moving things and people and events. A general tide sweeping all of creation toward some grand, just outcome. Perhaps because she had magic in her blood, born of people who worked with magic, this tide had pushed her to where she was now? The current of justice and purpose and perhaps fate, or destiny, was pushing her to where she needed to be? Toward regaining the station in life she should have had all along? Who knew where she would be in this world right now, physically and in terms of her education, and the type of home she would have grown up in, if her parents hadn't joined that effort to defend the land from that devastating tidal wave? Was there magic, as she believed, in simply being an orphan? Or some sense of recompense for losing her parents and the life they would have given her?

Was she being moved toward the enemy whom Blaz suspected was on the hunt for her? Was she fleeing some evil overlord of magic right now, and didn't even know it? Was she being lured by roundabout means to her doom at the hands of the enemy who had killed her parents?

Such thoughts occupied her during the long silences between the ring's stories and the ensuing discussions. And then even more so after Morris shared stories of vampire history and culture and lore. She couldn't shake the odd notion that he was trying, subtly, to convince her his was a better life, more lyrical and philosophical and serene. She was grateful, when she curled up to rest, that Fang cuddled close and Morris left them alone. He said he was foraging for something they could eat, but for the first day of their journey, she always started alert at the slightest sound, sure that a horde of vampires was coming down upon them. Then after the fifth or sixth time that she sat up and Fang grumbled at her for waking him, she finally figured out that if the bunny wasn't worried, she had no reason to be so. Certainly, the ring would warn her if danger approached.

That realization allowed her to rest more completely. Physically, at least. She spent most of the quiet time thinking, perhaps too much time, in the three days she and Morris, Fang and the ring traveled underground. They splashed through trickles of water and climbed over massive ripples in the cavern floor, and slid down slopes worn smooth by flooding, sometimes pausing to look upward at sunlight filtering through crevices and sink holes high over their heads.

"Do you think you will look back on this journey with nostalgia?" Morris asked after a long period of quiet, on their third day of travel.

Ash had to take his word for it that two days had passed. She had no sense of time down here, with the soft glow of the cave growths and the muted chimes of running or trickling water, and always the smell of wet rock in her nostrils.

"Nostalgia?" She had to think to understand the word. "Fondness? Yes, I think so. This has been interesting. Despite all the walking, it has been peaceful. And somewhat comfortable. No worries about shelter."

"No, I was thinking more of longing. Wishing to go back."

Fang, hopping somewhat lazily a few paces ahead, stopped and turned to look at them. His left ear stood straight up, and his right ear bent in the middle, bobbing slightly as it pointed straight at Morris. Ash had no idea what that meant.

"I don't know," she finally said, when she couldn't think of any response that wouldn't anger or sadden him. She knew better than to relax and be careless, despite all this time walking safely in his company. Despite the ring's certainty he would fulfill his promise. Morris was a vampire, after all.

"There is still so much of the world to see," the ring responded, when the silence that stretched between them started to feel tight and strained. "So many amazing places to explore, stories to investigate. And Justiciar Camwell could send soldiers to find Ash if she doesn't make some effort to fulfill the conditions of the quest. He is a powerful man, and just petulant enough to be feared, even if he is rather more genial and generous than most in his position."

"Of course," Morris said. "A fair answer."

"Why did you ask?" Ash said. And regretted it the moment the question left her lips. She mentally slapped herself for continuing this topic that now sent chills of warning across her scalp.

"Hope."

Fang squealed and hopped away, glowing a soft bluish-white. He vanished around a bend in the tunnel, and the echoes from his thumping leaps changed, though Ash couldn't quite discern how. She just knew there was some difference in the quality of the echoes.

"What's ahead?" she asked.

"Outside." Morris shrugged.

She almost said, "Daylight?" but held back the word. If there was daylight, there would be some reflection, a bit of glow against the bend in the tunnel wall. Ash shivered a little as she realized that indeed the cavern had been shrinking around them. The ceiling had been lowering so it was no longer two stories overhead. Now, it was close to Morris's head and the cave growths weren't as numerous or colorful. The glow they gave off was mostly greenish, tending toward yellowish-white. The walls had been creeping closer on either side as they walked, and she hadn't noticed.

"Fang?" She fought down a sudden breathless sensation when the echoes of his big feet slapping against the stone stopped suddenly. "What's happened to him?"

"He's out, I suppose."

"Out? But—"

Then she heard it, through the fluttering of her heart and the soft breaths of the breeze that had accompanied them from the first moment of this long walk through darkness. It was little more than a whisper, but she felt the power in it. The promise of energy. It could become a roar if she gave it a chance, if she listened and let it draw her closer.

"The waterfall?"

"It makes a door harder to penetrate than any fortress could hope for." Morris sighed again.

She was starting to get tired of that. He had been sighing since she woke up from the last rest stop. What was his problem?

"Fang?"

What was she doing calling for him? He couldn't hear her through the roar of the waterfall. Had he gotten through? Was he outside in the fresh air? Was it night out there? Was that why she didn't see any reflection of light? How far away was that bend in the tunnel, where she could see the way out? Suddenly Ash ached to get moving. She didn't care how powerful the waterfall, how heavy the force of the falling water, she couldn't wait to step into the wet, get drenched, wash the smell and taste of stone out of her mouth and lungs and hair. She couldn't wait to get outside and find something to eat other than mushrooms and slightly slimy lichen, and blind cave fish Morris had brought her. He had been kind, finding dry hunks of wood that had fallen down through the gaps in the cavern ceiling, so she could cook the fish. Still, there was something odd, almost repulsive about cave fish, and she never wanted to taste it again.

"He's probably past the waterfall by now, enjoying himself." Morris gave her a sad smile that made her ache. If one of the younger children at Fairhold had given her that look, she would have hugged him.

Ash shivered deep inside, sensing that hugging Morris right now would be the most dangerous thing she could ever do. While he insisted that vampires fed from the wrist, she had heard too many tales of people who had been bitten in the neck, with perfect aim so one long fang pierced the thick vein and drained their life blood in moments. It was an image she couldn't shake, no matter how hard she focused on other things.

And now Fang had left her entirely alone with Morris.

"It's a beautiful world down here, isn't it?" he said.

When had they stopped walking? That bend in the tunnel ahead of them seemed hundreds of paces away.

"I need to check on Fang. What if he fell? He's always bouncing around like a maniac. This would be just the right time to lose his balance and hit his head and—and drown." Ash took two steps.

Morris caught hold of her hand, drawing a yelp from her. His hand felt cold now, even though she had held his hand dozens of times along the way when he helped her climb.

"Did I tell you of the prophecies? The promises, glimpses of the future? Of a time when, with enough magic brought into the bloodlines, we would be free of the darkness?"

"No ..."

Magic in blood? Was he going to drain her blood for its magic?

Ring? What is he talking about?

"I haven't heard that story," the ring said. The prickles of heat that accompanied his words scorched Ash's finger.

She was grateful. Morris had been holding that hand, and now he yanked his hand free.

"Where does that story come from?" the ring continued. He glowed now, and his glow was brighter than the cave growths, making them look skimpy and weak.

"Does it matter? It is one of our most precious treasures." Morris fell into step with Ash as she started forward again.

She shifted the pack on her shoulder to her other hand, putting it between them, keeping her hand full so he couldn't take it again.

"Our most ancient visionaries foresaw a day when we would have enough magic in our bloodlines that we could walk again in sunlight, with no need for stopgap measures, such as bloodweed should have been. Whenever we find a mortal with magic in their blood, we ask them to join us, to become one of us, and the children born of those unions are children of promise. I would be proud and honored and ... pleased, yes, very pleased, to make you one of us, Ash." His lips parted as he smiled, and she had the awful suspicion his fangs were twice as long as they had been the last time he smiled at her.

Did vampire fangs extend and retract? Was that how they were able to bite and drink without ripping out the throat of their victims? Ash called herself an idiot for believing him for one moment, when he said that civilized vampires preferred to drink from the wrist.

She would never call them nightborn again.

"Lady Ashlyn has a duty and promises to keep," the ring said, his tone frosty. The heat prickling out of him increased, biting her finger. Ash wouldn't be surprised if she found blisters under the ring.

"She is a servant, treated like property, out there," Morris snapped, and gestured ahead of them.

Was that a hint of light? Or if not light, then a less dark shadow?

Where was Fang?

"Here, in this world we have created, she will be a queen. She will be adored. I adore you already, my warm, bright, witty Ash," he declared, with that fervent purr in his tone that made her feel chilled again. Just like the first time he had spoken to her.

He raised his wrist to his mouth and bit down hard. Then he thrust his bleeding hand toward her, making her stumble backward until she hit the tunnel wall.

"Sweet, lovely Ash, drink from me. Then let me drink from you. Stay here with me. I am so cold, and you warm me. Let me share all the riches of this world. Let me give you a life of centuries, millennia, and all the glory of music and poetry and stories, with time enough to read every book, sing every song, play every instrument. Live forever. With me," he finished on a rasp of such pain and longing, it wrung a sob from her.

Run, the ring shouted in her mind, with such force she felt as if her head would split open.

Ash lunged at Morris. Smiling, he spread his arms. She dove, sliding between his legs, rolling and vaulting to her feet in a move she was sure she would never be able to repeat. Her heart thundered in her temples, deafening her.

"No! My love!" Morris howled.

Yes, that was a faint glow of light. She stretched her legs as far as they would go, willing herself to move quickly, ready to shrug out of the straps of her pack and let it fall, sacrifice it for speed and lightness.

"Stay with me! Be a queen. Let us worship you. Give us your magic, and give your children, our children, the power to rule the world!"

Everything in her shrieked to look back, to see where he was, how close he was. Ash knew better. That was how she had always lost races against the boys at Castle Fairhold. This was too important a race to lose. If he was catching up with her, she didn't want to know.

Why, why, why had she dumped out all those bloodweed-infused stakes? Why hadn't she kept one, a short one, just in case? It wouldn't kill Morris, but it could make him sick. Couldn't it? Slow him enough to let her get out past the waterfall?

Unless it was night. Maybe that glow was the moon. What good would it do her to get outside if Morris could follow her?

Why was it taking so long to get closer to the opening and the waterfall and freedom from the tunnel?

Ash's left foot skidded out from under her. She went down, sliding on wet stone. Her chin cracked against the ground. She tasted blood. Her ribs screamed at her. She twisted, trying to get on the side that didn't hurt, desperate to get back to her feet.

In the glow from the ring, she caught movement and looked up. Morris was right overhead, moving on all fours on the roof of the tunnel, eyes wide and bright with tears, his face twisted in agony.

Fury shot through her, driving away the aches, the fear she had broken something. He had no right to be upset. Keeping her head tipped back to watch him, refusing to turn her back on him for a second, she struggled to her feet, slung her pack back into place, and fought the urge to clasp her hand around her throat. She refused to let him see her fear, even if she knew he could smell her fear. She hoped he smelled her fury, as well, and it stopped him. She hoped it made him ill.

"Please. Stay with me. It won't hurt. You'll laugh soon and wonder why you feared."

Morris scrambled across the ceiling, moving faster than any of the long, many-legged creatures she had imagined living in the darkness down here. Ash's gorge rose at the mental comparison, and she turned, nearly tripping over her feet in her haste to keep him in sight.

She ran, terrified he would get ahead of her, drop down and block the way out of the tunnel. The sound of the waterfall grew stronger, louder, closer, but not nearly loud enough to drown out the furious racing of her heart, the wheezing of her breath, the shrill whimpers at the end of every inhalation from her aching-burning ribs.

Morris dropped down from the ceiling, yanking a shriek out of her. He turned a graceful, liquid somersault, and spread his arms and legs, taking up most of the width of the tunnel. Damp mist filtered around him, past him, caught on a breeze that moved inward from the waterfall.

Was the light brighter, coming through the water? Did she see movement? Ash couldn't be sure, with the glow of the ring interfering. Was that dawn light through the water? Whatever it took, she had to get past him. Growing daylight would protect her.

How could she get past him?

"Stay with me. I adore you."

Morris held out his wrist to her. It had healed, no sign of the bite except a few streaks of drying blood. He glanced at his wrist, and a brief flicker of sheepishness mixed with annoyance nearly wrung a chuckle from her. She was too out of breath.

"Hasn't anything I've told you, anything I've showed you, made you curious, made you hungry for what could be? Think of the power, the chance at immortality, everlasting youth. Drink of me, let me drink of you, and we can be together forever." He shrugged. "Won't that be nice?"

"Nice?" She choked, caught between stunned and pitying and frustrated, when Morris nodded, grinning. Had he perhaps hit his head crawling across the ceiling, and knocked himself witless? What made him think any girl could be persuaded by such talk?

Chapter Fourteen

His mistake, she realized in a moment of breathless clarity, was giving her a choice. He should have ambushed her while she slept, put his bleeding wrist to her mouth while he bit her wrist, and presented her with the deed done the moment she woke. The only maidens she knew of who had choices were the ones in fables, in grand adventures, and usually they faced choices that guaranteed heartbreak no matter what choice they made. Servants had more freedom to choose than the nobles they served, when it came to marriage, but those choices could be torn from them in a moment to serve the needs or whims of the nobles who held the power of life and death over them.

Ash vowed in that moment, she would never marry unless she could choose, and if the man chose her and wasn't forced to take her.

That pause to think was a mistake.

Morris bit his wrist again and leaped at her. Ash yelped and ducked out of the way, and her wet boot slipped. She went to her knees. Morris tumbled over her.

Fang burst through the wall of water into the tunnel, chattering furiously. Sparks shot off his claws where they scraped the stone. His wet fur emitted a reddish glow that turned more bloody with every heartbeat.

"No, no, no!" Morris howled as he leaped to his feet and bent to reach for Ash.

Fang hit him dead center of his chest. They went tumbling. Ash heard the thudding of his massive feet pummeling Morris in belly and chest. Morris shrieked as Fang's front teeth clamped down on his wrist. His eyes glowed red, his jaw extended, and his incisors shot out, three times longer.

Morris bit into Fang's neck, wringing a shriek from him.

Ash leaped to her feet and swung her pack with all her might. One strap tore free as it slammed into the back of Morris's head, knocking him forward, knocking Fang loose.

The bunny flopped down limp on the floor of the tunnel. Morris's head slammed into the floor and he collapsed.

Ash didn't think. She snatched up Fang under one arm, the other hand clutching her pack by its one remaining strap. She ran. She leaped, plunging through the curtain of the waterfall.

And fell.

The pool at the base of the waterfall slammed into her like hitting the paving stones of the Great Hall. Ash knew what it was like to be one of the rare, shattered glass goblets Lady Beatrice had wept over. She couldn't breathe. Which was good, because she was over her head and didn't know which way was up.

Swim. Kick. Don't give up now! The ring shouted in her head, repeating the instructions until they finally made sense. Ash's body obeyed before her mind understood.

When her head broke the surface, still too close to where the waterfall pounded into the pool, she almost didn't know what to do with the air. Gasping, sputtering, then groaning with the aching through her entire body, she nearly let herself go back down and under. Something heavy pulled down on her arms.

Fang. She still managed to hold onto Fang.

That's it, the ring said, his voice soothing inside her aching head. *Kick, hold onto him, just a little further. There, now you can put your feet down.*

Feet? Ash sputtered and kicked a little. Why was thinking so hard? Testing, she stretched out her aching legs, half-afraid she would find them broken. Her feet touched something solid. She pushed up. Blinked water out of her eyes.

Daylight. She gasped, laughing at the relief spilling through her, though she couldn't quite remember why it was so vitally important to see daylight.

Just a step further away was the edge of the pond. She lifted Fang with protesting arms and shoved him onto the rocks and moss, then stretched her arms out and put her head down, holding on and catching her breath.

Get out of the water now, you little idiot.

Irritation stirred her when nothing else could penetrate the daze that made her want to just lie there and let everything fade away. Ash clawed awkwardly at the stones and pushed with her feet, and nearly let her pack slide off her shoulder before she remembered what it was. It was so heavy.

It's full of water. Get out of the water and empty it out, the ring told her.

That made sense. At least, she thought it did.

Finally, Ash was completely out of the water, on her hands and knees, the pack lying beside her and a stream spilling out of the opening at the top. She could barely hold herself up on one arm so she could wipe hair out of her face. There, that was better. Being able to see did make a difference.

She struggled to her feet and then nearly toppled over again when she bent, at the ring's urging, to pick up Fang. She sobbed with the effort and clutched him to her chest, and began the slow, staggering walk away from the pond. Not exactly sure where she was heading, or where she should go, except she knew she had to stay out of shadows. She had to stay in the daylight. Where she would be safe.

~~~~~

The smell of smoldering fur penetrated the haze that had wrapped around Ash's mind for the last few hours. She turned her head and winced. Every muscle and every bone in her body ached. She wanted to just sit perfectly still, but sitting hurt, because even her bottom was bruised. She thought she should laugh at the ridiculousness of that, but the thought of laughing hurt, and she was afraid to inhale, and find her ribs cracked and her chest full of bruises. She feared opening her eyes.

Her finger hurt, especially.

Good. You're awake. Sorry, the ring said.

She remembered she was getting extremely tired of the ring saying he was sorry.

You really do need to get up and do something. Fang needs your help.

"Hmm? Wi' wha'?"

Thump. Something big and hard whacked against her leg.

"Oww!" Her eyes opened and she twisted aside.

Amazingly, that bit of movement didn't hurt as bad as she feared. It still hurt, and she toppled over on her side. Now she was eye-to-eye with Fang. The bunny scowled at her.

Smoke slowly wreathed around his fur. As it thickened in the air between them, his scowl turned to surprise, then to something she supposed was fear.

Ash took a deep breath. Yes, that hurt as much as she had feared. She choked and coughed. That hurt too. She pushed with her arms, trying to sit up and get out of the smoke.

Where was the smoke coming from?

"Fang. You're on fire!"

He's not burning, technically. And there are no flames. But ... I'm very sorry, Lady Ashlyn, but it seems your bunny is at least partially vampire now.

"What do you mean, partially?" Somehow, she struggled to her feet and stared down at Fang, who flopped limply from one side to the other, visibly attempting to stop the smoke. Or was that steam? Whatever it was, it came out of his fur.

He's not going to burst into flames on contact with the sun, the ring said, *but he's going to be miserable. I imagine it's worse than sunburn, especially under all that fur. You could try covering him.*

"Yes. Of course." Ash bent, groaning, and dug through her pack until she found her cloak. It was sopping wet and she winced at the thought of all her other possessions still dripping wet in there. She pulled it out and shook it, snapping water out of it. Some showered on Fang. At least the drops didn't hiss on contact. His eyes widened in momentary relief.

A long, sighing whimper escaped him when she spread the wet cloak
~~~~~

over him. He smiled and closed his eyes just as the cloak completely hid him from sight.

Ash went to her knees and gingerly settled down where apparently she had been sleeping for several hours. Long enough for the sun to climb up straight overhead and shine down into the little clearing surrounded by bushes.

"Now what do we do?"

The ring was quiet so long, Ash nearly fell asleep again.

Common sense says to avoid people who will automatically assume you are a vampire because you are accompanied by a bunny who is a vampire.

She was a little surprised that sleep crept so close, with all her aches and the pinching, hot emptiness of her stomach. Right now, she wouldn't have minded some mushrooms or that spicy moss Morris kept insisting she would enjoy, once she got used to the furry feeling in her mouth.

Morris. She had to get as far away from the waterfall as she could. Just how fast could he travel when night came? Could he transform into something with wings, and chase her? How desperate was he to make her stay with him forever?

When had he decided he wanted her to transform into a nightborn? From the first moment he heard her admit she had magic in her blood? Or when they had laughed together over some of the more ridiculous stories people told about vampires?

Lady Ashlyn?

"Please don't call me that. Don't put ideas in anyone's head. Especially mine." She moaned and leaned forward and hid her face in her hands.

I was just going to assure you that you don't have to be afraid of Fang. He won't try to drain you in the middle of the night, although I do believe his teeth are longer, and have moved further apart. He likes you, and now that both of you have saved each other to some degree or another, he will risk his life for you. There's all that complicated code of honor the bunny clans hold to. He won't abandon you.

"Meaning ... you're telling me not to be afraid and try to abandon him? No, not for anything."

A chirping sound came from under her cloak. The sprawling lump that was Fang rose. She choked on a chuckle, watching it creep slowly across the mossy ground toward her.

"So, Fang, what are we going to do? Is there any way of ... I don't know, curing him? Is there a cure?"

Since he's only partially transformed, I should think so.

"How can he be only partially?"

She shuddered, reliving that moment when Fang had sunk his teeth into Morris, to defend her. Then Morris's head had changed, his teeth had grown. He had become something huge and capable of biting Fang's head off. But he hadn't. Ash played with the idea that would have been better for the bunny, who now seemed condemned to skulk in shadows to avoid smelling of scorched, wet fur during the day, and itching with sunburn.

"All right," she said, thinking aloud. "The same magic that allowed Fang to partially transformed also … what? Stopped him from completely transforming? Or are some of those ridiculous stories Morris was laughing at true, and Fang has to be buried, with all proper rituals, for the transformation to complete?"

I shouldn't think so. At least, I hope not. It's very confusing. Morris all but admitted that much of the false lore about vampires is the fault of the vampires themselves, to spread misdirection and make the fearful and vindictive waste time on rituals and defensive things like holy water, to give vampires time to flee for their lives. I think until we can find a magical library with reliable information, books that are spelled to only allow the truth to be recorded, we should simply avoid the entire subject of vampires.

"So how do we move about in the daylight? I need to put several countries between me and Morris. He's going to follow me, isn't he? At least, try to get me to come back?"

I'm afraid so. He's rather … pitiable. I think he … well, he's smitten with you.

"That's the last thing I need. A lovelorn vampire on my trail." She covered her eyes and leaned back and considered banging her head against the stump until she woke herself out of this truly frustrating, confusing, frightening dream.

Please, please, let this all be a bad dream? A fever dream?

Fang attempted to move about with her cloak covering him. It kept snagging on roots and low branches. Ash dug through her pack, pulling out everything to inspect it for water damage. She ended up turning it inside out, because the outside was drier than the inside. She spread everything out in the sunlight while she worked on adjusting her largest shirt to cover Fang. He looked rather cuddly, even cute with the shirt draping him so the tip of his nose peeped out, and the tips of his claws. The hem of the shirt puddled around him on the ground when he sat still. His ears were the problem. They kept popping up and pulling the makeshift hood off his head. Finally, the ring suggested they cut holes in the hood and use the remnants of the sleeves of the shirt to make tubes to cover his ears.

By that time, most of her belongings were dry enough to go back into the pack. Ash turned it inside-in again and repacked. The last of her dried fruit had vanished into the empty pit of her stomach. She had been relieved when Fang gobbled down his share without hesitating. There was that lingering fear he might try to snack on her, despite the ring's assurances. The dry bread had crumbled into inedible mush when the sack filled with water. The sweets had melted into a sticky lump that she had tossed aside. Fortunately, the journals Blaz had given her had been wrapped up tight in something apparently water-resistant, so none of the paper and leather and carbon sticks had gotten in the least wet. Ash made a promise to herself that once they had found a safe place to stay, she would write down a brief record of everything that had happened to them since they emerged above ground in Nordwell.

"Where are we, anyway?" she asked.

The ring had been busy all this time studying the maps Blaz had given them, deciphering information, trying to make sense of the blurred and smeared ink. The maps had not been made of spelled material and had gotten rather soggy. Ash had spread them out to dry in the sunshine.

So much of the cavern network wasn't noted on the maps, meaning no one has been able to explore it and report to anyone, the ring said. *However, judging by the glimpse of the last of the stars when we emerged at dawn, and the sense of the time currents as we were traveling underground, I believe we are in Ynderweil. It's west of Nordwell.*

"That's good?"

If the soldiers don't think to head west to look for us. If we're lucky, they've written us off as lost. Well, you and Fang, drained of blood, starting to rot to feed the cave creatures. They didn't notice me.

"They're kind of stupid, if you think about it. I'm clearly a servant, so why didn't anyone question why I would be wearing a ring made of gold and silver and ebony? Far too expensive to belong to me."

Hmm, yes … actually, only those with magic in their blood should be able to see through the glamour that Camwell orders all the rings to wear, once we're on someone's finger. It wouldn't do for someone to see us and try to take us. And when they can't take us off your fingers, resort to cutting them off.

Ash winced at the mental image. "Does that happen often?"

Far too often. That's why the glamour is necessary. The ugly, unfair fact of the matter is that the spell to keep us from being removed means we'll just pop out and pop back in again on another finger. Some thieves and other folk aren't very bright. They see that bit of magic and are even more determined to possess us, so they … well, they keep cutting.

"All right, that's more than I wanted to know." She busied herself arranging the maps and trying to put them back in their original creases. As she had done many times over the last two hours, she tipped her head back to study the sky. "We need to get moving. Put a few hours between us and Morris. And keep moving once it gets dark."

Or find a well-lit place to stay, with sturdy locks on the doors and sturdy shutters on the windows.

"Wouldn't that be lovely? Fang? Are you ready to go?" Ash pulled herself to her feet, swallowing down a groan. Maybe once she got moving, the aches would fade. She certainly felt like a hundred-year-old granny who sat huddled by the fire for days on end.

The bunny came hopping out of the underbrush, with several sticks clutched in his mouth. Enormous clusters of nearly-ripe raspberries hung from the ends of the sticks. He fluttered his lashes at her and dropped the sticks.

"For me?" Tears touched her eyes as he bobbed his head rapidly and hopped away. "Thank you!" Ash snatched up the sticks, carefully put them in her satchel, and slung it across her chest, leaving the top flap open. She muffled another groan as she slung her much lighter pack over her shoulder. She had fastened the cloak to the outside, to allow it to keep drying, and also keep it handy if Fang resumed steaming and smoldering, once they left the shelter of the trees. "And ... we're off."

She ate the berries slowly as she walked, waiting until the taste of one had faded from her tongue, then taking a long drink of water from the limitless flask before she ate another. It wasn't nearly as satisfying a trick as she had hoped, but it was comforting to crunch each one and feel the juice trickle down her throat. She put the last two in her mouth and tossed away the last of the sticks after she stepped from a dirt path to a road. A real road, of crushed stone, and signs of recent repairs. No huge ruts dug in the mud, and puddles wide enough to be small ponds. She wasn't sure what this said about the state of maintenance in the kingdom of Ynderweil, or the politics or the wealth of the people. She wasn't even sure if it was safe to travel a road, but it would eventually get her to a town and doors with locks on them. She wouldn't have to fight her way through brambles and underbrush. That would save her time and energy.

Ash took three steps, and the echoing thud-crash-stomp of Fang somewhere nearby didn't follow. She looked back at the place in the trees where she had emerged. No sign of him. She looked ahead. No Fang leaping ahead of her, enjoying the freedom to bounce high without hitting branches. She looked back.

Fang sat on the edge of the packed stone, ears slowly bobbing forward, as if they might touch the road in a few more bobs. His teeth were definitely farther apart than they had been yesterday. At least they didn't have those red stains that had gotten them both in trouble with the soldiers in Nordwell. She thought she saw some dirt smeared on her remade shirt, and his teeth, and a few crumbles falling from between his claws.

"It's all right," she said, even though she suspected their situation was far from it. "We'll be able to hear people coming from a long ways off, and you can duck into the trees to hide. When night comes, you can take off that shirt and finally move freely and ..." She shrugged. "Well, we'll figure that out when the time comes. Just … we're in this together, right?"

Fang bobbed his ears a little faster, and he nodded. He hopped up next to her, and she resumed walking. She wished she hadn't stopped for those few seconds, because her knees and ankles protested moving again. Fang kept pace with her for several minutes, then he leaped ahead, bouncing higher. He seemed to be in better spirits.

"It must be nice to find some joy in just bouncing," she muttered.

I've been contemplating your question, of what we can do, if we can reverse the transformation, the ring announced.

"It would take quite a bit of very strong magic, wouldn't it? And the help of a very wise, talented enchanter. Maybe several."

Indeed. And access to a vast library filled with magical books.

"How vast?" She thought of Blaz's shelves and piles of books.

Enough books that the combined magic stored in them makes them awaken, makes them aware. The ring sighed. *And possibly dangerous. The only thing more cranky than a magic book that isn't allowed to nap is a magic book that has napped too long, to the point of being neglected, allowed to go to dust on the edges. To go wild.*

"Where could we find that many magic books? And if they're aware and awake, would they be willing to help us?"

If we ask politely. And if we give them a challenge. I should think turning a rather crazy bunny back from half-vampire would be a challenge worth bragging about.

Ash hoped he was right. The idea of books being aware enough to not only help create transformative magic but want to brag about it rather boggled her imagination. "But where would we find that many books?"

Perhaps over the ocean.

That wasn't encouraging at all, but she chose not to say that. They had enough challenges to meet right now. She chose not to waste energy, and give herself a headache, by worrying about things they wouldn't have to face for days, weeks, months. Hopefully not years.

Chapter Fifteen

Ash walked, trusting Fang to warn her of problems and dangers ahead of them. Every time he bounced away out of sight, around a bend in the road, hidden by the trees that clung close to the sides of the road, and he didn't come back after two minutes, she worried. Her pace sped up. Then when he appeared she took a few gulps of air, always chagrined to find she had been holding her breath. Her steps slowed to a more reasonable, energy-conserving pace. Fang looked back at her, waving his ears in that pattern she chose to interpret as his all's well signal. Then he would bound away, out of sight, sometimes bouncing so high she could see him above the tops of the trees. That proved to be amusing. Most of the time. Until he again vanished utterly from sight and sound.

Somewhere late in the afternoon, she grew tired enough that she didn't pay attention to her surroundings. Maybe that wasn't wise, but that was what Fang and the ring were for, weren't they? To help her, guard her, warn her? She was doing all the hard work, after all. Dealing with Fang's problems, being half-vampire. Doing all the walking. Carrying the ring. Fulfilling that wretched justiciar's foolish quest that certainly seemed to be inspired more by his curiosity than by anything she had actually done wrong.

That thought swirled around in her head a few dozen times before she did something about it.

"Do you have any idea what Lathia has been doing?"

The ring chuckled.

"Is that good news for me?"

The silly girl hasn't gotten to the border of Alfordia yet.

"Has she realized that her ring can talk to her?"

It's not a matter of realizing, it's a matter of letting the ring speak. My friend is quite peeved and jealous that I was assigned to you. Lathia talks constantly, to herself if she can't get someone with visible ears to listen. Whining, complaining, and daydreaming about sweets and finding a magic to clear up her spotty skin and make her thin. She's jealous of her sister, and considers it totally unfair that she can't be thin and have boys drooling over her like they do over Leena. And even more unfair that to look like her sister she has to be active and ride horses and get exercise and fresh air and give up constantly filling her face with sweets.

Ash laughed. Her ribs didn't hurt even a tenth as much as they had that morning, and her stiffness and bruises had faded.

"Why hasn't she gotten out of the country yet?"

Oh, they wasted quite a bit of time searching the castle for you. Lathia insists that since this whole mess is your fault, you should be her servant. And the servants assigned to help her on the quest are even more determined to find you. The ring heard them plotting the night we left, to find you and drug you, sneak you out of the castle, then claim you had fled. They would set off with Lathia, and when they got to the place where they had left you tied up, they would drug both of you and make their escape. So when the two of you woke, you would be burdened with each other.

"Thank you, Hazel and Fang."

Indeed!

Laughing with the ring and imagining Lathia's frustration proved to be energizing. Ash looked around and was startled to see the sun's upper rim perched on the tops of the trees where the road curved to the right ahead of her. And still no sign of a town or even a farm. No shelter for the night. How soon until Morris came looking for her?

Please, please, A'theosius, make him despise me just enough to give up? Make him leave me alone?

Something huge crashed among the trees to her right. The shadows were thick enough, she could only make out movement, low along the ground, but not what the thing was.

"Fang?" She turned, looking in all directions, even though common sense said she should be looking ahead, not behind, and certainly not in the trees on either side of the road. "Where could he be?" She put her hand on her belt knife. While the blade was a good, handy size, it felt pitifully small to face whatever that big, lumpy, dark shape was, bumping and squirming through the shadows toward her. Maybe she should run?

Or would that thing prove to have a thousand legs, like the many disgusting night-dwelling creatures in the cavern, able to race with the speed of light once it hit the even surface of the road?

The ring chuckled.

That was getting almost as irritating as having him say he was sorry.

There he is. And I believe he has found dinner.

The ring was right. He was right often enough, and especially now, Ash decided she could forgive him for when he was irritating.

~~~~~

Two hours later, Ash leaned back against a convenient fallen log, toasty warm from a massive, horseshoe-shaped fire, and her stomach full of roasted venison.

Fang had brought down a ten-point buck. That was the huge, lumpy, creeping, dragging, noisy thing. The deer was six times his size, making it difficult to drag the carcass from wherever he had wrestled it to the ground and bit out its neck, to catch up with her on the road. But Fang
~~~~~

had done it. He was inordinately proud of himself, and even more proud every time she thanked him.

The ring provided enough sparks to build the fire. Under his direction, Ash created her campsite, surrounding herself with fire on three sides, and plenty of sharpened sticks at the ready to set on fire and defend herself, if Morris should catch up with her. Then, as the fire grew, she butchered the deer. What was left of it, anyway. Fang contented himself with the ribcage and all the internal organs. He did have a passion for red and juicy and messy, and being half-vampire now certainly brought that out. Ash was quite happy with the hindquarters. She intended to roast as much as she could after she had eaten her fill and contrive some way to carry much of the meat with her. She had learned the hard way that depending on finding generous people or comfortable inns was not a wise plan to follow.

When her stomach was so full, it ached nearly as much as it had when it was empty, Ash forced herself to her feet and gathered more wood. She needed to keep that fire going. While it would draw people to her, and possibly Morris, and hundreds of night insects, it would also protect her. And there was something deliciously decadent about being warm and surrounded by light, after those interminable days in the cool and damp and dark underground. No matter how beautiful the lights and colors of the cave growths, she couldn't imagine herself enduring an entire, extended lifetime as a nightborn.

Please, A'theosius, keep him away from me. Discourage him.

To Ash's dismay, she fell asleep. She remembered looking at Fang and finding something humorous and disturbing in the sight of him curled up in the rib cage of the decimated, devoured buck, fast asleep, purring in contentment. Then the next thing she knew, she lay curled up in her cloak, coughing as the smoke from her dying fire surrounded her.

Nothing had touched the makeshift racks she had placed over the coals to cook and dry long slabs of venison. No one had entered her campsite to attack her or steal her few possessions. Morris hadn't appeared from the darkness to woo her with a bloody wrist and his fangs growing long.

Thank you.

She nearly took back that repeating litany of thanks when she pushed herself upright and discovered that sleeping on the forest floor wasn't quite as comfortable as the stories of adventures inferred.

Fang was nowhere to be seen. Well, at least something was constant in her life. Ash set about washing, then took a long drink. She wondered how long she could keep drinking the water that tasted as fresh as it had been when she filled the flask. Sooner or later, even its enormous capacity had to run out. When she found a spring or a well, she had to make a point of adding water to the flask. When she ran out of the venison, she would have to rely on water to fill her stomach, if by that time she hadn't come among people again and found some way to earn her keep. After all, what were her chances of running into more magical people who would help her from the kindness of their souls? That happened in adventure tales, but Ash knew better than to expect such luck in real life, in the real world. After all, the real world had people like Winston and Lathia, as well as Lady Charlotte and Lady Leena. The real world had Captain Creiklan and Morris and greedy fools who didn't consider magical rules and problems, such as Branley.

Ash allowed herself a piece of meat the size of her open palm for her breakfast. She packed away the rest in the remains of her extra shirt, mixed with handfuls of several kinds of leafy herbs that the ring pointed out to her. They would fight decay and keep away insects that would want to share her food. Ash found some satisfaction in the bulges in her pack and told herself she didn't mind the extra weight. She would walk it off and eat it off and build some muscles along the way. She had to get stronger, although she despaired of ever being as strong as Lady Leena and the other maiden warriors she had seen. Still, the better able she was to defend herself, the safer she would feel.

Under the ring's direction, she scattered the smoldering coals of her fire, then buried them in dirt. Some of the things he said about forestry practices and burning off deadwood went right over her head. She tried to listen but didn't even consider asking questions. It was nice to have the ring talking to her as she worked, cleaning up her campsite and doing the best she could to make it appear that no one had spent the night there.

Except for the remains of the deer, of course. Insects and smaller animals were already moving in, or hovering in the shadows, waiting for her to leave, to judge by the sounds. Ash trusted most of the evidence would be cleared away soon, so anyone who stepped a bowshot off the road into the forest wouldn't realize what had happened here.

"That's going to be the way of it for a while, isn't it?" she said as she tied her cloak into a neat bundle and attached it to the back of her pack. "Sliding by in the shadows, staying unnoticed as much as possible, hoping people don't realize I'm there. At least until Fang is cured."

Perhaps, the ring said.

"Perhaps?" She laughed softly. Softer than she would have in the castle. Already, this life of stealth and watchfulness was affecting her.

You are growing and changing. You were growing and changing before that selfish snot attacked you and set you on this path. Who knows what path you would have followed if she hadn't come along? You can't blame all your changes on Fang.

"True. And do you have any idea where he is?"

A chirp startled her. She turned and saw Fang sitting halfway between the campsite and the road. He waved his sleeve-shielded ears at her and rose up high on his hind legs. Ash was pleased to note that he had not only gotten into the adjusted shirt without her help, but he had groomed himself and removed all that blood that had soaked into his fur during his rather messy, loud feasting on the fresh deer carcass.

"Well, shall we get going?"

Fang chirped and bounced up high. He turned a somersault in mid-air, startling a laugh out of her.

After several days of Fang and the ring keeping watch, and no sign of Morris hunting her, Ash was willing to avoid people to protect Fang, as he would protect her if necessary. For Fang's comfort, she kept them to the less traveled lanes, and even opted for cutting through small woods and skirting around farms and villages. She chose her route to let him move in shadows as much as possible, first, and then to stay out of the sight of people. The sight of a rather large bunny with rather long teeth and an unusually large gap between them was bad enough, but seeing one bounding along wrapped in an oversized shirt was sure to garner dangerous attention. Avoiding people gave them freedom to forage for their food and sleep under hedges, without anyone accusing her of being a thief or runaway servant or apprentice. And wouldn't let anyone get close enough to realize she was a girl disguised as a boy.

When it was impossible to avoid places with too much traffic for comfort, they found a place to sleep during the day, and started walking at sunset, until they had either passed by that troublesome area full of people or they found another safe hole to hide in. Fang was quite good at finding all sorts of edible roots and berries and herbs that Ash learned to enjoy raw. He found great delight in hunting, and she had some difficulty convincing him to avoid larger prey, such as deer, when they were within earshot of people who might hear the struggle and come to investigate. She didn't mind his growing taste for bloody food when they were far enough away from people that she could cook enough provisions for several days. At least Fang had proven to be a rather fastidious creature, taking great care to clean himself of all evidence of his messy meals.

And all the while, the ring taught her about the plants and animals they passed, and the geography of the kingdom they walked through, even tidbits of history if he had had access to documents relating such information. Ash learned more than she had ever hoped to about herbs and healing practices and history. And magic. It was all theoretical, of course, but the ring taught her the signs to look for of magic being practiced nearby, of magical objects performing their tasks, of malfunctioning spells that either needed to be avoided or dealt with. And most important, signs of her inborn magic finally awakening.

Ash didn't look forward to the day when some troublesome magical talent or potential grew strong enough that she needed to find a teacher. What mattered to her was performing the tasks Camwell assigned to her and being free of his oversight. He hadn't checked in on her yet. The ring had promised to tell her when the justiciar opened up the link between them, to try to observe through her senses and track her progress and location. She was relieved to have gone through two caverns and crossed two borders, and already learned the list of rankings of magic users. Her quest was already halfway completed. Hopefully Lathia would be so troublesome and uncooperative he would focus all his attention on her, prodding her to get moving, maybe even sending questions for her to answer constantly. She liked the idea of Lathia finally realizing someone was always watching, but not to attend to her every need. The more Lathia took up Justiciar Camwell's energy in oversight, the less attention he would expend on Ash. Despite that, the day of reckoning would catch up with her eventually.

"How do you think he'll react when you tell him about the bloodweed and the soldiers and being forced into that cavern and walking with Morris and learning so much true lore of vampires?" she mused one sleepy-warm afternoon.

The ring had helped her find a rather comfortable perch in an oak, high above the ground, among foliage so thick she couldn't see the people who passed by unless they walked directly under the tree. Ash had fashioned a sling with her cloak so she could lie down and sleep without fear of falling. Right now, she sprawled out quite comfortably along a massive limb twice as wide as her torso. When her eyes grew heavy enough, she would have to move into that sling, or all her caution would be for naught. Fang was some distance away, terrorizing any small prey animals he might see. He wouldn't catch and kill unless he was hungry, but he did find great joy in practicing his stealth skills, or just bounding high enough to drop down dozens of paces away and send creatures scattering in all directions in terror.

I fear he will insist you spend time with him narrating each step of your journey, submitting to thousands of questions for details. While his home is quite comfortable, and you will have the distinction of having your name listed in several books, depending on how he records the information ... The ring sighed.

"What's wrong?"

Well, he is an inveterate traveler. With you to do the physical work while he remains comfortably, gluttonously at home, you're likely to be forced to travel from one castle and estate and inn to another until he grows bored with your observations or whatever inhibits you. Traveling with and for the justiciar is nothing like this freedom and simplicity you're enjoying now.

Ash nearly snorted aloud. Enjoy? She wouldn't call living out in the open, getting drenched by showers despite her cloak or whatever shelter she had found, being chilled on unusually frosty nights, and baking during the day, and constantly walking enjoyment. Granted, she did enjoy lazy times like this. But she could do without constantly wondering when she would run out of food and have to either beg or find someone who would pay her in food, or steal.

Well, come to think of it, yes, she did rather enjoy this life. Despite the discomfort and bouts of hunger and thirst and not being able to wash regularly. She felt stronger, certainly, from all the walking and climbing. The ring's constant teaching had certainly expanded her education. She had thought the hundred or so books in Castle Fairhold's library were an amazing luxury and privilege and she had a valuable education. Now she knew better.

"What would be the difference?" she asked, when she realized the ring waited for her to respond. With more than a muffled snort.

You'd be constantly in attendance on him. Depending on his mood, he'll either keep you disguised as a boy, perhaps as an apprentice clerk, and entertain himself waiting for someone to realize there's something not quite right about you. Or he'll dress you up and make you look like a bit of fluff, just to astonish people when you recite and prove your extraordinary education. Just the fact you can read and write puts you equal to and even a few levels above many in the nobility. Far too many depend on their clerks and seneschals to handle all the records and accounts for them. And he could give in to a moment of whimsy and what he considers generosity and make you his ward, and then marry you off for his own political gain.

"Oh." She felt quite wide awake now, compared to moments ago when she had let her drowsy thoughts wander. Ash regretted bringing up the topic, yet at the same time, she was grateful she had. How could she defend herself if she didn't know what threats awaited her?

A snort escaped her. A vague resolution and a plan she had been considering at the back of her mind had just moved to the front and solidified.

"Please don't take this the wrong way, ring, my friend ... but I hope I'm far away from the justiciar when my quest is fulfilled –"

Quite understandable.

"And if you aren't magically taken away from me, but I'm able to take you off my finger, I will. Just so he can't track me any longer. We can still talk if we're together, even if I'm not wearing you?"

That possibility has never been tested. Usually because my previous wearers are all relieved to be free of me.

"I'd like to find a way to keep you with me. And not just to spite the justiciar. I want to make it impossible for him to find me, without being separated from you, or not being able to talk to you for long periods of time, or ever. Can we still talk if, say, I'm wearing you on a chain around my neck?"

I'm not really sure how much contact we need. I was able to talk to Blaz, and he wasn't wearing me.

"Blaz has magic."

So do you, my Lady Ashlyn.

She snorted and sat up, wriggling around so she was leaning against the trunk of the tree. "I wish you wouldn't call me that. Looking at me, I'm certainly no lady. And considering the lives ladies have to live ... I much prefer this."

There is more to being a lady than wearing fine dresses and jewelry and living as if every movement is about to be captured in a sketch or portrait, or A'theosius protect us, in a tapestry for the ages to admire and learn from.

That earned a chuckle from her, quickly muffled behind her hand. It was one thing to talk in low tones, but it was another to laugh. That was a sound people walking on the road a bowshot away from her might hear. Ash knew it was risky to talk aloud with the ring, but speaking to him in her thoughts gave her a headache after a time. She thought it rather strained something in her brain.

What you need, the ring continued after a moment of listening, waiting silence, when Ash assured herself no one was on the road, *is to earn enough power, you can live as you please.*

"What kind of power?" She shook her head. "I think I know. There is wealth, and there is military might, and there is land and political power, and the fear you can generate in other people. Any of that will take me so long, I'll be an old woman, and what's the use then? I won't be able to enjoy traveling and adventuring like this. Of course, people will just ignore me then. They'll just say I'm another crazy old woman. They'll lock me up, or they'll let me run loose and use me to frighten their children into behaving and doing their chores."

Or there is magic.

Ash held her breath, not quite sure why.

Use this quest to find what your magic is, grow it, make it useful, put yourself in a position where people will want your help, and be grateful, and protect you. Respect that comes from admiration and gratitude is far more potent than respect grounded in fear.

Chapter Sixteen

"Easier said than done," Ash said on a sigh, echoing something she had heard Lady Beatrice and Lady Charlotte say to each other many times.

If something is easy, you don't appreciate it when you achieve it. The ring tightened slightly around her finger. He had done it several times, during conversations like this, and Ash had decided to equate it with a friendly arm draped around her shoulders, to encourage her. *Don't you worry, my lady, we will solve this riddle together. And if A'theosius blesses us, you'll be powerful enough, or at least far enough away when you complete the quest, we can stay together, and Camwell will never be able to retrieve either of us.*

That was such an encouraging thought, Ash relaxed and entertained herself with images of the justiciar's frustration, until she could stretch out in the sling of her cloak and get some sleep.

Such conversations filled the quiet hours in the midday heat on days when Ash needed to hide and couldn't sleep. She found them rather enlightening, opening up places in her mind and soul she hadn't suspected were there. Would she have ever traveled such mental pathways if she had stayed in Castle Fairhold? Likely not. Especially as her body continued to betray her and make it harder to masquerade as a boy.

Several days after that conversation, she nearly laughed aloud at the realization that maybe, just maybe, she should be grateful for Lathia's "innocent" game of tormenting her "inferiors." After all, otherwise she wouldn't be traveling in kingdoms she had only read about, accompanied by a spirit ring and a partially transformed vampire bunny, on a quest somewhat like those she had read about and had filled her dreams.

Two afternoons later, Ash woke from a nap under a thick canopy of ivy, with rain dripping through to touch her face and heard two voices in her head. One was the ring, the other was a tired baritone.

"Ah, she awakens," the baritone said aloud. "Good. We have just enough time to reach my cottage before the rain becomes a real drencher."

Something tapped Ash's leg. She fought down an urge to scold the ring for not awakening her when this stranger happened on them. How had he found them? Muffling a moan, she discovered several bruised spots in her back where she had slid over in her sleep to rest on several hard things. She tugged her hood down enough to see a long, pale wooden staff. She followed the staff up to a thin, elderly man who smiled at her and nodded. Despite the shadows of her ivy shelter, she saw the thick, milky color of his eyes. No pupils whatsoever. He was blind.

"You're a seer?" she said, her voice cracking a little as she sat up.

"Cecil, at your service, Lady Ashlyn." A grin turned his deeply tanned face into a nest of wrinkles and crevices, like a walnut.

"Ring ..."

The ring laughed. *Go with him. You need what he can give you.*

"What do I need besides a bath? And maybe a nice thick slab of bread and butter?" Ash had meant to be flippant, but the thought of fresh bread after nearly a month of nothing but herbs and roots and wild-caught meat made her mouth water and her stomach twist, loudly.

"What do you say to all the books you could care to read?" Cecil said. Leaning on his staff, he stood up. "Oh, sorry," he hurried to say, as his injudicious movement jarred the ivy overhead, sending a cascade of drops down on them both. Then he laughed and tipped his head back. His hood slid down, revealing his balding head and fluffy white fringe of hair.

Despite his wrinkles and stooped shoulders and the creak in his voice, he seemed so much like a mischievous little boy, Ash couldn't be upset at the drenching. Besides, that was the magic word: books. If the ring trusted Cecil, then she would too.

Unless Cecil was one of those powerful seers who could not only see into the future and into the minds of people, but he could change their thoughts, their memories, and make them act the exact opposite of what they should do and be?

"Where's Fang?" she said instead, to get her thoughts away from that troubling idea. If Cecil was a danger, manipulating the ring against her, she didn't want him to guess she suspected him. If Cecil was exactly as he appeared, she didn't want to insult the man. Especially if she had a chance to read books for a few days and sleep in a real bed and maybe eat that bread.

"I suspect he's halfway down my row of beets and getting quite messy," Cecil said. "He seemed quite excited when I pointed out all the lovely vegetables and fruits in my garden that were red, or a lovely red-purple. We sent him on ahead, so you could sleep as long as you needed."

"Thank you." Ash wasn't sure how she should feel about that. While she appreciated others looking out for her comfort, it felt odd.

They walked in silence. She kept stealing glimpses of Cecil, half-expecting to find that the milky haze no longer obscured his eyes. He did walk without swinging his staff from side to side and ahead to feel the meandering forest path. No, he still looked blind, yet he didn't move like any blind people she had seen. Granted, most of them seemed content to huddle on a bench in some public place, stretching out their hands toward any sounds of people passing by, begging for charity and pity. Cecil walked with his head up and shoulders back, with confidence, and she couldn't envision him wanting charity. She could envision him laughing at pity, maybe scolding anyone who would treat him as if he were blind and helpless.

That assessment made no sense to her, when she thought about it, because she had just met the man only fifteen minutes ago.

Maybe he was as she had feared: one of those seers who could influence people's thoughts? If so, what kind of trouble was she walking into?

"If you're blind, why do you have books?" she asked, to change the course of her thoughts. Just in case he could peer into them.

"Ah, that is the price of my gift. I was a great seeker of wisdom in my youth. At least, I thought it was wisdom, when I thought everything worth knowing could be found in books." Cecil shrugged, and his grin grew wide enough to inhibit speech for a few moments. He chuckled. "Then I learned the difference between wisdom and knowledge. I lost the use of my eyes so my soul could see more clearly. Now, I share my books with those who need the knowledge contained in them, and I share my wisdom with those who need my help. A'theosius speaks to me in the night quiet and my dreams and the whisper of the wind and rain, and my visitors tell me more stories than I could read in a dozen lifetimes." He shrugged. "I am content. Most of the time."

Ash decided that little confession made a huge difference.

He mourns his books, the ring said.

"Indeed. But my loss is to your benefit. We will trade, yes? You can read to your heart's content, and read to me what I have forgotten, to refresh my memory, and together we will try to find something to help your friend, Fang. What do you think?"

"That is ... very generous of you."

If Fang wanted to be helped, of course. Ash thought about the bunny's gusto when he leaped on prey, the bigger and more difficult to bring to its knees, the better. He enjoyed getting messy-bloody, in the hunt and killing as well as the eating. What if he didn't want to be cured? He was like her, in some ways. Shoved out of their comfortable homes, accused of crimes they hadn't committed. What if Fang decided he liked being a half-vampire more than the chance to fix his teeth and mannerisms, so he could go home to the warren and be like all the other bunnies? Maybe the limited bunny magic and longevity weren't enough for him anymore?

Such thoughts swirled around in her head, and Cecil let her think in silence on the rest of their journey to his cottage. After half an hour of walking, she marveled that he had found her hiding place, quite a distance from the local roads and pathways. Then again, he was a seer. He had probably gone searching in response to a vision or dream.

She was relieved to note that Cecil's cottage looked large enough to comfortably house a family. A loft, if not a second story, hid under that sloping, thickly thatched roof. It had four windows, two on each side of the solid front door, and the walls were stone, not wattle and daub. Smoke curled up from the chimney. A lean-to off one side and several barrels up on a platform nearly head-height indicated the incredible luxury of a shower for bathing. She quite preferred that to sitting in a tub, because there was the mess of emptying the bathing tub, and the risk of spilling dirty water all over her clean clothes and body. A wall of sticks, loosely woven together with rope, curved around from the back of the cottage. It allowed glimpses into a garden large enough to feed Cecil and several others. Ash wondered if anyone else lived in the cottage with him. There was plenty of room. Then again, she had seen huts in her month of travel where ten people lived together in space a third of the size of this cottage.

A squeal warned her just before Fang jumped up from behind the garden wall. He leaped over it and bounced three circles around Ash and Cecil before coming to a stop. He wrapped his messy, redly juicy forelegs around the legs of the seer, hugging hard enough to almost knock the man off balance, then attacked Ash the same way. She laughed and bent down to give Fang a good scrubbing between his ears and down his back. He wriggled happily, chirping and squealing, then bounded away, back to pillage the garden more.

"I'm sorry," she began.

"Oh, no, don't be." Cecil gestured toward the cottage door with his staff. "I actually loathe most of the messy red stuff he's been devouring. I had no idea why my dreams directed me to plant those things this spring. Tomatoes make me itch, and I am overrun with the wretched things. Fang is welcome to all he wants to devour."

He opened the door and gestured for her to go in ahead of him. Lanterns lit of their own accord as soon as she crossed the threshold. Then she saw the treasure lining the walls, and she didn't hear the next few things he said. Ash trembled at the sight of the books, neatly lining the shelves up to the wooden plank ceiling, shelves built into the walls between and around the windows. More piles of books sitting on two tables pushed to the far end of the room. More books in crates and spread across a table near the fireplace.

Then the aroma of mutton stew, heavy on spices and sweet with carrots, reached out on a plume of steam from the cauldron simmering to one side of the roaring fire. She became painfully aware of how damp and grimy her clothes were, how her boots squished, and the earthy, sweaty, metallic odor of her own body.

"Which would you like first? To eat or to put on dry clothes?" Cecil asked.

I should think she would rather make a nest out of some of those books, the ring said. *She has lovely table manners, but I think Ash is about to drool.*

Ash laughed. Then she nearly burst into tears when Cecil pointed out the second cauldron on the other side of the fireplace, full of steaming water. He gestured to the little door leading to the bathing lean-to.

"While I'm sure the clothes waiting for you will be the right size, I can't guarantee the color. You might look rather garish."

"Clothes? You put out clothes for me?" She had to shake her head a few times, as if that would change what she had heard.

"I obeyed my visions, that is all. I did not know I would meet you today. I merely obeyed the instructions to find spare clothes and get food cooking and water heating. My only knowledge was that I would have a guest, and perhaps someone to read to me." Cecil let his cloak slide off his shoulders, catching it with a flourish, and stepped over to the wall on the left of the door, where a number of hooks waited to take it, and where he leaned his staff.

Ash found the ladder to climb up to the loft and put her pack and satchel down. There were four cots waiting under the eaves, and four chests to store possessions, and lanterns that lit of their own accord. And more shelves full of books. When she climbed back down, Cecil told her where to find some thick cloths to protect her hands, to take the hot water to the bathing lean-to.

Ash nearly burst into tears when she found bars of soap, smelling of rosemary, and scrubbing brushes, and thick towels waiting for her. She gladly peeled out of her dirty, damp clothes, and wished she could just stomp on them until they vanished through the slats in the wooden platform that allowed the water to drain out of the lean-to. The clothes hanging on a peg were somewhat faded, but that toned down what had probably been an eye-searing shade of orange and a rather uncomfortable shade of green. The cloth was thick and promised warmth; shirt and vest, trousers, stockings, and some odd, ankle-high shoes made of felt, with pointed toes.

She scrubbed hard with soap and hot water and held her breath when she pulled the rope that opened the sliding latch to allow water to pour down and rinse her. It was chilly, but refreshingly so. To warm up, she washed again in the hot water. Then she dunked her dirty clothes in the cauldron and swirled a bar of soap through it, up and down several times, before it occurred to her that maybe Cecil would want the rest of the hot water to wash himself. He had been out in the drizzly chilly rain too, after all. She worked out the wording of her apology as she swirled her clothes around and wrung them out, and swirled them again, then spread them out on the wooden platform and pulled the latch to rinse out everything, including the cauldron of dirty, soapy water. Then, shivering and grateful for the thick towels, she dried off and hurried into the borrowed clothes.

"I'm sorry, I didn't think," she said, stepping through the little door back into the cottage. She halted as the stars embedded in her flesh stung, just for a heartbeat.

Magic at work?

Music greeted her. Cecil sat curled around a large lap harp, plucking strings that shimmered with colored light. Ash held her breath, watching as thin tendrils of light played around the cottage. A book slid across one table, pushed by a streak of yellow light, and flipped closed. A large spoon wrapped in pink light stirred the cauldron of mutton stew. A blue tendril of light slid a pitcher across a short shelf, to rest under the spigot of a barrel, while a second tendril of light, pale green, turned the spigot and amber liquid spilled out to fill the pitcher.

"Can you play the flute?" Cecil asked.

"I don't know."

"Would you like to learn?"

"Yes, please."

He chuckled and strummed across several strings. A thick streak of violet light shot out, to a shelf over the barrel, picked up a flute as long as her forearm, and brought it over to her. Ash took the flute, careful not to touch the light. The instrument was made of some pale golden wood.

"Good. It's been years since I had someone to play with me. For some odd reason, people feel rather uncomfortable when I make music." Cecil sighed and bent forward, sliding the harp down to sit on the floor at his feet. Then he straightened up. His sorrowful expression twisted into mischief.

This is going to be great fun, the ring said.

Ash almost said what swirled through her mind and seemed to plant roots in her heart: *I think I want to stay here for always.*

In that moment, with the last streaks of magic light fading from the air, she remembered something Lord Digory had said, years ago, on a harvesting trip to a valley a day's journey away. She couldn't remember the name of the valley, only that they had been working under Hazel's direction to gather various rare herbs that only grew every five years. Everyone had gathered around campfires in the open meadow at night and told stories. Lord Digory had delighted the castle's younger servants with stories of magic gone wrong, and the absurd things people had to do to set the spells aright. Several stories had warned about the foolishness of thoughtlessly speaking wishes. Especially when magic hung in the air.

If she was wise, Ash knew she should learn precautions from Cecil for however long she could stay with him. If she had magic in her blood, and it awoke without warning, she could cause herself a great deal of trouble by speaking without caution. This was an entirely new aspect to the proverb Myrtle often repeated in the castle kitchen: *Best to be quiet and appear wise and thoughtful, rather than speak everything in your mind and prove nothing worthwhile resides there.*

"Thank you," she said, when she realized the silence had grown too long. "I'll do my best. I'm sorry, but I used up all the hot water. Should I get more heating for you?"

"No need. Let's have our dinner. By the time we're done, and we've agreed on our plan of attack for the next few days, the rain should have stopped, and you can hang your clothes outside to dry."

Ash nearly asked how he knew she had washed her clothes. Then she decided he had probably heard the noise she made, swishing and wringing and rinsing multiple times. Then she wondered if he knew because he was a seer, and not because of sharp ears.

There was a great deal she needed to learn.

~~~~~

Cecil gave Ash chores to do. His ability to do most everyday chores amazed her at times, because it certainly seemed as if he could see. Yet every once in a while, his blindness seemed to slap her in the face. She didn't mind the little details that required the magic lanterns to shine brighter so she could see into corners and underneath furniture. There were tiny repairs to make. Cecil certainly couldn't mend his clothes, for instance, and he did like to look nice even if he couldn't see what he was wearing. He had an image as the local seer to maintain, after all. They worked out a system where she sewed letters into the inside of the necks of his shirts and jackets, and the waists of his trousers, to tell him what colors they were. Cecil laughed when she suggested that trick. None of the other people he had asked to help him organize his clothes and other possessions had ever thought of such a thing. Then again, Ash was one of the few who took shelter with him who knew how to read.

She did the same with his cooking spices and bags and jars of ingredients, so he didn't make unfortunate mistakes with seasonings when he had a cold and couldn't smell the difference between spices that certainly felt the same when he stuck a finger into the pot or bag.

Her favorite chore was organizing his books for him. Over the months, piles had toppled over on the floor, or slid off the tables. Helpful people put books back on the wrong shelves. Cecil had an extraordinarily organized mind when it came to his books, although some of his classifications didn't quite make sense to her. He liked to organize history books by the time periods as well as the kingdoms they covered, except when there were multiple books by the same author or groups of scholars. Then they had their own shelf and organized by time period of subject within that shelf. She couldn't quite understand why he cherished a quite
~~~~~

extensive collection of illuminated volumes by clerics at the Retreat of the Echoing Caves. While the illustrations at the start of each chapter, and along the tops and bottoms of many pages were beautiful, after all, he couldn't see the striking colors.

Many times, as they went through his library, shelf by shelf, he had her stop and read to him. Thin braids of thread in multiple places throughout each of his favorite books marked his favorite passages. Sometimes he asked her to mark new places after she read to him. There were several days when she read aloud the entire book to him, and they were both surprised when one or both of their stomachs, or Fang, interrupted to let them know they had gone the whole day without eating. The lanterns stayed lit all day, until Cecil strummed a note on his harp to make them dim. Until Ash's throat grew dry and her voice raspy, they often weren't aware of the passage of time.

As the days sped past and she grew to understand how Cecil's mind worked when it came to organizing his books, he gave her some freedom to rearrange. If she explained to him what she was doing and why. Sometimes they argued over her reasoning. She liked those times, which surprised her. Perhaps because she had avoided conflict as much as possible, at Castle Fairhold.

"That's because you didn't want people to notice you long enough to really look at you," Cecil said, when Ash voiced that thought. "The problem with trying to go through life invisible is that you soon fade in your own mind and self-perception. It's hard to have adventures if you're skulking in the shadows. It's also hard to have people come to your rescue if they don't know you're there."

That gave her several nights of sleeplessness and restless thinking. Ash found she liked that too, in retrospect. Not at the time it was happening, though.

Chapter Seventeen

Ash worked out a system for marking each of his books, and the shelves, so that if people who could read came to consult his books and didn't put them away, or didn't put them back on the proper shelf, Cecil could do it himself. She didn't expect to stay with Cecil forever, as much as she would have enjoyed that. There was the problem of finding a cure for Fang, after all. And the ring didn't have to remind her that Justiciar Camwell would check on her soon. If she hadn't moved along, if she hadn't crossed another border or explored another cavern, he might look in on her more intently than she would like. Such as trying to see through her eyes or even examining her thoughts. Or worse, her memories. The thought of employing that blocking and blanking spell Blaz had worked out for her made her uncomfortable. Sort of itchy inside her head. She didn't want to forget any of the things she had learned so far. It wasn't enough to write them down in the journals Blaz had given her, because words weren't quite adequate to record smells and sounds and tastes and emotional reactions during conversations or funny or sad or frustrating or terrifying moments. Yes, the words helped her remember, but she didn't want to need help remembering.

The day came when all of Cecil's books were on their shelves in proper order and he didn't have any adjusting to do. He even had two new shelves, which hung from the ceiling and could be lowered and raised on pulleys. Ash had enjoyed the days they had spent experimenting until they figured out that device. Cecil had laughed nearly until he cried, when she pointed out that the space underneath the tables was wasted, so why not ask Max the local carpenter to build boxes on wheels to slide under the tables, to store books. That reduced the danger of piles toppling over.

After all the books she had looked through, focusing on references to magic and curses, vampires, and magical healing, Ash hadn't found anything to cure Fang of being partially turned into a vampire. Nearly two months had passed since Cecil had come to find her and bring her to his cottage. She wouldn't mind if she stayed all summer and fall and through the winter, but should she? More pressing than the chance Justiciar Camwell would intrude and make her move on, she might need to go somewhere else, with more magic books, to help Fang. He now slept during the brightest part of the day and did most of his prowling and hunting in the forests surrounding the nearby village and farms at night. His eyes had grown bigger, his claws longer, and his teeth had moved farther apart, so he most certainly deserved the name of Fang. His bouncing and bounding didn't appear quite so carefree and joyful. He didn't go off at odd angles. His mannerisms struck her as more intent and purposeful. There was something predatory about him, even when he was sitting quietly, drowsing in a corner, listening to her and Cecil discuss a book of history or lore or fables or philosophy.

Ash didn't like being just slightly afraid of Fang. Afraid that he might turn from the forest animals that he hunted with such glee, and try to sample human blood. Cecil had been teaching her small, simple magics with the flute, strong enough to make her stars itch sometimes. She was sure she could defend herself if Fang attacked. Put him to sleep. Pin him to the ground, moving something heavy on top of him, if necessary. She didn't want those tactics to be necessary. She wanted her manic, sometimes silly companion back.

"Yes, I can see where that would concern you," Cecil said, when she explained her problems and concerns to him one evening. "Have you asked him what he wants?"

He laughed when she sat back, blinking rapidly for several moments as she let those words bounce around inside her head.

"Does Fang want to be cured?" he asked while she still struggled to figure out what she felt and thought.

"Well ... why wouldn't he?"

"He seems rather happy as he is." Cecil shrugged. "When he comes back in the morning, ask him."

She did, and Fang went so still, she feared he had stopped breathing. He didn't blink, his ears didn't twitch, and they were always twitching. Ash had learned to use his ear twitches, the angles and the speed, to interpret his thoughts and moods. They had worked out a sort of sign language between them, as the flexibility and dexterity of his ears increased.

Then he sat up and his ears snapped back, so they were nearly lying flat, straight out. A definite no.

"You don't want to be cured?"

His ears snapped upright, then back. Three times.

"You ... like being this way?"

Fang grinned, close to his original manic grin when they had first met. He waggled his ears upright, forward hard enough, rapidly enough, to generate a small breeze. A definite, happy sort of yes.

"But I thought you didn't like how you were before, when you were accused of being a killer."

Fang's ears twitched multiple times, different directions, so rapidly she couldn't interpret them.

"Ring, can you help us?"

He thinks …

The ring paused and felt a little warm on her finger, indicating he was focusing quite intently on Fang, touching the bunny's mind. Since the transformation after Morris's bite, Fang hadn't been quite so easy for the ring to read. That had worried Ash, but she hadn't really considered the implications until now.

He likes being this way much more than before. He likes being different, and strong. He likes eating meat, rather than being afraid he will be meat. He likes confusing, more than scaring. The ring sighed. *I'm sorry, that's the clearest impression I can get. His mind has changed. I wasn't able to look into Morris's mind unless he allowed me. Since Fang is partly a vampire, I am partly blocked.*

"Like trying to read a book at twilight," Cecil said, when Ash reported the conversation. "Well, Fang, if you're happy, and if you promise not to dine on your friends, why should we try to change you back? You weren't really happy before, were you?"

Fang stood up on his hind legs and shook his head so hard he wobbled. He took a few tiny hops up to Ash, sitting on a stool next to Cecil, and reached out both his forepaws to her. She grasped them, and he bent his ears forward enough to make an 'X' over his chest.

I think that means he crosses his heart, the ring reported.

~~~~~

That evening, Ash was climbing up to the loft to go to bed when Cecil let out a groan, followed by a thud. She jumped down and hurried to his side. He had sprawled halfway into his tiny closet of a bedroom. It was barely large enough to hold his bed. She worried he had hit his head, the way he was rubbing it when she reached him.

"No, I'm fine. I'm fine. Some of that nice herbal mixture you've been refining would help, though." Cecil held out his hand. His staff, which had rolled away out of reach, now slid across the floor to him. He bowed his head and took a few more deep breaths. "Give me time to think, to sort out … I'm sorry."

"For what?" Ash paused in crossing to the fireplace, where the smallest cauldron was always hung to keep water hot.

"I don't know yet, but I know there's always something to be sorry about when I get a vision."

"Is that what happened? Does it hurt?" She reached for the wax-stoppered jar with the herbal mixture she had tried to recreate from one of Cecil's oldest, most faded books. Some of the names for ingredients were nearly impossible to read, or else were mangled spellings, or the name for the plant had changed over the centuries. Ash was quite proud of the soothing qualities of the potion she had come up with, and even
~~~~~

more proud of how good it tasted. Her experience with healers and their potions in the past had made her believe that the more vile the potion tasted, the faster and more effectively it worked.

"Having a vision is like having the top of your head pried open and someone writes right on your brain with a quill dipped in flaming wine. Fortunately, the sensation only lasts a moment ..." Another sigh, as he positioned the staff and pushed himself to his feet, pressing his back against the wall. "However, I have learned that it hurts most when the vision deals with someone I am fond of. This time, I fear the vision is for you."

"Me?" Ash shook her head, and nearly dropped the mug she had sprinkled the mixture into. "I'm sorry."

"Oh, don't be. Visions are necessary, if their warnings and guidance are obeyed. They are a gift from A'theosius." He smiled and made his way a little slower than normal to his chair by the fire.

"I'm sorry you had to take a vision for me. My experience with visions and omens and such in the past hasn't been very pleasant. I'd rather avoid them, if I could."

"Hmm, yes, that is a wise attitude, I fear. But when a vision comes for you, it's always best to listen instead of running away." He chuckled. "Unless of course the vision warns you to run away."

He bowed his head and rubbed at his temples. Ash hurried to dip up hot water into the mug, and covered it with a small plate, to preserve the essence of the herbs. She waited, trying to think of the right words to beg A'theosius, or whichever guiding spirits might be listening, to please take away Cecil's pain, first, and second ... well, how exactly could she say, *'Thank you but no thank you, I'd rather not be important enough to have a vision aimed at me,'* without insulting the higher powers?

Cecil sipped at the brew when she judged it strong enough. His color improved, which just made the stab of guilt repeat. She had done this to him, even if she hadn't asked for any guidance.

"You need to remember this," the seer said after several slow sips. "Every castle with a touch of magic wants a princess. It needs a princess to be fulfilled in its purpose. The enchanted castle in the enchanted forest? Even though it has swallowed many princesses over the decades, it is never satisfied."

Cecil shuddered and closed his eyes and took several deep breaths. Then he sat up and tipped his head to the right, as if he were listening. His face wrinkled with a frown of concentration.

"Hmm, that's odd."

"What is?" Ash nearly whispered.

"I know I had several visions, one after another. But once I spoke that warning ... well, it's as if all the pressure is gone. I think all the visions meant the same thing. Which is rather frightening, because what is so vital that I had to see it multiple different ways?"

"What does the castle have to do with me? I'm not a princess."

"Hmm, no. Not right now." A small grin caught up one corner of his mouth. "There are many ways to become a princess, and not all of them require you to be born a princess or to marry a prince."

"It doesn't matter, really, because I've been warned enough to avoid the castle." She leaned forward to look into his mug. "Do you want more to drink?"

"I think that might be wise." He held out the mug, his hand shaking slightly.

That stabbed her again with a sense of guilt.

"What exactly did you see in the visions?" She silently pleaded with A'theosius that Cecil had been mistaken. That the visions didn't apply to her, and he had misread them because of the pain of the delivery. Having his head opened up and the message written with a flaming pen sounded awful. Ash sprinkled more of the herbal mixture into his mug without dumping out the dregs from the previous batch and spilled in more steaming water.

"That's ... the problem." His smile grew. "Sorry."

Ash nearly snapped that she was tired of hearing that, but she couldn't yell at Cecil because it was the ring that had become so irritating with his apologies.

"For what?"

"It doesn't happen all the time, but quite often, as soon as I speak the message of the vision, it fades. I can't picture it in my mind any longer."

"So nothing other than that the enchanted castle wants a princess?"

"Oh, and a very strong impression that you need to be careful of your seventeenth birthday."

"Why?" She couldn't imagine why that would be of any concern. She had turned fifteen just before she fled Castle Fairhold. Why give Cecil a headache to warn her about a birthday two years in the future?

"For those with magic in the blood, especially princesses—"

"I'm not a princess, and I never will be."

"That you know of. There's no predicting the future, even for seers. As I was saying, the seventeenth birthday is pivotal for those with magic in their blood, or those of royal blood. It is doubled if they have both kinds of blood. It's a turning point in their lives, and for the people and countryside around them. How many stories and legends and histories have we read, when something devastating struck near the seventeenth birthday of a noble, or someone who turned out to be the descendant of a powerful enchanter or sorcerer, or even a hedge witch?"

"True." She flinched, and thought she caught herself before she inhaled too sharply.

"You thought of something." Cecil wagged a finger at her.

"Well, I just thought, what if I was wrong, the healers were wrong about my age when Lady Charlotte brought me and the other orphans home with her? What if I wasn't three, but I was four or five? That means my seventeenth birthday will come sooner, and I won't be aware of it until some disaster strikes. And even more of a bother, I don't really know when my birthday is. The healers guessed my age and assigned me a birthday."

"Hmm, sorry, but I'm not in any shape to request details like that, to help you out. Maybe the next seer you encounter, or maybe a magic mirror can seek the answer to that."

"Next seer?" Ash shivered a little at those words.

"That's the other part of the visions. A strong impression that you need to move on soon. Not now, but soon." He frowned. "Hmm, you need to move on before you are forced to move on. That's not very helpful, is it?"

"I don't want to leave." She hoped he wouldn't say she needed to leave right now, this very night. Not just because it was a chilly night, threatening rain, or because it was dark out there. She worried about Cecil.

He reached out with that uncanny accuracy that still startled her at times, to catch hold of her hand with one of his and pat it with the other. "Nor do I want you to leave. If it weren't for these dratted headaches, I would quite enjoy keeping you here as my apprentice, to take over the duties and visions for me."

"You can transfer the ... the ... gift?" The word tasted wrong in her mouth, but she couldn't think of another word. "You can just choose to pass it on to someone?"

"Hmm, not always choose but yes, the guiding spirits come and oversee. Well, it doesn't matter, because you are to move on, and I am to stay here." He took the mug she pressed into his hands and raised it so the steam wreathed around his face. After a testing sniff, he raised the mug and sipped. "You will make me a triply large batch of this before you leave, won't you? And write down the recipe? And I do hope you don't have to leave before we finish marking all the books and the shelves. It will save me so much time and trouble in the future. Some people who come to me for help are rather sloppy, or perhaps more accurately, they're rather careless about inconveniencing an old blind man. Would you believe that some people have accused me of faking my blindness?" He *tsk*ed and shook his head, an impish curve to the edges of his mouth.

"I can believe it. You're far too canny. You have different ways of seeing, and that keeps you out of trouble."

"Hmm, not nearly enough trouble." Cecil tipped his head back. "I'm going to sit here by the fire and let it warm a few bruises out of my side. Go to bed. We're going to be very busy tomorrow."

Ash obeyed, because she really didn't have a choice. She heard the unspoken words: *Because we have no idea when you will have to leave.*

"Do something for me, Ash?" Cecil said, when she was halfway up the ladder.

"Of course." She started to climb back down.

"When you, *if* you become a princess, try not to be the wrong kind? If you can't avoid becoming a princess, be the right kind?"

"I'll try." She continued up the ladder.

"That's all I can ask."

~~~~~

Two nights later, the ring woke her with pinpricks of fire, tightening around her finger to the point Ash feared the bone might break. She woke with a yelp and lay still, feeling her finger throb.

"What was that for?" She managed not to yell.

Camwell has checked on you. He didn't talk directly to me. Perhaps he fears we've become friends. He has to know that you're clever enough, alert enough, to realize that I'm alive, not just a tool and servant. My impression is that he's upset you've been sitting in one place too long.

"Can't you explain ..." She sighed and rolled over on her side and curled up with her knees nearly touching her shoulders. "No, that won't do any good, will it? That would just reinforce his worst fears."

Most definitely. I think he's going to send men after you. I'm sorry, my dear girl, but you really do need to move on. Before his hunters find you, force you to move on, and choose the path for you.

She couldn't do anything but agree. That was the warning in Cecil's visions, after all.

Dawn was still several hours away, but she couldn't sleep. She crept down from her loft and whistled a request to the lanterns not to light, except the smallest one that hung in the air near the ladder. Ash beckoned for it to follow her, and gathered up her clothes, to examine them and make whatever repairs she would need. Cecil had given her several changes of clothes, and she had to decide which ones she could fit in her pack and which she had to leave behind.

It's entirely too bad Cecil doesn't have a bag of accommodation, the ring commented as she got to work. *You could pack a month's worth of provisions and books to read and all sorts of lovely things to make your travels easier. You wouldn't feel the weight, and the bag wouldn't be any larger. It wouldn't be stolen, because anyone who saw you would think it was empty.*

Just before dawn, Cecil woke with a groan. He hit the door of his little room several times before emerging, and Ash guessed he was getting dressed. She debated with herself if she should offer to help, but the door
~~~~~

flew open before she could make up her mind. Cecil gripped the frame of the doorway and tipped his head back, inhaled deeply, then paused. He exhaled even more loudly.

"Ash? Are you down here?"

"Yes."

"Good. I didn't like having to wake you, but we are pressed for time. He's coming. Again." He slammed his right fist into the door frame. "When will that idiot learn? It's not like I can print a dozen or a hundred books or buy that many since the last time he raided me. Unless he knows ... oh, please, A'theosius and all the guiding spirits, please don't let someone have betrayed me."

"Cecil, what's wrong? Who's coming?"

"Ruprick. Come, we have work to do. Hopefully with your help we can get it done in less time, and you can fix any mistakes I make."

"Get what done?"

Cecil didn't explain until they had cleaned off the handcart tucked up against the back side of the bathing lean-to, then filled it with the first load of books, and headed into the forest.

Ruprick of Rathelshiffen was on his way. More accurately, his men were on their way to confiscate more of Cecil's books. He had grand plans to build a center of learning. The rumors couldn't agree if it would focus on magic, or just higher learning in general. Therefore, it didn't matter if the books were history, philosophy, literature, or dealt with magic.

Last time, Cecil had had enough warning to get most of his books into hiding. Ruprick's men had taken everything that hadn't been hidden. Nearly thirty. Two of the three had laughed when Cecil told them they were foolish to risk the wrath of a seer. They said he wasn't much of a seer if he collected books he couldn't read. Then they knocked him over and broke his staff in half. An hour later, he had a vision of them boarding a ship to sail home. The ship shattered and sank. One man survived, the one who hadn't laughed at Cecil.

A year later, Ruprick sent a message to Cecil that he was responsible for replacing the books that were at the bottom of the ocean, because he hadn't warned the men to take a different ship. Cecil had responded by telling him not to trust in ships any longer, and if he was going to keep collecting books, he should start using them. Or better yet, learn how to use the enchanted forest to travel from one continent to another without sailing.

Chapter Eighteen

By this time in the story, Cecil and Ash had reached the hollow oak tree in the center of the forest, where all the seers before him had hidden their valuables. He tapped the tree with his staff. The oak obligingly split its trunk open, revealing a staircase that went down as well as up, and shouldn't have fit inside the oak, yet did.

"And he's just contrary enough, that thieving, self-righteous braggart actually listened to me. He's found a way, or rather, some weak-willed, greedy scholar found a way to chart the shifting of the portals into the enchanted forest, and how to get from one continent to another. And now he's coming after the rest of my books." Cecil sounded more weary than worried, which was only slightly encouraging.

"How long ago did that happen? Because Friar Ipswich told me that King Ruprick of Rathelshiffen stole books from Castle Fairhold, but several generations ago." Ash paused in lifting the first sack of books off the handcart. "How long did it take for him to get through the enchanted forest?"

"Oh, not the King Ruprick who robbed me. This one is his son. Nearly every Ruprick revives the dream of his predecessors, to build the biggest library in the world and establish a collegium. This one is focused on a collegium of magic, where all the most powerful enchanters, sorcerers, wizards, visionaries, seers, and what-have-yous will come to share knowledge. The gaping hole in all the Rupricks' reasoning is that none of them stop to wonder why all these powerful magic-wielders haven't done so already. The answer is, they don't want to. Which is why the plans for the collegium keep falling apart with each new Ruprick who comes along. And the great dunderhead, of each generation, expects them to be grateful and gladly do his bidding and make him the most powerful king in the entire world." Cecil huffed a little as he led the way up the stairs, with a heavy sack of books clutched in each hand.

As soon as Ash stepped onto the bottom step, four below him, the trunk of the tree snapped closed with an echoing, hollow bang. She yelped.

Then the steps rose upward, carrying them. The movement wasn't entirely smooth, making Ash wobble several times as they rose up, seemingly higher than the topmost branch of the oak, before coming to a stop on a platform made of what looked like alabaster, as thick as her arm, and stretching out apparently forever, in all directions. Cecil instructed her to put the bags she carried next to his. A pillar of light rose up from the alabaster floor and expanded to surround the sacks of books. When Ash reported what happened, Cecil nodded, looking grimly pleased, and led her back to the steps.

They descended the same way, and in less than a minute the oak tree trunk creaked open again, letting them out. They made eight trips with the handcart before Cecil declared they had moved enough books. He had been careful to leave a good forty books in the cottage, spread across some of the bookshelves, in an attempt to take up more room than they needed.

"You can't depend on those muscle-headed brutes Ruprick employs to be dense enough to look at the shelves and not wonder why I have so many shelves, and so few books," he explained to Ash, as they moved the shorter shelves into the bathing lean-to, the loft, and under Cecil's bed.

The built-in shelves were a problem. Cecil had Ash put neat piles of clothes on the shelves, his harp and her flute, dishes, pots, and all the spare blankets from the loft. Anything that could take up space and make the absence of books less obvious.

Ash had a moment of panic when she thought of all the books in the loft. All it would take was for one of Ruprick's men to climb up high enough to see into the room.

"Not to worry. Everything up there is a duplicate of my books on the shelves down here." Cecil sighed and gestured around the room. "At least, the ones that used to be here. I've only left the duplicates of duplicates, or books that I've found to be useless because the writers were proven to be so greatly wrong, nothing they taught or theorized can be trusted. And, if you'll be so kind, play that new melody I taught you a few days ago. The one for opening clouded eyes. Play it backward and focus on the lanterns in the loft. That will keep them from lighting, if anyone climbs up there. Then we'll paste some don't-look-at-me spells across the ladder, so no one will even think to climb up. If you don't see a ladder, you don't think there's a loft, do you?"

She had to agree, no, she wouldn't look for a loft unless she saw a ladder. Then again, Cecil's cottage did have a rather high roof, so someone looking at it from the outside might anticipate another room tucked up under the eaves. After all, she had.

By the time they had made all the adjustments to the cottage, it was halfway between noon and dinner time. Cecil sent Ash to run to the village, to warn Oswald the blacksmith, Healer Jasper, and Lucinda, the headwoman. They had libraries of their own they were greatly proud of. It didn't matter that they had perhaps twenty books among the three of them. That was still an enormous library compared to most other villages and villagers. They were constantly borrowing books from Cecil, and once a week, they joined him and Ash in the evening to sit by the fireplace and discuss history or philosophy or whatever Ash had been reading to Cecil. They could be trusted not to reveal the quantity of books in Cecil's library, so they deserved fair warning to hide their own books.

"That selfish rotter," Lucinda growled, when Ash gave her the warning. "I heard when his father came through here. Before I was born." She stepped backward into her cottage, beckoning for Ash to follow. "My father was the village teacher, as well as the headman, and they took the readers the village had just bought for the children. Thirty pages each, teaching them their letters and how to add and subtract, and those idiots had to take those books too. Just because their king said every book they could get their hands on. Didn't matter what was in the books. What half-wit takes a children's primer? What good will it do him, when it's clear enough to me he doesn't have the brains to learn to read in the first place?"

"They deserve what happened to them," Ash blurted.

"Eh? What's that?" Lucinda paused in reverently placing her armload of books in a hole lined with oilcloths under the floorboards.

"Those men the last time laughed at Cecil and got what they deserved."

"That's a story I haven't heard."

So Ash told her what Cecil had told her. Lucinda carefully wrapped the oilcloth around the books, then sealed up the hole in the floorboards. She rubbed dirt into the seam lines, so the hiding place wasn't that obvious, and covered the spot with a rag rug. She laughed when Ash got to the end of the story. "Good man, our Cecil."

"Oh, but he didn't do anything. The vision came after they left."

"I wouldn't put it past him to be strong enough to resist the warning, so he couldn't give it to them. A curse of blindness on those rotters and their thrice-rotten king and all his descendants."

This was a gruff, spiteful side of Lucinda Ash hadn't seen before. Yet she could understand her fury for anyone who would steal someone else's books, especially children's books.

When she returned to the cottage, Fang had emerged from his sleeping place, a fur-lined box sitting on top of the bathing lean-to. He was hopping slowly around the outside of the cottage, tracing the tracks of the handcart and Cecil and Ash. She was surprised now that all their work, back and forth to the hollow oak and rearranging the interior of the cottage, hadn't awakened him. While Fang only faintly steamed or gave off puffs of smoke in the daylight, awakening him before dusk made him exceedingly cranky. When she stepped into the clearing around the cottage, he waggled his ears at her, bending one down to point at all the tracks and the places where the wheels of the handcart had dug ruts through the moss.

"We had a great deal to move today." Ash stumbled a little as she stepped over to the bench sitting to the right of the cottage door. "We have to move on, Fang. The ring says the justiciar is looking for me, and he's going to send men to make me get moving again. So we need to do it before he sends them."

Fang jumped up on the bench and leaned against her, purring softly, the vibration moving his entire body. She smiled, blinking back some ridiculous tears, and stroked him where he liked it best, from just in front of his ears, between his ears, and down his back. His fur felt slightly hot and prickly on the outer edges, meaning he wasn't on the point of bursting into smoke, but close. Fortunately, the shadows were visibly thickening as sunset turned to dusk. His fur would cool soon, and he was in no danger.

Out of the thickening shadows of the trees stepped six men. They were dressed alike, with swords sheathed at their waists, leather caps with metal rings sewn all over them, and leather tunics over their clothes. So, the current King Ruprick had sent twice as many men as his father had sent. Did he think Cecil was less blind after all these years? How long had he waited, and built up his courage and self-righteous wrath, before coming after more books? Ash wondered if Cecil was wrong, and someone in the village had indeed betrayed him, reporting that he had ten times as many books as the ones the previous Ruprick had stolen. Or had one of the many visitors who came to Cecil for advice during the intervening years come as a spy?

There was no such thing as gratitude or loyalty any longer, she feared.

"Where's the old man?" the biggest and reddest of them said.

"The seer has had a long day and he's tired. I'm going to make his dinner soon. You can come back tomorrow with your questions." She stood and took a few steps forward.

Her fingers prickled, with what she imagined was magic ready to be used, and her two stars stung, harder than they ever had before. Was this a sign her magic was about to awaken? The problem was that she didn't know how to direct it. Whatever magic was in her blood and bones hadn't made itself known to her. Now was not a good time, because as Captain Reginald had often said, what good was a sword in an untrained hand?

All her reading with Cecil had been rather discouraging, because magic was specific to the user, manifesting in limited ways. One person could move things with magic, another could heal, a third could create illusions. Very few people had enough magic in them to do all three things, and even fewer could do more besides. If she had the flute in her hands, she could use music magic to throw things at these men, or perhaps use it to seal the door shut. The problem with music magic was that while she was playing, she would be distracted, and it wouldn't be hard for these brutes to attack her, knock her down, take the flute from her to stop the magic, and worse, break the flute, and her, in retribution.

"We don't have questions," the leader of the six said with a sneer. He looked Ash up and down, and he didn't get that slight widening of the eyes or another "ah ha" or "what?" expression, meaning he didn't realize he was talking to a girl under the grubby boy clothes. "We're not asking for anything, we're taking."

The door opened and Cecil peered out, braced against the door frame, his face wrinkled in pain and his sparse whisps of hair standing out at odd angles.

"Ash? Might I trouble you for some more of that lovely brew? I've just had another … Oh. There you are." He pulled himself upright and sternness wiped away his discomfort as his milky gaze appeared to sweep over the six men. "I've been expecting you. Don't expect any more joy in this errand than your predecessors had."

The soldier on the far right growled a string of curses and launched himself across the clearing at Cecil. Ash braced to lunge and intercept him, though she didn't expect much success.

The leader of Ruprick's brutes stepped forward, an arm outstretched, and clotheslined the man. He went down with a crash.

"You want to bring a whole gob of trouble on us?" he growled. "The king said no roughing up the old man. That was the mistake the others made."

"Weren't no mistake," the man on the ground snarled. "I got a right to get some back for my grandfather, don't I?"

"Tell me." Cecil stepped out of the doorway, leaning with one arm against the front wall of the cottage. "What is the difference between roughing up a seer and stealing from him? Both are causing harm."

"Ain't stealing," a third man said. "We're confiscating on the orders of King Ruprick."

"He's not king here," Ash said. "He's got no authority. Did the king of Ynderweil give him permission to steal from his seers?"

"You shut your gab, boy!" The leader pointed a beefy finger at her. The man closest to Ash stepped forward, ready to enforce the order.

Fang shrieked and bounced up high, so his ears brushed against the lower branches of the overhanging trees. All six men tipped their heads back, watching his upward and then downward arch.

"What is that?" the man on the far left blurted, followed by a string of curses Ash couldn't begin to understand. She wondered if the man was speaking another language.

Someone started to laugh. Someone else said something about a crazy rabbit. Then Fang landed in front of the leader, bounced at a sharp angle, and slammed both feet into the man's face. He went down with a scream four octaves higher than his speaking voice. Before he hit the ground, Fang bounced off him and ricocheted off a second man to hit a third. In seconds, the air was filled with dust and grunts and yelps and curses and thuds and Fang's furious shrieks. One of them tried to crawl out of the growing, thickening cloud on his hands and knees. He raised a hunting horn to his lips. Fang landed on his head, smashing him flat to the ground. But not before the horn let out a single blurt of sound. Then Fang's left fang dug into the man's wrist, wringing a shriek from him.

The scent of blood joined the fracas. Ash froze, stunned by Fang's sheer speed as he bounced from man to man. Cecil reached out a hand to her and they clung to each other, staring, as heads and hands and feet emerged from the whirlwind of dust and cursing and shrieking, and a few bleating calls for, "Mama!" Fang muttered and growled as he punched and bit and thumped with his hind feet, and Ash could almost make out words. If she wasn't mistaken, he was cursing. Did bunnies curse? She supposed they had to know how, if they were magically endowed.

A horn sounded in the distance, in the direction of the village. Followed by the approaching sounds of hooves. People shouted. One of the men fell out of the tangle of fighting and landed on his back. He was bleeding from multiple scratches on his face, his clothes were torn, one eye was starting to swell. But he tipped his head back and laughed, somewhat brokenly.

"That'll teach you," he said, his voice strained and ready to break. "Think we were stupid enough to come with just a few this time?"

A troop of mounted men broken through the trees into the clearing surrounding Cecil's cottage. They were all armed. One had a squirming little girl clinging to him, clawing with one hand at the sack hanging off his saddle. Several men stared, goggle-eyed, at the dying cloud of dust and blood and struggle. Two burst out laughing, until a glare from their leader silenced them. Ash thought he had to be their leader because he wore some chain mail instead of just leather for armor.

"What are you idiots doing?" the man in the chain mail barked.

"Fang, stop!" Ash called and held out her hands.

As if Fang had ever listened to her? She doubted he would listen now. From the glimpses she had had of him, he was enjoying himself far too much, despite the fury that made his eyes glow red through the dust and debris.

She was as surprised as anyone when Fang bounced up high, came down hard on the red-haired man's chest with a loud snap that wrung a broken shriek from him, then bounced at a sharp angle, right into her arms. She stumbled back from the force of the impact. Fang stank of blood and dust and mud and sweat and the bitter tang she supposed was anger. Or else vampire bloodlust.

In those few seconds of Fang calming down, and a lot of gasping and staring and muttered curses, the villagers caught up with King Ruprick's mounted men. Cara the baker stomped up to the man with the little girl clinging to him and yanked her free. She also managed to yank the sack free. The man cursed and reached for the sack, but the woman's furious gaze stopped him.

"I told you, Ox, leave the children's books alone," the leader said without turning to look at the man.

"His majesty said all books," the man retorted.

"Did he? You were there in the throne room when I got my orders?"

That didn't get a response, other than a few other men chuckling.

"What is that?" Lucinda said, somewhat out of breath, and pointed at Fang.

He clung to Ash, trembling in fury, or maybe exhaustion. He smeared her shirt with blood and mud, and judging from the sharp stabs, tearing holes in it with the claws of forelegs and hind legs.

"That is a vampire the boy and I have been trying to cure," Cecil said. He glared at the downed men, who were wobbling and staggering as they struggled to their feet or contented themselves with crawling toward their fellow soldiers. "It's very hard to do when what few books of magic I used to have were stolen, and I have to rely on memory."

"You can't read, you stupid old duffer," one of the mounted men shot back. "What does it matter?"

"I don't need eyes to read magic books," he said, drawing himself up tall and straight, and glaring directly at the speaker.

That earned fearful looks and mutters from villagers and soldiers alike. Fang muttered, but Ash was sure that wasn't fear. More like he was working himself up into another fury, to attack.

"Just hand over the books, seer, and we'll be on our way," the leader said. He sounded tired, rather than irritated. Ash didn't know if that was a good sign or not. "And promise us you won't put any curses on us."

"I don't call down curses. I merely report them."

"Yeah, right, like you reported what was gonna happen to me old granddad," a bloody, dusty, torn man grumbled.

"If you get any visions about us on the way home, you'll tell us," the leader said.

"If I don't have a vision about you before you leave," Cecil responded after a moment of thought, "then how can I report it to you?"

Several people laughed. The mounted men looked around, but Ash didn't think they identified who had laughed. She doubted that would make a difference. King Ruprick's soldiers were the usual low-grade bully boys she had seen when traveling on errands for Lady Charlotte. Lord Digory had never allowed their type into the castle, when they came looking for work. Usually, such men sought a new master and home because they had either failed abominably and been cut loose, or their previous master had faced the king's justice. Either way, they weren't the sort to work well with the soldiers under Captain Reginald's command. Men like them didn't need an excuse to beat on someone, and they didn't need to know who was guilty when they punished. They just struck at whoever was handy.

"Maybe we should just stay here, enjoying the hospitality of the village, until you do get a vision," the leader said after a moment of thought and studying Cecil through narrowed eyes.

"That will take some time, because I just had a vision, and it will be several weeks before I'm well enough to have another one." Cecil slumped forward and reached to brace himself on Ash's shoulder. "I was just coming out to ask my apprentice here to brew me a restorative tonic when your men so rudely interrupted. And freed the vampire bunny while they were at it. Don't any of you have the sense of a rock, not to barge into and break the wards around a seer's home, and set loose all sorts of imprisoned and partially tamed demonic creatures?"

Many of the soldiers stepped back toward the dubious shelter of the trees and thickening shadows. Most of the villagers retreated as well.

"Vision, eh? And what was in the vision?" He rested a hand on the hilt of the sword at his hip, in very clear threat.

"Forget about the vision." Lucinda pointed a slightly trembling hand at Ash. "What do we do about that vile creature of darkness?"

She meant Fang, not Ash. That was no relief. Despite his peculiarities and bloodthirsty aspects of his nature, Ash was rather fond of the manic bunny. Besides, he was half-vampire because he had been defending her.

"That is in the vision," Cecil said. "Ash, you need to take a three-day journey into the forest, to the glade that you saw in the silver scrying bowl. When you get there, find the hidden spring. Wait until the water turns red, then put the vampire bunny into the water and hold him down until the water runs clear again. He will be cured."

Fang squealed and chattered, the sound muffled against Ash's shoulder. Several villagers let out yelps and curses and more fled back out of sight among the trees.

"If it's a vampire, why ain't it drinking from the boy?" one of the bedraggled, bloody soldiers grumbled.

Chapter Nineteen

"That's one of the few wards you imbeciles didn't break when you came barging in here. What kind of two-bit magicians work for your King Ruprick, to work such badly designed magic that interferes with wards and knocks the magical humors out of balance, and endangers everyone in the village?" Cecil groaned, hunched his shoulders, and pressed his free hand against the side of his head.

Ash caught her breath. That wasn't play-acting. The wrinkles of discomfort forming around Cecil's eyes and mouth were real. He needed the healing brew and should have had it long before this whole idiotic encounter began. So was his vision also true?

She couldn't imagine him speaking the instructions of a vision meant for her to everyone in the village and these bully boys, serving a king who had no authority in Ynderweil.

"You need to leave," Lucinda said. "Haven't you done enough damage? Barging into people's homes, taking what ain't your king's right to take? Don't you give me none of that celestial right of kings garbage. Ruprick ain't our king, and I know if we go to King Steffan, he'll agree that Ruprick has no right here. You're nothing but a bunch of bully thieves."

"Maybe we are," leader turned his horse to face her now, with his hand still on the hilt of his sword, "but who's going to stand against us?"

"Well, the longer you sit there, making your demands, the more time the soldiers from Fort Paxus have to get here and teach you some manners," Cecil said. His hand gripped Ash's shoulder a little tighter. "The moment you rode through our village wards, an alarm at the fort let the soldiers know we were being invaded. They were on their way before you broke down the first door. And yes, you really should have listened to your leader and not tried to take the children's books. Imagine how embarrassing it will be for your King Ruprick, when he can't even read a book made to teach the children how to read?"

Several someones snickered and chuckled. Ash saw at least two of them were Ruprick's soldiers.

"I don't know if I should believe you." The leader glanced back and forth between Cecil and Lucinda.

"But you can't afford to take the chance, can you?" Lucinda's tone was smug, if not her expression. She took two steps closer to the man, fists jammed into her hips, and glared at him.

Cecil let go of Ash's shoulder. She turned, shoving Fang out of her arms, as the old seer went to his knees. She tried to hold him up, but she was too slow, and he knocked her off balance. They both went to the ground as she shouted his name.

In the fuss of getting him into the cottage, two soldiers shoved their way through the door. They swept clear three bookshelves, knocking most of the books to the floor. Fang let out a long, furious, howling shriek, and leaped through the door. The soldiers gathered up what they could and fled. Fang followed them out the door, and Ash heard him shrieking and stomping and bouncing back and forth in front of the cottage.

She splashed hot water into a mug, then dumped in twice as much of the herbal mixture as she needed and stirred it with her finger. Lucinda and several others got Cecil into his closet bedroom and stretched out on the bed. They jammed up in the doorway, because there just wasn't enough room for so many in there. The angry, frightening whinnies of horses and the sounds of retreating hoofbeats and the curses of men, both soldiers and villagers, filled the air. She ignored the chaos outside while she blew on the brew and willed the herbs to steep quickly and release their healing power into the hot water. Maybe it wasn't as strong as she would have liked it, but Ash thought it was strong enough to do Cecil some good, by the time everyone cleared out of his tiny bedroom and she could guide the mug to his mouth for the first sip.

By the time nearly half the mug had gone down Cecil's throat in small sips, everyone else had left except for Lucinda. Ash heard her moving about in the main room of the cottage, picking up the scattered books and putting them on the shelves, then closing the door with a loud thud.

"Sorry," the village headwoman muttered, although Cecil hadn't reacted to the sound. A moment later she appeared in the doorway. "How is he?"

"Much better." Cecil opened one eye. "Thank you for not giving me away. Seers aren't supposed to lie, which I depended on to make them believe me. If you had reacted in surprise, that would have ruined everything."

"Oh, you mean about the soldiers coming? Funny thing, but I prepared a message and alerted our fastest boys to be ready to run, as soon as Ash told me about those bullies coming back. They were already on their way to the fort before those brutes could figure out which building was the schoolhouse." Lucinda chuckled.

"Doesn't it have a sign that says school?" Ash wrapped Cecil's fingers around the mug, sure he could drink without her help now.

"Yes, it does," Cecil said, "but it's almost a law that despots like Ruprick never hire men who can read. Or use basic logic and common sense. I wonder if he will ever understand the irony of sending illiterates to steal books."

Lucinda snorted. "So, you're on the mend now?"

"Much better getting all that animosity out of the magical atmosphere. I wasn't joking about badly made magic accompanying them. The current Ruprick decided to be a little more cautious than his father had been, when it came to earning the ire of seers."

"Not cautious enough to stay in his own kingdom." She sighed and seemed to deflate a little, leaning against the door frame. "So … you did have a vision? I know from my father that they do try to knock your brain out through your ears, but I've never seen you right after you had one." She nodded to Ash. "Good thing you have the boy here, looking after you." She winked. "Whatever the reason for the disguise."

Ash blushed a little. She had been experimenting with bands around her chest, to flatten what was, fortunately, taking a long time to blossom. Obviously, she hadn't done a good enough job.

"Yes, I had a vision. And I swear before A'theosius … half my pain is from lying about it." He let go of the mug with one hand to reach for Ash's shoulder. She sat on the edge of his bed, ready to take the mug when he was done. "I saw you go through an archway of roses, into a tunnel of roses and thorns, all covered with snow."

"Me or the roses?" Ash asked without thinking.

"Both. That's what worries me."

"So … just avoid roses that bloom in … Oh …" Lucinda nodded.

"What does that mean? What don't I understand?" Ash tried to keep her voice soft, for Cecil's sake.

"Roses, blooming in the winter? That's a sign of magic at work. Strong magic. And maybe something you can't escape if it's aiming for you." The headwoman shook her head. "Even I can read a sign like that clearly enough."

"And you really do need to leave, Ash. As soon as possible. Those soldiers will talk about Fang, and you know they won't admit it was just one angry bunny that made fools of them and got the better of them. They'll have an entire troop of vampire bunnies, as big as cottages, and you'll be painted as a dark warlock, whipping them to a frenzy and driving them before you." Cecil shook her once. "Get Fang and get out of here before there's a frenzy to hunt down every rabbit and hare and bunny from one border to the other."

"I was planning to leave, thanks to the justiciar, but … not so soon." Ash looked to Lucinda.

"Don't you worry, I'll take good care of him," the headwoman said, with a nod and a frown that was as good as making a vow.

"The arch of roses. Am I supposed to go in or is it a warning to stay out?" she asked as she stood. Already she was thinking about all the things she needed to find, where she had left her mending, what provisions she could take without shorting Cecil. And most important, if Fang had headed into the woods for his evening hunting, or he had retreated to his basket on the roof. What was the use of fleeing if he wasn't with her?

"I don't know," Cecil said after several long, thoughtful, frowning moments. "You were just there, standing in the archway. I didn't see you go in. I suppose this is just a warning sign, look for the arch and the roses in winter, and be prepared for something to happen."

Ash didn't think that was any help at all. Certainly not worth the headache Cecil had to suffer to receive the vision. She knew better than to say so. With a nod to them both, she headed across the room, to the ladder to the loft. The disguising spells had faded, meaning the threat truly was gone. She decided to take the flute, and a bag of the healing herbal mixture, and a wooden cup and bowl, but she would have to leave behind almost everything else Cecil had given her, for the sake of swift flight. She was still better off than she had been when he found her. Other than the ache weaving through her chest. It hadn't hurt this badly when she fled Castle Fairhold.

Fang was waiting for her when she slipped out of the cottage less than half an hour later. Lucinda had offered to have her husband give Ash a ride in his wagon to the king's highway, to give her a good head start. Ash had declined. She had seen the look of mixed confusion and horror from Dominic, when the cloud of dust from the battle had settled and he had gotten his first good luck at Fang. She couldn't ask the goodhearted man to take Fang in the wagon, and she couldn't ask Fang to go by foot while she rode.

The bunny nodded to her and kept pace with her with sedate, short hops as she headed into the thickening shadows of the trees. His ears twitched in the fading light, the signs clear enough to read.

"No, I'm not angry with you at all. You defended Cecil. They were entirely in the wrong. And besides, we were getting ready to leave anyway." She reached out to stroke between his ears. Fang stopped to let her get in a few strokes, purring hard enough to make her leg vibrate when he leaned against her. Then he hopped away, leading her into the forest and the night.

~~~~~

Eight days later, the ring announced that Justiciar Camwell's men had arrived at the village. They were distracted by tales of the vampire bunny and the apprentice seer who controlled the magical creature. They didn't connect the stories with their quarry until someone let slip that the only newcomer to the village in the last three months had been the apprentice seer. When they finally thought to ask Cecil for help, which
~~~~~

they should have done the moment they arrived, he told them Ash had headed into the forest to perform a ritual he had found for her, to free the bunny of his vampirism. Half the village had heard him tell her what to do, after all, so Camwell's men had to believe him, with all that supportive testimony. The justiciar's men were not only able to read, but they knew how to ask the right questions and not simply make assumptions. Cecil convinced them he was still exhausted and aching from the last vision. His weakness was exacerbated by his fear for Ash, that the ritual had failed and she had been savaged by the vampire bunny. The last anyone knew, the men had headed south instead of north, thanks to a few misdirection spells that Lucinda had deployed, using several charms hidden among the village's secret treasures.

"How do you know all this?" Ash asked, after digesting that announcement for a few moments.

She and Fang had stopped to sleep the hottest daylight hours away in a thick clump of blackberry bushes. Her fingers were just as stained with the juice from the enormous fruit as Fang's chest and face and paws. He enjoyed messy food, period, not just red, messy food.

Oh, their leader was wearing another spirit ring, linked to me, therefore linked to you. The justiciar is under the mistaken impression that certain rings have authority over others. We allow him to continue in this error to protect ourselves, quite frankly. My friend was quite accommodating and took his instructions literally. To follow your trail to the place where you had come to rest. He didn't tell them you moved on, how long ago, or what direction you're going.

And the man wearing my friend is too vain to want help so badly he will ask the ring to volunteer information. He only wants information when he asks for it, and exactly what he asks for, nothing more. That is his error. We spirit rings have learned over the centuries not to inflict advice on those who will resent it. For some reason, the leader of the justiciar's hunters has a rather large, ingrained distrust of magical items. He's apparently of the seen but not heard school of magical mastery. It's rather odd, the large number of people who are disturbed when magical items become old enough, full enough of magic, they become aware. As if the only souls A'theosius grants are to upright bipeds.

The ring's words and tone made Ash laugh. She was grateful. She needed some humor after that bit of disturbing news. Any frustration that landed on Justiciar Camwell and his men suited her just fine, because she quite resented having to leave the comfortable spot she had been making for herself. Yes, she had known she would have to move on, even before the ring let her know what his ring friends had reported. Still, there was the possibility, not exactly discussed between her and Cecil, but hinted at between them, that she could return someday. She had made friends among the villagers. That friendship might have been tainted by Fang's presence and actions, and she suspected she would either have to find a cure for him or he would have to leave her before she could be fully welcomed back to the village. Still, other than the awful headaches seers suffered as the price of their visions, and yes, going blind, there was something comfortable and secure in the idea of being Cecil's heir. He had called her his apprentice numerous times. That meant something. One of the oldest rules of magic, and one of the first Cecil had taught her, was that when something was said often enough, and believed hard enough, it became real.

Now that there's proof you're on the move again, the ring said, breaking into her ruminations, *hopefully they will report to the justiciar and leave you alone.*

"Hopefully," she muttered. Then she grinned into the shadows of her fruity shelter as a new thought came to her. "So, have you heard anything from your friend saddled with Lathia?"

Hmm, the last I heard, she was grumbling about how much silence there was in the silly girl's head. When she wasn't complaining about how unfair everything and everyone was.

"Has Lathia figured out that there is a person inside the ring?" Ash chuckled. "Or am I totally wrong, and you're not really inside the ring, it's just an illusion? Maybe you're somewhere else and your voice just comes to me?"

Silence.

Fang's ears twitched a few times, but he had gorged so heavily on berries a short time ago, he was in a stupor almost equivalent to heavy drinking. Ash suspected she would have to shout several times to awaken him. She knew better than to disturb him, though.

"Ring? I'm sorry. Did I offend you?"

Hmm? Oh, no. Not offended. It's just a question no one has ever asked me, or anyone else I know. To be honest, it's not something I've really thought about … and to be even more honest, I'm not sure I can answer. I perceive through the ring, but if I have a body other than the ring, if I am anchored somewhere else and only have the illusion of traveling on your hand … I really can't say. He chuckled. *How interesting. You've given me and my friends something to research and discuss and argue over for possibly years.*

"Is that a good thing?"

Oh, yes, indeed. Intriguing questions and knowledge and philosophical discussions are the wealth of beings like me, since we don't really need homes or food or much of anything else physical.

"I haven't asked outright before. I thought maybe it would be rude, but … what exactly are you? Some of the stories I read in Cecil's books hinted folks like you are originally from other lands. Other magical traditions and magical rules. Are you a form of jinn?

Another long silence.

It's rather funny, and a little sad to admit it, but I don't really know, he finally said. *My impression is that we, or rather many of us, were something else entirely. Something huge and powerful and we … trespassed. I don't know if that's the correct word. Isn't that funny, that I can't find the right words or concepts to apply to myself? We went where we shouldn't have gone, tried to do something we were forbidden, and we have been reduced. Yes, reduced is a good word. Limited. Constrained. We are much less than we once were, and greatly less than we could have been by now. We are being redeemed through forgetting and through service. Hmm, that's interesting as well. I never really thought of it that way before, but it makes quite a bit of sense. We are being redeemed. We lost our souls … no, that isn't the right way of explaining, but it's as close as I can get right now. We are earning back our souls, I suppose.*

"I'm sorry. That doesn't seem quite fair."

Oh, my dear Lady Ashlyn, when will you grow up enough to realize that very little in this life is fair? The ring chuckled, taking the sting out of his words, although his tone had been light, amused, not at all condemning. *Look at it this way: Whatever crimes I committed before the great hazy wall in my memories, I have most likely paid for them, because how else can you explain my great good fortune at being paired with you, your delightfully inquisitive, sensible mind, and the adventure you have been sent to pursue? These are all gifts from A'theosius.*

"If you say so," she said on a sigh.

The ring was silent for a few moments, then he chuckled. *Oh, my dear girl, I'm not laughing at you now. No, my friend is responding to my question. We haven't talked in a while. What she's telling me is quite astounding. And rather amusing and satisfying. That petty little snot got her comeuppance, it seems. My friend says the telling will take some time. Rather than tell you each bit as she tells me, I'll wait and tell you everything once she's told me the whole tale, if that's all right?*

"Yes, please." Ash busied herself adjusting the drape of her cloak among the brambles of the berry bushes, to create shade as the sun traveled across the opening overhead. It wouldn't do for Fang to wake up, smoking and steaming and prickling with sunburn. He had made it very clear that his fur didn't protect against sunburn of the vampire variety, and just made the sunburn worse.

The ring was still silent when she had harvested several more handfuls of berries and put them on a rag by Fang's head, for him to snack on when he woke. She gathered more for herself and tempered the sweetness with a few bites of cheese. Then she curled up to sleep the day away, as much as she was able.

Naturally, sleep didn't come right away. Her brain was too full of the new things she had learned from the ring. She had half a pot of ink left from the supplies Blaz had given her, so now she recorded her thoughts and questions in the second of the journals. She took the time to calculate the seasons. Spring had come several weeks early to Castle Fairhold, when her troubles and adventure had begun. She hadn't been paying attention to the months and dates, but from the phases of the moon and the steady heat and clear skies every day, the end of summer approached.

What was she going to do when the fall rains hit, followed by winter? That was probably a question best left for the ring when he was free to talk. Should she alter the path Blaz had helped her plot out, and find a more temperate climate to spend the winter? Ash had read enough to know that the weather patterns weren't the same in every country. Some lands were warm all year round, while others had more than their fair share of snow. She knew better than to hope she could find another friend and mentor and shelter, like she had enjoyed with Cecil. Especially if Justiciar Camwell again sent someone to give her a shove back onto the road if she sat still for too long. She wouldn't put it past him to have his hunters do something awful, to drive her away from new friends. Remembering the fear on some of the faces of the villagers still stung. She could understand their fear, seeing Fang for the first time, at his messiest and bloodiest and most vicious. But hadn't he been justified in turning into a miniature tornado of destruction in the face of the threat from King Ruprick's thugs?

Ash didn't want to have to go through that again. Common sense said to get the quest over with and fulfill the list of conditions before she settled down somewhere for the winter. The problem was that she might just lose the ring's company and guidance, once the quest was over. She didn't want to risk that. She needed to find a way to break Camwell's mastery of the ring, maybe all the spirit rings he used for spying on travelers, to free her friend before she freed herself.

How? Where could she find enough magic to accomplish that without exciting Camwell's interest in her actions so much that he would change the conditions of the quest, and keep her bound to him indefinitely?

Chapter Twenty

The sun had descended toward evening until only a finger's width showed above the top berry brambles, when the ring woke Ash from a drowsy, sweaty, headachy stupor. She was grateful, because she sensed bad dreams waiting to pounce once she fell far enough into sleep.

Do you want the entire story, step by step, or do you want me to gloss over the boring details and give you the important bits? The ring's voice rippled with amusement.

"Give me the important bits now, and then you can tell me all the details when we're walking."

Sensible. Well, first of all, Lathia lost her two escort servants within the first fortnight.

"They ran away?"

They tried, but her father had Hazel put a linking spell on them. He was so rude and said so many untrue things about you, she decided to add a just desserts spell, to allow Lathia to punish herself, combined with enough conditions to allow the servants to escape, if they wanted. Oh, and they wanted, very badly, before they even crossed the border of Alfordia.

"So how did they escape Lathia?"

The silly clunch triggered the just desserts spell before she was more than an hour from Fairhold. That guided her to a nest full of nasty spells once she crossed the border. One of them was to separate travelers from their companions. The servants were set free and dropped fifty miles away, in the opposite direction they were heading. They've made no effort yet to return to Lord Winston or find Lathia. They're in another kingdom altogether, so Winston has no authority to have them brought back. As for Lathia, she got herself trapped in the dungeon of a wannabe ogre, forced to cook and clean for him. It's the usual servitude and instruction and personality improvement curse, meaning she would be imprisoned until she showed compassion on several other prisoners and broke their spells. Which would have, or rather I should say, should have, resulted in them freeing her as well.

"No compassion?"

She's constitutionally unable to hear their pleas for help. She certainly couldn't see there was anything unusual about a talking hen and a pot of flowers that changed color and perfume. No, Lathia was such a bad cook and even worse at cleaning, she frustrated the ogre so he shoved her out of his underground lair and told her to never come back. She's just as much a thief as she is a liar, and she stole several items of gold. All enchanted people. The moment they were out of the ogre's lair, the enchantment broke, and they expressed their gratitude by helping Lathia on her way.

"But?" Ash grinned and settled back with a handful of berries to nibble on. The richness of his voice hinted the story was only going to get better. Well, better for her, worse for Lathia.

She can't tell the difference between gratitude and flattery intended to trap her. Two of the people she accidentally freed were twin halflings, sons of a minor faerie princess and a prince who rescued her from a three-centuries-long sleep. They took Lathia home to their grandfather's court, where she promptly attached herself to the kind of court officials that think everyone is out to get them because they are out to get everyone else. They used her to try to steal several valuable items from the faerie king's treasure room.

Lathia was foolish enough to try to keep several baubles for herself. She got herself enslaved to a particularly nasty creature that steals people's bodies for a few days of what it considers fun. She spent that time locked up in a nesting doll, all six layers. When the creature returned her body, much worse for wear, she made such a nuisance of herself with her complaints, the faerie king had her banished.

"And?" Ash prompted, when the ring let out several nasty chuckles.

With green hair, ears like a donkey, and forced to go about on all fours until the full moon freed her. Even worse, for the people who found her, at least, she was shoved out of the faerie kingdom on the shores of Welladee.

"Wait." She nearly crushed the last three berries in her hand as she sat up and thought hard, trying to place the name on a map of the world Cecil had showed her. "That's ... that's on the continent of Marcocia. That's on the other side of the world." She grinned. "They don't speak our language there, do they?" Then she popped the last three mangled berries into her mouth and bit down hard, squirting juice down her throat so she nearly choked.

No, they do not. Unfortunately for the people who found her, the clear signs of enchantment convinced the local prince she was a princess under a curse. He brought in every enchanter and wizard and seer and magician he could find, to set her free. Someone was foolish enough to whip up a translation spell, so Lathia could tell her story. The ring snorted. *Her version of the story, you can be sure. With little resemblance to the truth.*

"No. Oh, no ... don't tell me." She closed her eyes, and nearly rubbed her face with her berry-stained hands.

I'm sorry, but yes, the prince married her. He did take the precaution of making sure she really was of noble blood. It didn't matter to him how diluted that noble blood was, and how far away her noble family was. My friend believes he was relieved to learn how far away her interfering relatives were from his kingdom.

"That's so unfair!" Ash had a hard time keeping her voice down, and not letting it turn into a wail. "How does she end up with a prince and a castle and a kingdom and far enough away nobody knows the truth of what she's done and … and … and … it's just not fair." If she were a few years younger, she might have thrown herself face-down on the ground and drummed at it with her hands and feet. There wasn't enough room to do that in the tiny blackberry bush bramble clearing, so she hugged her legs to her chest and scowled at the ground in front of her.

Be honest, you silly girl. Do you want a prince and a castle and a kingdom and all the responsibility that goes with them?

Ash took a deep breath and held it until her heart thudded faster in her ears. She let it out.

"No. But that doesn't make it all right for her to get all that."

What makes you think that a prince and a castle automatically equate to happily ever after? Think about all the fables where being royal and rich ensures people face all sorts of curses and invasions and enemies.

"Hmm, that's … true. I suppose." She took another breath, let it out slowly. "I'm being silly. You're right. I'm sorry. It's just … she's free from the quest, isn't she?"

Well, she certainly crossed enough borders, and she went through several caverns. Not enough to fulfill the terms of the quest, certainly. However, nothing will convince Justiciar Camwell to send men to the other side of the world to nudge that selfish brat into moving on again. And he won't want to come up against her prince. He's one of those lazy, self-satisfied princes who never do enough to get into trouble so a faerie or enchanter will beat some sense and courtesy into him. He does everything he can to avoid being a hero, and surrounds himself with all the help money can buy. Soldiers and servants and magical folk. Look at how he paid a dozen other people to figure out Lathia's cure, instead of making some effort to rescue her himself.

"Why did he marry her?"

Princes like that are desperate to ward off quests. Especially the kind that have a princess under an enchantment at the end. Like enchanted castles that desperately need a princess, or a maiden to turn into a princess, princes without princesses attract quests with a princess at the end, or a series of trials and dangers that will try to turn them into heroes. If he married a maiden of noble blood, then he's effectively shielded from such things latching onto him and pulling him out of his comfortable, sedentary life. He enjoys dealing with facts and figures and administrative tasks and delegating all the real work to others. He's also the kind who would never consider the possibility that he should make any effort to make his wife happy, or that love has to be earned and protected.

"Please stop," Ash said, "you're starting to make me feel sorry for Lathia."

Then that means you have grown, thanks to this quest. I'm proud of you, Lady Ashlyn.

"And stop with the Lady Ashlyn. The last thing I want is to become a lady. I've read enough histories and fables now, even a hint of noble blood, especially a noble title that's been given as a gift, well, that just encourages something magical to target me and give me trouble. Am I right?"

Yes, far too right. The ring was silent for a few moments, then he laughed.

Ash grinned. She couldn't deny the silliness and ridiculousness of the conversation, and there was something nastily satisfying about learning Lathia had indeed gotten her comeuppance. In a sideways fashion. The problem was that Lathia was so self-centered and dense, and unfamiliar with truth and reality, she probably hadn't realized yet what a mess she had gotten herself into. She might spend the rest of her life thinking she had triumphed over everyone who had ever contradicted her.

Ash's bright spirits drooped when she and Fang had been on the road for a few hours, quietly making their way through the darkness. Except when he hopped away to do some quick hunting. Some time after midnight, when the moon had started its downward plunge toward dawn, she realized something. If Lathia was beyond Justiciar Camwell's reach, that made Ash his only source of entertainment until the quest was completed.

The ring's warnings took on extra weight. She needed to be even more careful now, and not become too entertaining, or Justiciar Camwell would ensure the ring would never come off. While she preferred keeping the ring's company and guidance, the thought of Camwell forever able to look over her shoulder or through her eyes, or examine her thoughts, gave her the queasies.

<center>~~~~~</center>

Common sense said Ash couldn't spend her entire journey foraging for food, sleeping in underbrush or in the branches of trees. Especially as the weather turned unfriendly. She also couldn't sleep through the day and travel at night constantly. At the very least, she needed to talk to people who knew the roads, who could point out the way to go when the maps Blaz gave her were no help, when local roads didn't appear on the maps that kings and soldiers and magic users used. She didn't want to run into any more vampires, for instance. There was no telling what sort of communication channels the nightborn used. She didn't want to risk going into a cavern and finding someone with the same ambitions as Morris waiting for her.

Then there was the risk of running into an ogre or other magical creatures looking to capture someone with magic in her blood. Ash had read enough in Cecil's books to know she was in a vulnerable position, unsure what her magic was, when it would emerge, and how powerful she would be. The greatest danger she faced was encountering someone who knew how to tap her magical potential and either enslave it or drain it away entirely. Until she had freed herself and the ring from Justiciar Camwell, she couldn't return to Cecil and resume the lessons that might just be vital to her safety and freedom, or perhaps even her life.

Yes, the ring was right. The world was an unfair place, and she was a fool to wish it were otherwise.

~~~~~

Blaz's map disagreed with the markers at the crossroads Ash reached late in the morning. She had been on the road again nearly a month now. Five roads met in a large open area that looked like it had been a campsite recently. There were fire rings and places churned up by wheels and hooves, the dusty remains of horse droppings, and bits of discarded pottery and rags. The map Blaz had put together for her showed only three roads meeting at this point. The signposts at this crossroads looked like they had been carved and erected fairly recently, perhaps this spring. The names of the towns they pointed to only agreed with two of the three names on her map.

The ring speculated that some political upheaval had occurred since the last time Blaz had any information on this part of the continent. Perhaps two kingdoms had merged through a marriage alliance, and a third had been formed where the two met, to allow the newlyweds some practice governing before they took over from their fathers. Or more likely, the heir to a throne had argued with several younger siblings for control or fought with an uncle who didn't want to give up being regent. One or two countries had split into several, which explained the change of names as well as the addition of roads established to avoid going through unfriendly territory. The roads here were little more than dirt packed down by the passage of many feet and wagons, and if travelers were lucky, they were improved by the addition of gravel to protect a little against becoming muddy bogs when it rained.

There was no help for it. Ash had to go into the nearest town to find someone who could verify she was on the right road. While she was here, common sense said she should find some work, to earn a few coins, hot food, and a real bed under a roof for a few nights. Or as long as she could stay until Fang got careless in his hunting and skulking at night, and someone saw him and bizarre stories started to circulate.

When she reached the nearest town, which was marked as Capper's Creek on the map but now called itself River's Edge, it was market day. Ash approached a man sitting in front of a stall full of all sorts of items carved from wood. Eating utensils, bowls, plates, pegs of various sizes, decorated shelves, walking sticks, and more. Ash reasoned someone who worked with wood needed help cleaning up all the debris, so she asked about work.

"What for you be wanting work?" a woman said, before the man
~~~~~

could respond to Ash's question. She reached past her and caught hold of the girl's wrist. "When you be wearing such a pretty bauble?"

Ash didn't understand for a moment. Then she realized the woman, who smelled as brown as her teeth, meant the ring. She thought people without magic couldn't see the ring. She hadn't felt any sting or burn of magic in her stars, so a spell wasn't helping the woman see the ring. What was going on?

"I'm not allowed to take it off. I have to deliver it …" She sighed. "It's not for sale." She looked at the woodcarver, who was watching her with a half-smile and one eyebrow cocked up in what was clearly doubt. "I want to earn my keep."

"Do you now?" a man said from behind her.

Ash turned to see several more people had approached the woodcarver's stall. The man who spoke looked prosperous, meaning his clothes looked newer. He wore several rings on his hands and his gaze kept dropping to the ring on her hand as he spoke.

"I'm always looking for a clever boy who doesn't mind hard work. I'll gladly provide bed and board while you stay with me and learn what's involved in the business." He smiled, a stretching of his thin lips that didn't reveal his teeth. "Of course, with all the valuables in my shop … let's say you leave the ring with me as pledge until you've proven yourself trustworthy. Or you decide to move on, that you don't want to stay and learn the trade."

Ash had no doubt that when the time came for her to move on, or more likely the man shoved her out the door as unsuitable, the ring would have vanished. He would call her a liar if she went to the local magistrate to retrieve the ring. He might even accuse her of stealing from him. Muttered comments from the people standing around the woodcarver's stall reinforced that suspicion. From the narrow-eyed way the woodcarver watched the well-dressed man, he wasn't well-liked or even respected. Feared, maybe, but not liked, or trusted.

Not that she was going to accept the offer. Only a fool would expect the man to deal honestly with her. He hadn't even said what his business was, only implied that he expected her to steal from him.

He's going to accuse you of stealing me if you linger too long, the ring told her.

How can he see you at all? How can anyone?

There must be some low-level magical energy drain, cancelling the illusion spell. Or … someone around here is employing multiple charms, and warding against illusions of any kind. That implies someone extremely paranoid, with a dangerous secret to hide or a filthy conscience.

How does that help us?

It doesn't. Not until I do some intensive searching. The ring sighed. *The problem is, if you turn and leave right now, he'll accuse you.*

And when they try to take it off my hand ... Ash shuddered at the image of someone holding her down while someone else cut her finger off. What would they do when the ring vanished and reappeared on another finger on her hand? Keep cutting?

That's the answer, the ring told her.

Let them cut off my fingers? She nearly yelped that aloud.

Prove I won't come off, so they can't accuse you of stealing, because how could I come off someone else's hand? Essentially, tell them the truth. Just not the whole truth.

"Sir ... I would be glad to stay and learn a trade." Her brain felt like it was running in tight circles as she scrambled for the words to play out the image the ring put in her head. "However, you don't want me to stay very long. It wouldn't be good for you or maybe even this town." Ash held out her hand, wiggling her fingers to make the sunlight dance on the silver strand of the ring. "I'm under a ... well, a curse. I have to keep moving forward. I'm not allowed to take the ring off. I can't take the ring off. Here," she blurted, and held out her hand when the man's eyebrow cocked up even farther. "If you could take this off me, I would gladly stay and learn your trade. In gratitude."

The man reached out a hand that looked plump and pale. Ash feared it would be mushy and damp. Whatever his business was, he obviously didn't do the work himself, but paid others. Or more likely, he brought in apprentices and enslaved them, and when they complained or learned too much, he accused them of stealing, enabling himself to dismiss them without the pay and supplies to set up in their own business, as tradition and the law normally required.

"No, your hands are too dirty. I might catch some disease from you." He pursed his lips and fluttered his fingers in distaste.

The woodcarver snorted and winked at Ash. The well-dressed man flushed and anger sparked in his eyes. Ash held her breath, waiting for him to start shouting that she had stolen the ring from him.

"Eryk, your hands are made for tasks like this. You take the ring off him." He fluttered his thick fingers at the woodcarver. When the other man opened his mouth, clearly about to refuse, he snapped, "And I'll give you an extra month to find those ... items I was looking for."

"You will, will you?" Eryk the woodcarver sat back on his stool and crossed his arms. "What items are those? I don't recall agreeing to find anything for you."

"You know what I'm referring to." His face flushed darker.

Are you sure this wouldn't be a good time to slip away, while they're arguing with each other? Ash asked the ring.

Before the ring could respond, Eryk flashed a grin at the well-dressed man, then winked again at Ash. "I'm always up for a challenge. Especially if the ring is cursed, like the boy says."

The other man snorted. Several people around them chuckled or made comments that made Eryk's grin widen, and the well-dressed man flush even darker. The woodcarver held out his hand, beckoning to Ash.

You had better be right about this, she told the ring, as she gave her hand into his grasp and the woodcarver's fingers wrapped around hers.

His skin was hard, smooth, like saddle leather, hot, and adjusted to a nearly crushing grip around her ring finger. He spread her fingers, to wrap his forefinger around the ring. And pulled. His smile faded. He pulled harder, and kept pulling, until Ash nearly went forward across the worktable between her and him. He grimaced and adjusted his grip on the ring, with forefinger and thumb. The joints of her hand ached as he tried to wrap several fingers around the ring. Still, it wouldn't slide off. It wouldn't even shift its position at the base of her finger.

Eryk yelped and jerked his hand back. Ash stumbled backward, so she landed on her rump and slid a few paces away. More townsfolk around them in the market stopped and stared for several seconds.

"Cursed indeed," the woodcarver gasped, and rubbed at his fingers.

What did you do? Ash asked.

Bit him. The ring sounded like he was having fun.

She could almost have been angry with him, but the woodcarver's doubt shifted to awe. Then what she suspected was admiration.

"What did a boy like you do to get saddled with a cursed ring?" the man asked.

"Cursed? A likely story," the well-dressed man said, his face twisting in a sneer.

"He was in the wrong place at the wrong time," the ring said aloud.

Ash nearly choked from the effort not to laugh, and not to grin at the man's wide-eyed confusion, how he looked in all directions except at the ring on her throbbing hand. Eryk certainly had a crushing grip, which only made sense.

"What is that?" the man said.

"I am the spirit of the ring, the boy's advisor. He has been given a series of tasks to perform and must complete them within a specified period of time, or else the curse will strike everyone in his village. If he does not return by midnight on the last day of winter, all is lost."

Chapter Twenty-One

Ash choked on laughter, recognizing the words from a favorite story.

"Heh. You expect us to believe you?" The brown woman spat for punctuation.

"It's a magic ring," Eryk said, with a sigh and a groan. "It's got no reason to lie."

"If I find out you lied to me, that this is all a trick …" The well-dressed man glared down at Eryk, then at Ash.

"If you're going to try to change in midstream and claim the boy stole it from you," someone said from the people standing behind Ash, "there's too many of us for you to bribe or threaten into looking the other way. Give up, Bydeen."

"Claim? I have no need to make claims." The man thrust his chest out, growing even redder. He opened his mouth, clearly ready to make the accusations Ash had feared from the moment his gaze landed on the ring.

The ring flashed a pale green light that glistened on the man's rings and the silver pin holding his neckcloth. Bydeen's eyes widened, and his high color drained away. He opened and closed his mouth several times, then backed up, stumbling over several people who didn't get out of his way quickly enough.

"Yer an idjit," the brown woman muttered, shaking her head. She winked at Ash and tottered away through the marketplace.

In moments, the people who had gathered around to witness the little encounter dispersed, leaving Ash alone with Eryk.

"What sort of help do you need, boy?" the woodcarver said, when the normal traffic and background noises of the market had resumed.

"I just want to earn some coin for the journey, and a roof over my head for a few nights." Ash thought of Fang. He would only let her stay in the town for a few nights, then he would come looking for her. He had grown very protective of her since that encounter with Ruprick's bully troops.

"How far do you have to go by the last of winter?"

"It isn't how far, but the things I have to find." She could see that didn't satisfy him. "I have to return to Alfordia."

"Alfordia?" The woodcarver whistled. "How long have you been traveling, boy?"

"It feels like forever."

Eryk gave her a disk with an oak tree carved into it, and what she assumed was his sigil on the back, and told her to go to the Silver Acorn tavern. The owner was his sister and would feed her. He chuckled, and suggested that Ash ask for a bath, as well.

The tavernkeeper, Ellien, took the token, then took a step back and frowned and looked Ash over head to foot three times. She grinned and gestured for Ash to follow her. Into her private quarters upstairs from the main room.

"Eryk will either laugh or stomp off in a huff when I tell him," she said, and shut the door with a hard click to emphasize her words.

"Ma'am?" Ash held tighter to the strap of her pack. *Ring, am I in trouble?*

"What's your real name?" Ellien led her to a room that looked like it had been tacked onto the side of the inn, where a balcony had been.

"Ma'am?"

"This—" she opened what Ash thought was a cabinet, revealing a series of vertical ropes, "—goes down to the kitchen, and a vat of hot water. Pull up as much as you need, and soak as long as you want. I imagine you haven't had a decent bath in months."

"Do I smell that bad?"

That earned a chuckle. "No, lass, but I've had to masquerade a time or two to save my skin, and the bath always suffers first."

"Lass." Ash decided to be amused that Ellien had known what she was after just a few seconds.

The hot bath was glorious, with lemon-scented soap. Even better was the thick stew, full of beans, chicken, and herbs, and fresh bread dripping with butter. Her only regret was that she had to turn down the dress Ellien offered her. Better to stay with the disguise of a boy, especially since she had to sit in the main room at the tavernkeeper's table with her, to eat that incredible meal.

"You could be a castle cook, and have a much easier life," she said, after nearly inhaling the first half of the bowl.

"Had experiences with castle folk, have you?" Ellien said.

"I grew up an orphan and a servant, until some troubles came and … basically picked me up and saddled me with a ring and a watcher and a deadline." She clenched her fist and turned it to look more closely at the ring. As if she didn't have every twist and glimmer of the three strands memorized.

During her bath, she and the ring had worked out the story she would follow, while in this town. However long that stay would be. At least a few days. But not too many. She would get too many questions, raise too many suspicions, if she vanished once her stomach was filled.

She needed to make friends, find out what she needed to know, chart her new route to the next cavern and over the next border, and then come up with a good reason for leaving.

"Where was that?" Ellien smiled as she asked, but something tightened in Ash's chest. A now-familiar sense of teetering on the edge of trouble. Just over a simple, friendly question.

The further along on this quest she went, the less free she felt to trust people. Look how trusting Morris had led to that attack on the edge of escaping the cavern, and Fang turning partially vampire. Look how settling in and getting comfortable with Cecil had led to trouble. He wouldn't have had that vision-generated headache and been partially incapacitated when Ruprick's bullies showed up. Camwell's men wouldn't have come to the village at all. Lucinda and the others probably despised her now, with a justiciar chasing her from one land to another.

And now Ellien wanted to know where she had spent most of her life. Was this to find out if her story was true, and she was who and what she claimed to be?

Ash couldn't give those details. Bad enough she had already told Eryk she had to return to Alfordia. The story she and the ring had agreed on worked best without names and times. Fortunately, the ring had come up with the answer that he promised most people would accept, and hopefully generate some pity for her. Sympathy was always good for greasing wheels and smoothing trails. The people who wouldn't accept the story were usually looking for trouble and didn't trust much of anyone.

"I'm sorry, I'm not allowed to say." Ash held out her hand, flat now, and the ring obligingly shimmered, to give silent verification of what she had just said. "Revealing names is ... forbidden. I don't want to bring more trouble on the people who gave me a home."

"Ah, yes. The gossip got here while you were washing. A curse, is it?" Ellien nodded. Ash couldn't tell if she believed her or not. Tavernkeepers needed to keep neutral faces and voices, after all, to avoid offending people or warning miscreants that the local law was about to pounce on them.

"Many-layered curse." She tried to smile. Suddenly all that good, solid food she had eaten didn't sit well in her belly.

Between the glorious luxury of the hot bath and clean clothes and now the meal, Ash needed to curl up and sleep long and hard, get rid of the heaviness in her belly, make herself alert and light on her feet again, ready for attack. She couldn't do that, out here in the open, among all these people. In the forest, hidden in the underbrush or safely up a tree, out of sight, yes, she could sleep. The ring and Fang would keep watch. Fang was too far away and what could the ring do except glow and spark and prick her finger and shout to distract attackers? What if Bydeen had built up his courage and came looking for her, or someone else decided to claim she had stolen the ring?

That brown woman didn't strike Ash as the sort who would quietly walk away and keep her suspicions to herself. She was the sort of unpleasant creature that skuttled along the outskirts of every town and village, ignored until trouble struck. Then she was in the middle of things, shouting false accusations and stirring up suspicions and rousing people to grab torches and pitchforks and ropes for hanging.

"What's it like growing up in a castle?" Ellien sat back and reached for the pitcher of spiced cider sitting on a serving shelf by the door into the kitchen.

The tavern was large enough and prosperous enough to have a woman in the kitchen and three serving maids, to deal with the customers. There was one large room for eating, another just for drinking, and a third, where Ash and Ellien sat now, that appeared to have been a large hallway between the two rooms at one time. Half the wall had been taken down. Where the tavernkeeper sat, she could keep an eye on everything going on, both in the kitchen and in the rooms where customers sat and talked and ate and drank. It was a clever setup. Ash felt tired just considering all the work Ellien had to do overseeing everything going on in her tavern.

"I don't really know, because I haven't known anything else. Until now. I can't compare it to anything."

"True." The woman chuckled. "So what was an ordinary day for you?"

That was a safe question to answer, with mostly the truth. The closer to the truth she kept her story, the easier it would be to stay consistent. She wouldn't have to strain her brain remembering all the lies and keeping them from tangling and knotting.

Ash went through what had been her ordinary day at Castle Fairhold. Washing and dressing to serve in the dining room. Cleaning up. Hauling linens and clothes to the laundry. Running errands for Lady Charlotte. If she had free time, stopping in the library to read, or having a short time of lessons with Friar Ipswich, if he wasn't occupied with research. Then setting the table for the noon meal, serving, cleaning up. And the afternoon repeating the morning's cycle. Sometimes there would be exercises and chores to see where the servant children's talents lay, to determine what their future, adult occupations would be. Sewing. Cooking. Tending to the castle's horses. Going out to the farms owned by the family, to tend livestock or raise crops. Weaving. Traveling with the merchants. Training as a soldier. Learning to cipher to assist the seneschal and other servants who oversaw the efficient operations of Castle Fairhold.

She was surprised to realize how little time it took to relate the ordinary course of her days. There was still half a mug of cider remaining, and she had taken only two bites of the juicy apple tart Ellien had divided between them once the stew and bread were gone. As she paused to take a bite of that tart, because treats like that should never be allowed to dry out, Ash felt the weight of someone's gaze on her. She looked around, ready to scold the ring for not warning her, and met Eryk's friendly gaze. He was sitting on the half-wall to her right, leaning back against a support post, one leg cocked up and resting on the half-wall. It looked like a comfortable pose, and she wondered how long he had been sitting there.

"How did you get in so much trouble that you're out here, so far from Alfordia?" Eryk said.

"As I said earlier," the ring responded, and gave off a silvery burst of light that pulsed in time with his words, "the wrong place at the wrong time. It's not Ash's fault at all, this whole ugly quest. Everyone is best served, especially my charge here, if those details are left unspoken."

"Who can argue with a magic ring?" He nodded.

Whispers echoed those words, and a chill washed through Ash when she realized that people in the rooms behind her, beyond the half-wall, were listening.

I'm sorry, the ring said. *I should have been more aware and warned you to never sit with your back to the room. It's a beginner's mistake.*

"Spirit ring," Ash said. "There's a difference."

"Is there?" a gruff voice said. A moment later, a bald head rose from behind the half-wall, slowly revealing bushy red eyebrows and big gray eyes in thick nests of wrinkles, then a red-streaked white beard surrounding a scowling mouth. Thick fingers like sausages gripped the top of the wall, as the man rested his chin on it. Ash guessed he had been sitting in a chair set against the wall. That scowling face warned her it wouldn't do her any good to point out that listening in on conversations he wasn't part of was rude.

"Magistrate Blosi," Eryk said, gesturing to the man.

"You claim that's a magic ring, do you?" Blosi gestured at Ash's hand.

"No, sir." Ash fully regretted eating too much. How was she going to run if this situation turned problematic? As if it wasn't already problematic? She had just pointed out it was a spirit ring, yet the man insisted on calling it a magic ring.

"Ash doesn't have to claim anything. To claim means there is some doubt as to either the truthfulness of the one speaking or the story being told," the ring said. Now his glow had a faintly reddish tint among the silver. As if he were angry.

"Well, isn't that interesting?" The magistrate pushed himself up a little higher against the wall and hung both arms over the side. He held out his hand. "Give it here, I need to examine this thing. My duty demands I protect our lovely village and its people from any inimical magic that might come among us."

"I already told you, Magistrate," Eryk said, "the ring won't come off."

"You don't have magic in your fingers. Well, your talent is a kind of magic," Blosi said with a nod and a totally flattering smile for the woodcarver. His smile faded as soon as he turned his gaze back on Ash. "But I have enough magic to overcome any weak little tricks such as this boy might try to use on those without training in real magic." He held out his hand. "Give me the ring."

Ash braced herself for his magic to awaken, and for some unpleasant reaction in her stars. She certainly didn't want to put her hand into that thick-fingered, huge hand. The room on the other side of the half-wall was two steps down from Ash's side, but the magistrate was apparently shorter than the average man. He was also thicker. Short and heavy-set rarely equated to jolly and friendly. She had to comply. After a moment of hesitation, she put her hand with the ring on the magistrate's open palm. The man frowned at her.

"Think you're being smart, do you?"

"Sir, the ring won't come off until the quest is complete. If you can take it off me, then please do. Maybe I'll be free, and I can ..." She shrugged. "I don't know what I'll do, because I don't dare go home without completing the quest, but—"

"Yes, yes, I suppose that makes some sense. Very little," he added, and caught hold of her wrist with his other hand. His hands were hot and slightly damp, and very strong despite being so thick. Perhaps the man was more muscle than fat.

Cold fire stabbed deep through Ash's stars, arching through flesh and bone to meet somewhere behind her heart. She gasped, unable to breathe for a moment. Tears touched the backs of her eyes.

Ouch! The ring flared a darker silvery-red. *That was uncalled-for, you brute. I'm not maintaining the bond, so torturing me won't do you any good.*

Brute, am I? The magistrate's voice was in Ash's head, not her ears. He bared his teeth and wrapped his fingers around Ash's ring finger, pushing her other fingers back and aside so she cried out in pain. Her legs tried to fold, but he yanked her upright, as if he might pull her over the wall in another moment.

He yanked harder. Fire wrapped around the ring, green flames that flung the man and Ash apart, so she hit the table, slid across it, knocking her empty bowl onto the floor, and crashed into the next table. She lay sprawled across the downed furniture, feeling like a rag doll that had been left out in a thunderstorm. Her hand throbbed, and when she tried to close her fingers, fiery stabs shot up her arm. Her stars echoed the throbbing, making her chest and bottom spasm. She cried out, and curled into a ball, gasping for breath. Beyond the thudding of her frenzied pulse in her ears, she heard laughter.

We have to get out of this village. These people are insane.

Absolutely. The ring sounded rather breathless. *I'm sorry, my lady. I should have detected sooner the charms he has hidden under his clothes.*

She lay limp where she had landed for several minutes while everyone gathered around Blosi, drawn by his screams and thrashing and curses and the stink of burned cloth and hair and melted metal, thanks to the destruction of his charms. Then Ellien and Eryk picked her up, careful as they could be about her hand, and carried her upstairs, without asking if the girl could walk. She couldn't, until her lungs remembered how to work. It was all she could do not to burst into tears, when every movement made her stars and her hand send jagged stabs of icy fire through her body. Ash had nearly lost consciousness twice from the jarring, and then hitting her injured hand against the door at the top of the stairs.

The magistrate had broken the fingers on either side of her ring finger, in his zeal to remove the ring. The front of his vest and the shirt underneath were burned away in the destruction of the charms he wore sewn into a second vest. He had blisters on his very hairy chest in the exact shape of the charms, according to Griselda, the local herb-mage, who came to tend Ash's hand. She didn't have to say what she thought of the magistrate. Her eyes gleamed with amusement, except when she sniffed with disgust and warned Ash she needed to get out of the town as soon as possible. Once the magistrate stopped whimpering and thrashing about in pain from the dozen or so small burns, he was going to have her thrown into the stocks and whipped daily.

"I gave him the weakest burn ointment I had on me," she added, as she wrapped wet cloths around Ash's hand.

Ash had no idea what good wet cloths would do her hand when the fingers were visibly crooked. She held her breath and tried not to whimper, because Griselda very clearly was doing her best to be gentle. Nothing could persuade her to be as selfishly pitiful as the magistrate.

"Unfortunately," the herb-mage added, as she settled Ash's hand on hers, palm to palm, then spread her other hand over the top, "I infuse my healing power into my ointments and tonics at the time I make them. Otherwise, I promise you, I would have withdrawn every bit of power before I gave the jar to that bootlicker assistant of his." She sniffed for emphasis. "Imagine, the gall of that man, condemning people all these years for illicit use of magic, for claiming to have more power than they did, and holding himself up as the standard of what true magic use and authority should be. And all this time, he's been a big fat arrogant fraud.

Every bit of his magic came from charms. Magic that other people loaned to him for coin. Nothing earned." She smiled and stroked Ash's bound hand. "You've done this village an enormous service, my lass." Her smile faded. "Too bad you need to flee before the other bootlickers decide to punish you for their fall from power."

"How?" Ash caught her breath. The pain was fading.

"Eryk and his friends are good men. They'll find a way." She winked and leaned closer, as if about to tell a secret. "They're rather clever, getting around the pompous, self-righteous types like the magistrate. Former magistrate," she added with another sniff. "Once the territorial overlord hears about this, he'll send someone to investigate. Wouldn't doubt that destroying all those charms set off some magical reverberations, or at least enough discord to make the man himself come running to investigate. Don't you worry. We've got some good, skilled smugglers in this town. They'll get you out of the territory in broad daylight, and no one the wiser." With a sigh, she took her hand off Ash's, then with the other hand lowered her wrapped hand to the table. "Now, how does that feel?"

"Fine. I think."

There is some swelling, the ring told her. *But it is diminishing. Please pass on my compliments to the lady healer? I'm still somewhat sore myself from that assault, and it's hard to be audible right now. The defensive magic didn't come from me, but it did draw on some of my strength to defend us. Some of those charms were of a very nasty type. It's slanderous to call it dark magic. More accurate to call it lightless magic.*

"Well, that's interesting," Griselda said, nodding slowly, once Ash passed on the ring's words. She made a little bow toward Ash's hand. "Thank you for that helpful bit of knowledge, sir ring. I hope you'll be up to full strength soon, to help our lass here with her escape. A'theosius blessed her, I think, when she was partnered with you for what sounds like a highly unfair quest."

Ash agreed, strongly enough she thought she might cry. She didn't though. If she hadn't cried at the breaking of her fingers and the huge bruise down her side and the back of her head, from hitting the table, she couldn't let herself get teary over feeling overwhelming gratitude.

Chapter Twenty-Two

By the time Eryk and his smuggler friends packed up Ash to get her out of town just before dawn the next day, no response had come from the territorial overlord. She was impressed to hear that not only was he in charge of magical use, but government officials and military patrols to keep the roads safe. This was a very progressive and civilized kingdom. She wished she didn't have to leave. Eryk's friend, Nissia, took her down a tunnel under the tavern and to the riverbank half an hour of walking away. On the way, she told Ash Magistrate Blosi had a tendency to get louder the more in pain he was. Half the village had heard his vows he would cut the ring off her finger and have her handed over to one of the traveling gangs of chained criminals who worked off their debt to society with hard labor. The messier and more brutal, the better. He also bragged about powerful friends who, according to him, shared his "enlightened" mindset about who had a right to use magic and keep magical items, and who didn't.

"The big blowhard has made trouble for quite a few powerful people in the surrounding ten villages." Nissia chuckled. "Wouldn't doubt he's on the outs with all of them very soon. The territorial overlord has been looking for such a list of names for years. Enlightened mindset, faugh!" She spat, then chuckled again and patted Ash's shoulder. "Wouldn't doubt that a number of folk are going to be a little braver standing up against that blowhard, now that all his magical talent he boasted about has been uncovered. And scorched right off him."

They came to the end of the tunnel then, and spent a good hour crouched behind the overhanging ivy and broken branches and other growth that hid the mouth of the tunnel from sight. The time passed too swiftly for Ash, because Fang hadn't caught up with her. The ring assured her that he had recovered his strength enough to call to the bunny. The problem was that she had no idea where they were in relation to the place in the forest where she had left Fang to sleep away the daylight.

Then there was the problem of what Nissia would do when Fang jumped down into the tunnel to join them. The smuggler woman made no effort to hide the knives tucked into the top of one boot, the long knife hanging at her waist, and two stilettos that served as pins for the thick knot of hair at the base of her neck. She was ready for trouble. Even if she really wasn't ready for the kind of fight Fang could give her.

Ash was too grateful for the help that had surged up around her to want any harm to come to anyone.

Success, the ring reported. The first glimmers of dawn on the water sparkled through the curtain of grasses and ivy.

Meaning?

Fang is following the boat that's coming our way. You need to be ready to catch him and cover him, because the sun will be above the trees before our friends get here.

Ash felt slightly queasy at the thought of trying to explain a smoking bunny to the armed smugglers who were helping her. True, they were clearly finding much satisfaction in frustrating Magistrate Blosi, but just how reasonable would they be, how willing would they be to keep helping her, if they found out Fang was partially a vampire? Did it matter that he was only partially a vampire? She could see how some people wouldn't care about degrees of transformation. An oversized bunny with enormous teeth was a visible threat. And these people had knives and swords and who knew what other kinds of weapons.

She felt like she could breathe freely again when the sound of oars dipping in the water and thudding against the sides of the boat reached her. Nissia pushed aside the screen across the tunnel mouth and grinned at her before leading the way down the steep side of the riverbank, to the water's edge. Ash strained her ears for the sounds of Fang thudding and bouncing among the trees. She couldn't decide if that was her heart racing, or the manic bunny catching up with the smugglers.

"Quickly." Eryk leaped out of the prow of the boat. It had a single mast and a small sail that hung limp, waiting for a breeze. The two other smugglers in the team grinned and nodded to Ash while Eryk pulled the longboat up along the muddy, pebbly shallows.

The front portion of the boat had a makeshift deck, probably creating a hiding place for whatever was being smuggled. The back portion was crowded with barrels in among four sets of benches, wide enough for two men on each, with long oars strapped to the sides. Ash tried to imagine how fast such a boat could go with sixteen strong, determined, perhaps frightened men rowing for their lives and freedom when the wind and the sail failed them. And the river patrols chasing them, or perhaps soldiers racing along the riverbank, trying to beat them to the next shallows or the next bridge, to catch and stop them. There was a time when she would have read about some adventure like this, and cheered for the military, enforcing the laws. She had never thought she would be on the other side of the law. Then again, she hadn't really considered how right and wrong changed color and shading when the authorities weren't upright men who obeyed the laws themselves.

This quest was turning into quite an education for her, in degrees and aspects she had never considered before.

"Don't worry." Eryk grunted, giving the boat a hard shove out of the shallows, and splashed a few steps before hauling himself over the side and back into the boat. "We'll be long gone before Blosi stops whimpering and starts following through on his threats. He has too high an opinion of himself and expects his friends to come running to check on him."

Nissia snorted. "The only news going about right now is how all those illegal charms of his turned on him, and how he tried to steal a spirit ring from a defenseless little boy. Who wasn't quite so defenseless."

"Little boy?" Ash finally turned her gaze off the riverbank. "Is that what they're saying about me?" Maybe she should have taken Griselda and Ellien's advice, and accepted a dress to wear for a few days, to further muddle the trail. Then the other words registered. "Illegal charms? Is magic against the law in this kingdom?"

"No, but there has been enough trouble with magic cheats, it's regulated," one of Eryk's friends called down from his position by the mast. He gave Eryk a thumbs up and set about pulling up on the ropes to raise the sail. A bit of breeze tugged at Ash's hair. She sat far enough down in the boat, the high sides hid her from sight as well as most of the breeze.

"Regulated." Somehow, that word just didn't feel like it belonged paired up with magic. "How? Why?"

"Just like with Blosi. People use charms to give themselves magic, then claim they're born with those gifts. To get power over people. To take authority they don't have a right to. He wouldn't be in half as much trouble as he's going to be with the territorial overlord if he just wore those charms openly." Eryk settled down on the bench facing Ash. "Whoever sold him those charms didn't register them with the authorities. How do I know?" he added, when Ash opened her mouth to ask. "Because if they knew Blosi was using them to carry out his duties, they would have reproved him for hiding them. That's the greater crime, hiding the source of the magic. Which means the source was illegal."

"He's going to get away with it, you know," Nissia said. "Unless they bring in a very strong, skilled charm weaver, to decipher what those charms were supposed to do, Blosi can always claim he was influenced. He can claim he was tricked into taking the charms, and he was forced to lie about them and hide them. And probably claim he was changed by the charms, to become the arrogant, greedy wretch he's been the last few years."

"Is that possible?" Ash said. "Charms changed him?"

"It's possible. And it's happened far too often. Which is why charms and other such things are regulated. So innocent people aren't duped, made into puppets for outside magical powers." Eryk frowned, turning quickly to look to the riverbank.

"I see it," the man at the mast said.

"See what?" Nissia said.

"Something's been following us since we passed Sky Trail bridge." He held onto the mast with one hand and leaned out over the water, as if that could give him a clearer view of what lurked in the bushes and underbrush along the bank.

Fang, the ring said, at the same moment Ash said, "I'm sorry."

Eryk and Nissia turned to frown at her.

"I have a … a friend. He has to stay in hiding when I go into villages for supplies. Is it all right if he joins us?" She looked back to the man at the tiller. "Can we get a little closer to the bank, so he can jump in?"

The man at the tiller looked to Eryk. Before he could open his mouth, probably to ask the questions she saw in his face, Fang let out a chortling cry and bounced up high. Ash cringed, seeing the smoke pluming off his fur, especially the tips of his ears. She snatched up a wad of rags sitting on the bottom of the boat near her feet and stumbled down to the front of the boat, where Fang was coming in for a hard, loud thud of a landing. He made a crackling sort of cry that she had learned to interpret as pain. Ash flung herself down on him, wrapping herself and the rags around the smoking bunny.

"What … is … that?" Eryk stood over Ash now, staring down at the wriggling bundle of fur and rags and wisps of smoke.

"His name is Fang, and he's a bunny. Bunnnies are magical, did you know that? That's what makes them different from rabbits and hares and … Anyway, his magic protected him, but not enough, when he protected me from a vampire and got bitten. So he …" Ash sat back and gestured at Fang, who had stopped smoking, fortunately, and huddled in the partial shade of the open hatch under the deck. "Well, he doesn't burn in daylight, but he smokes." She took a deep breath. "And if you want to put us off the boat right now, I don't blame you. But he's my friend and we protect each other."

"Kill me now." The man who had been at the mast was kneeling on the upper level, looking down at them. He grinned. "Now I've seen everything."

Ash dared to hope that grin meant no one would try to kill Fang.

At least, as long as he didn't try to snack on someone.

In exchange for the tolerance of the four smugglers and being allowed to stay on the longboat until dusk, Ash told them her real story. Abbreviated, and leaving out names and places. She had a duty to protect her friends, after all. Nissia laughed. Eryk shook his head quite a few times, and his smile faltered. The other two men, Bair and Jonas, muttered and swore, clapped once or twice, and generally seemed caught between amusement and uneasy wonder. Ash wondered if there was something wrong with her that she didn't think her adventures were that amazing or shocking or even frightening.

Maybe the magic in her blood protected her from too much shock? Or maybe magic bred a kind of insanity? It made sense, she reflected later, when she really thought about it. Enchanters and sorcerers had a tendency to turn cruel or reclusive or unbalanced under the weight of all that learning and all that magic power flowing in their blood. At least, according to all those books of Cecil's she had managed to read.

Or maybe that was further proof that her education was seriously lacking in essential, vital aspects.

When she left the boat at dusk, Eryk covered her in a cloak that smelled of tar and fish and led her along the docks. Wherever they had stopped, unnamed by her smuggler friends, this was a major center of commerce. Just looking around in the fading daylight, with torches and lanterns being lit in a spreading starburst, Ash saw they had come to a place where several rivers met. She wondered if they were anywhere near the sea, and these rivers led to the coast, to major ports. Bair pushed a cart with several barrels on it. One held Fang. They walked past the torchlight, into darkness, following a path that went from wood planks to gravel, cut through a small grove of trees, then turned from gravel back to wooden planks, and another pool of torchlight at another section of docks. These were large, seafaring ships, not river-navigating boats. The masts held multiple sails, and the docks extended out into the darkness past where the torches and ships stopped.

Eryk led her to a smaller ship, with only two sails on its single mast. He banged on the hull of the ship and climbed up onto the top deck without waiting for a response. He gestured for Ash and Bair to wait. Before she could get nervous or think of what questions to ask without getting into trouble, Eryk returned with the captain of the ship.

As a favor to Eryk, Captain Ayles would take Ash down the coast until the next evening, to leave her and her barrel at Willemsport, far enough to cross over the borders of two countries. No questions would be asked. Eryk handed her another wooden disk, with the oak carved into one side and several symbols she couldn't interpret carved into the other.

"I can't guarantee anything, but if anyone can help you move on in safety, rumors say you need Filby the hostler. After that, I think the debt we owe you is repaid," Eryk said. He held out his hand to shake Ash's. "You've taught me not to accept what my eyes show me. I'll have quite a few free drinks off this story, for months to come."

Bair chuckled. He clapped Ash on the shoulder, then held out his hand. When she thought he would shake her hand as well, he slipped several copper coins into her palm. She stumbled through her thanks, and Fang thumped three times on the barrel where he hid. The two men laughed, clearly taking the thumps as his way of saying thanks. Captain Ayles just raised an eyebrow and turned and went back to whatever he was doing when Eryk found him.

"Be careful, and if you can, send us word how your quest turned out." Eryk tipped off a salute and turned to leave.

"I can write you a letter, if you want," Ash said.

"You can read and write as well?" He grinned. "If I listen to enough amazing things, I'll be convinced the last two days were a dream, and nothing more."

He and Bair were gone, into the shadows beyond the edge of the torchlight, before Ash realized that he hadn't answered her.

"He can't read," Captain Ayles said. He stood on the upper deck, looking down at Ash and the barrel, tucked into a nook on the forward deck, out of the way of everyone and everything. "His sister can, though, if you really did mean to write a letter."

"I did."

"Well ... I'm starting to think I promised too hastily, when Eryk told me to leave you entirely alone." Then he nodded to her and turned away.

Ash lifted the top off the barrel to let Fang out. She settled down in the shadowy nook, and he sighed and curled up next to her. Before the moon had reached zenith in the sky, the ship pulled away from the docks. Ash watched the torchlight that seemed to slide past the ship as it traveled down the coast. The wind was strong, and the ship picked up speed as it pulled further away from shore. It rocked very little, so she could convince herself it sat still in the water and everything else around them moved. She dozed, so the night hours passed in a series of disjointed blinks.

When the first streaks of dawnlight spilled across the water toward them, Ash woke and struggled to lay the barrel down on its side. It was large enough for her and Fang to curl up inside, safe from the sunlight and view of everyone else on the ship. She worked on filling in her most recent adventures in her journal, trying to say as much as possible in as few words and as little space as possible. They both dozed the day away, conserving their strength, preparing for the next part of their journey.

The ring told her when they crossed one border, safe from any vengeful actions from Blosi. Then six hours later, they crossed another border. That started a conversation about the geography of this coastline, the many small kingdoms that all fought to keep possession of access to the sea, and the commerce that would come to their ports.

Since I've crossed more borders than required, do you think that will satisfy the justiciar?

We won't know until the magic binding us together lets go, the ring responded after only a few seconds of hesitation.

Do you think we can convince him that the smuggler tunnel counts as a cavern?

We can try. Certainly you've gone farther afield than he could have expected.

What do we do if he alters the conditions of the magic?

I've thought about that. The simplest course of action is to find someone with magic stronger than Camwell used, and ask them to shut down the spell.

That's simple? Ash nearly laughed aloud.

Well, simpler than finding a magical court willing to hear our plea and accept proof that he violated the terms of the spell and the quest, and rewrote them for his own personal curiosity and satisfaction.

How do we find a magical court, when it will be hard enough to find an enchanter or sorcerer or anyone else strong enough to revoke the justiciar's spell?

We will figure it out. Say your prayers, and believe that even if most kings and nobles are unfair, and life itself is unfair, A'theosius is fair, and will help you.

Ash thought about that, and then she thought about everything she knew about finding magic users and asking for help. Just how strong did someone have to be to overrule Justiciar Camwell's spell, if he did indeed rewrite the terms of the quest as she and the ring both feared?

At Willemsport, Ash listened to the ring's advice, and offered her help to the captain. She supposed she was strong enough, but rather than risk some accident that would reveal she was a girl, she didn't offer to do any of the heavy lifting. Especially as it was a hot day and the air was humid and she could imagine what she would look like after hours of getting drenched with sweat. The bands she used to bind her budding figure weren't as reliable as she would have liked. Since the captain had showed some interest when she admitted she could read and write, she offered to help him with tallying the goods leaving the ship, to ensure they were correctly labeled for their destinations. Then she helped check the manifests for the goods coming onto the ship, bound for the next port. Again, the captain joked that he had agreed too hastily to let her travel in exchange for a favor he owed Eryk. He thanked her for her work, which saved him some time, and freed the men who could cipher a little, to handle barrels and raising cargo nets and other physical work.

"You didn't have to do anything, but I'm grateful. You have a stronger sense of honor than many I've seen lately." He held out his hand. Ash thought it was just to shake, but when she clasped his hand, she found a coin pressed into her palm.

"Captain –"

"It's less than the wages you would have earned today if you were crew," he said with a wink. "After your passage is taken out, of course. I'll tell Eryk I still owe him that favor. And if you want to sign on ..." He shrugged.

"Thank you, but I'm ..."

Always tell the truth whenever possible. This is a good time to tell the three-

quarters truthful story, the ring urged her. *With maybe a little embroidery. Just in case. I think he's a little too eager to take on another crew who can cipher.*

"Sir, to be fair to you, you should know I'm under a curse. Of sorts."

Geas, the ring supplied.

"A geas. An order to fulfill certain conditions before ..." She shrugged. "Before disaster falls on me. I have to keep moving. There's no guarantee that staying on a ship would keep me safe from those who would come after me, if I don't fulfill the conditions."

"A geas. Is that so?" The captain rubbed at his bearded chin, studying her with half-lidded eyes.

The ring bit at her finger. Ash yelped, nearly dropping the coin. She stared at her hand, the reddish glow pulsing from the ring.

The captain stared as well.

"Leave Ash alone," the ring said, his voice metallic and somehow hot. "Don't interfere with his path or his pace. This is the only warning I will give."

"Well, that's something you don't see or hear every day." The captain stared at her hand until Ash jerked her arm behind her back. "What did you—no, I don't want to know." A grin twisted one side of his mouth. "You're an interesting one, Ash. I will wish you good luck, and good speed ... and the offer is still open, when you're free of the geas."

"Thank you, sir. That's very generous."

Sorry, the ring said. *I had to startle you to make it believable.*

Ash slung the sack holding Fang over her shoulder, nodded farewell to the captain, and strode down the gangplank. She waited until she had left the ship and the docks behind and was several streets into the port city proper before she looked at her hand. She could move the ring a little bit, just enough to examine the skin under where it usually rested. It looked normal and didn't throb or sting. She had expected to find it blistered.

Chapter Twenty-Three

As soon as she could, Ash let Fang out of the sack. They kept to back alleys as she made her way through Willemsport, asking for Filby the hostler. The unloading and reloading hadn't finished until late afternoon. Ash used the coin to buy food from a man who cooked over a grill set in a wheeled cart. She bought bread and fruit and enough sausages to make him shake his head. He kept looking between her slim frame and flat belly and the thick bundle of sausages, wrapped in cheesecloth and dripping grease.

"I've others to feed," Ash offered, and silently begged him to hurry up making change from the coin. Fang was waiting in a dark alley across the square, and his eyes had been red from hunger and impatience when she left, more than twenty minutes ago. She didn't want to contemplate the disaster that would result if he came looking for her. Or worse, decided to take his dinner from the different stalls and carts of vendors filling the square.

Fang did come looking for her, but he only got a few hops away from the shadowy mouth of the alley before she returned. He signaled her that he had found horses. Ash muffled a groan and hurried back to the shelter of the alley. She hoped she wouldn't have to have that talk with Fang again, persuading him that he could get along just fine on the food she had found, rather than foraging. She was sure by now he preferred freshly killed meat because it let him get in a fight. Taking down a horse would be an even bigger challenge than taking down a buck out in the forest. How could she persuade him that attacking a horse in the middle of a large city like Willemsport would not be good for either of them?

Ears twisting and folding and turning so fast Ash feared they would snap off his head, Fang repeated himself several times. Then he leaped at her, the moment they reached the shadows, and hooked his claws into the pouch where she put essential things, like her flute and coins. And the wooden disk token Eryk had given her.

"Filby the hostler?" she guessed.

The bunny rolled his eyes several times, then hopped up and down and pointed to the left with both ears.

"After we eat, all right?"

She had several reasons for the delay. First, the shadows of the city in full night would hide them better, if she had to cross streets or squares or walk any distance out in the open with Fang hopping and bouncing after her. Then she had an image in her head of a stable full of horses going into panic if they smelled a hungry bunny with a taste for fresh blood, coming into their sheltered area. If Fang ate, and if he smelled of cooked sausages, there was less chance of horses making an uproar, and getting herself driven out of the stable before she could present the token to Filby.

Fang agreed, without rolling his eyes this time. Ash gave him six sausages and ate two. She put the other six aside for later, tucked into the top of her sack, with the cheesecloth wrapped tightly around them. She wrapped the sack that had held Fang around them, to protect the rest of her possessions from the cooling grease. Then they stepped out into the early evening traffic of Willemsport. Ash relaxed a little when she saw that despite the thickening shadows, the lanterns hanging from signposts and at the intersections of streets hadn't been lit yet. That would make travel a little less tense for her. She doubted Fang worried about anything anymore. That was going to get them into trouble one of these days, and the only remedy she could think of so far was to get away from cities and large towns as quickly as possible. Hopefully, Filby would recognize the symbols on Eryk's disk and agree to help make that possible. Without asking too many questions.

Fang led her down one wide street that seemed to be a main thoroughfare. The various buildings on either side were either shops, closed and shuttered for the night, or taverns and inns, filling with people seeking food or shelter or both. Ash flinched every time she heard a door creak or a shutter bang open, or people's raised voices. Her shoulders ached from hunching by the time they got through another, larger intersection with a wider cross street, and the distinctive aroma of horses and hot metal reached her nose.

On the other side of that intersection lay a sprawling building, vanishing into the shadows on either side, and what looked like trees rising up behind it. Had they reached the far side of Willemsport? That was a relief. As she got closer, and could make out doors and angles and different shades of aging in the wood, Ash guessed this wide building had once been several, three at the very least. They had been joined together, as the owner grew more prosperous. One building had a wide, tall doorway, and she heard horses nickering and snorting and stamping now. The stables. The one next to it had a doorway just as wide, but not as tall, with a large sign panted on one side showing all sorts of little figures. When she had crossed the street, she got close enough to read the sign, but not step within the pool of lantern light that illuminated it. The figures looked like barrels and bales and sacks, and next to them were circles. Were those coins? She supposed this was a listing of prices for various items the hostler sold. It made perfect sense, because then there was no arguing or bartering. Everyone who came here knew what the owner expected them to pay. She had heard how this was done in the larger cities. No haggling and bartering and playing the game of beating down the price, as was done in the villages around Castle Fairhold and in her travels so far.

The last building hung open on two sides, and a dark red glow came from within. Ash made out shapes hanging from the ceiling, and several lumpy piles around an open area that surrounded the red glow of fire. From the smell of hot metal, she guessed this was the blacksmith's shop. So was Filby a blacksmith and farrier, as well as hostler, or had Fang brought her to a likely place that would prove wrong?

The middle building was three stories tall. Ash guessed that living quarters would be above that building, rather than the blacksmith shop or the stables. She took a deep breath and approached the open door. Fang had hung back, staying in the shadows on the other side of the street until now. She looked into the shadowy interior of the building. It stretched back into darkness, all neatly arranged in piles of barrels and crates and sacks and smaller boxes. She smelled the harsh tang of dyed cloth, cheese, the dusty perfume of grain, candles, lantern oil, apples, and other items that all swirled together inside her nose, almost overwhelming.

But she heard and saw no people, no hints of movement. She stepped further into the shadows, head pivoting back and forth.

"Hello?"

Silence.

She glanced back, weighed the possibilities, and gestured to Fang. He was across the street in two massive bounds, with a speed that surprised her. Maybe he was as nervous as she felt?

"Hello?" She stepped into the darkness, with Fang pressing against her thigh. Not enough to knock her off balance, but enough to let her know he was there. Somehow, that was encouraging. "Is anyone here?" she called, raising her voice. "I'm looking for Filby the hostler."

"Why?"

The voice, a woman's, came from directly overheard. Light spilled down. Ash looked up and saw an opening in the ceiling. The woman leaned further out and down, so she nearly hung from her waist, and held out a candle in a protective box. Her hair was a long braid of silver, her cheekbones high and sharp, pointing back toward her ears, just like her long, elegantly slanted eyebrows pointed at her ears. But her ears, exposed by her hair pulled back in that braid, were not elegantly tall and pointed.

Ash realized she was staring. Her face heated.

"Excuse me. I'm looking for Filby the hostler. Eryk the woodcarver at River's Edge sent me." She dug in her pouch for the wooden disk, although she doubted the woman could read it from that height.

"Oh, Eryk did, did he?" The woman chuckled. "Catch."

She tossed down the box holding the candle. Ash muffled a yelp and leaped to catch it. She cringed in anticipation, expecting it to be hot. She caught it by the large wooden ring on the side the woman had used, and grinned in relief when her fingers didn't singe. The woman caught hold of the side of the opening in the ceiling and went heels over head, letting go at the last minute so she dropped easily and landed silently on her feet. She wore trousers, tucked into boots that rose past her knees, a long vest full of pockets that went nearly to her knees, and a loose sleeveless shirt underneath it. Everything was in shades of rich brown and gold.

"Who might you be?" She beckoned with a flip of her hand for Ash to follow and sauntered into the darkness at the back of the building.

"I'm Ash." She hurried to catch up with the woman, and winced when Fang's bounds thudded on the floor, indicating a hollow space underneath, perhaps a cellar.

Each step just showed the massive room going back further, with neat piles of boxes and crates and sacks and pots and jars on each side.

"How old are you, girl?"

Ash nearly dropped the candle box. "How did you know?"

The woman laughed and held out her hand. Ash gave the candle box to her. "Here in the kingdom of Egalia, and quite a few around us, it's considered normal for women to wear trousers. So we don't assume someone wearing trousers has to be a boy or a man. It makes it easier to see what's really there, instead of what we expect to see. Where are you from, Ash?"

"Alfordia."

"Ah. Lovely kingdom, very modern and enlightened in many ways of thought, but some of the holy folk still think that the outside determines holiness, not the inside." She gestured into the darkness and resumed walking. "I am Filby, by the way."

"Oh, good."

"And what is that interesting creature hopping along after you, trying to hide between all the piles?"

Fang screeched and leaped over a stack of wooden boxes with pictures of grapes painted on their lids. He landed in front of Filby and bowed, arms spreading wide and back behind him, like Ash had seen some particularly pompous courtiers do when presented to Lord Digory and Lady Beatrice. Filby laughed, and curtsied. It looked odd, done in trousers.

"Well, hello. I haven't seen your kind for a dragon's age."

"Are you faerie-kin?" Ash asked. Her face heated more. That was a rude question, especially considering the woman's ears weren't pointed, even if her cheekbones and the shape of her eyes indicated otherwise.

"Half-blood. My mother named me Efilbiana, but when I settled here, I decided it was safer to keep my ears out in the open, so to speak, to reduce the number of rude folk who—"

"I'm sorry." Ash hurried to catch up with the woman, whose legs seemed to get longer, so she moved faster toward the now-visible back of the building without actually increasing her pace.

"Oh, no, I didn't mean you. I mean the ones who see my eyes and bones and assume I can grant wishes or perform magic for them. If they see my ears, they know I'm a half-blood. They figure I'm useless, with no magic worth mentioning or bothering me about, because if I had magic, I'd still be in the faerie side. Why do fools always assume that the faerie side is more fun and more interesting than out here, in the solid, real, physical world?"

Filby winked at her, then reached forward and caught hold of a massive ring of wood sticking out from the wall. She pushed hard to the right, and a crack appeared in the wall, revealing a floor-to-ceiling door that slid to the right. Light slowly appeared, streaks and spots in soft shades of the rainbow all over the walls and ceiling, growing like sunrise. Ash's two stars hummed pleasantly, just short of tickling. Filby stepped through the doorway and looked back, eyes narrowed as she watched Ash.

Fang hopped through the doorway. Light flashed, surrounding him, and he let out a squeal. Ash leaped to catch him, intending to pull him back.

"What did you do that for?" She went to her knees, pulled down by Fang's weight, and wrapped her arms around the bunny. He didn't seem hurt, just startled.

"Hmm, interesting." Filby's expression relaxed, and she went down on her haunches to rest a hand on Fang's head, between his ears. "You, my friend, have gone through some odd changes, haven't you? I sensed far more to your magic than your kind usually possesses, but I didn't understand the darkness." She snorted. "I still don't."

"He got bitten, defending me from a vampire," Ash said.

"Did he now? That complicates things. Vampire venom and magic, like an infection. That explains what I sensed in him. But the sacrifice he made, that's a strong kind of magic of its own, and it protected him, diluted the darkness. Was the vampire intending to feed on you, or change you?"

"He wanted to change me." Ash shuddered, remembering.

"Of course. He wanted access to all that untamed magic hiding in your blood. You two are an interesting pair." She chuckled as she got to her feet.

There was a grating sound as the door slid closed without anyone touching it.

"Poor Eryk. He probably thinks he sent a boy in trouble to me, never knowing all the magic and probably winds of prophecy working to guide your path. Then again," she said as she crossed the room and a door opened in the very air, so she vanished for a moment, "he doesn't know all the magic in me."

Ash shuddered at this very visible use of magic that didn't generate any reaction whatsoever in her stars. Not that she was complaining. Sensing every use of magic could be irritating, if not downright painful. This sudden lack just knocked her off balance. What kind of magic was this?

Filby's voice sounded hollow and distant. "Like everyone else, Eryk probably assumes I'm just an old woman who's very good at business and likes to help strays and those down on their luck." She emerged with a large basket filling her arms. "Here, this should fit you. No need to go about ragged and grimy to hide what you are. You're not exactly pretty, but there is something striking about you, hints of elegance. You should make use of it."

Ash let Fang slide to the floor and slowly stood. She focused on the things filling the basket and the last of Filby's words, because she didn't want to think about the first few things. Especially when it came to prophecy.

"You wouldn't have been able to see this place, much less enter, if you didn't have magic," Filby said. "You'll be safe here, hidden, while I give you some basic, essential lessons. Yes, your friend the ring has been telling me the gist of your troubles and travels. I understand that you need to move on, but you're coming to the end of your luck, in terms of delaying your training in magic and exploring just what your heritage is. You need to study and train and put a harness on all that strength waiting to burst out. It's only common sense. Magic without training is like putting an unbalanced sword into the hands of a child."

"I've had lessons," Ash protested, thinking of all those lovely hours of reading and research in Cecil's house.

"Theory? No practice?" She chuckled when Ash shook her head. "First lesson." She swirled her hand around in the air over the girl's head. The movement of air grew stronger, a breeze smelling of apple blossoms swirling around Ash's ears. "This is one of the housekeeping breezes and will show you how to find the door to your guestroom, and the bathing room beyond. Go get washed up, and Fang and I will have a nice chat and prepare dinner for all of us." Filby gestured off to the right, then turned and went left. Another doorway slit in the air opened. Fang hopped after her through the slit, and then both vanished.

The breeze and scent of apple blossoms grew stronger, tugging at

Ash's ear.

"Hello," she said, voice wobbling a little. She had a sensation of someone whispering, but without words. "What should I do? How do I find the door? It's not in the wall, is it?"

A whisper like a muffled giggle touched her ear. The breeze grew stronger and traveled down her right arm, tugging on her sleeve. Ash took a few steps, trying to let the breeze guide her. Something like a sheet of the finest, sheerest cloth rippled in front of her. It stung, just for a moment, then she heard a note inside her head, from an instrument she couldn't identify. It wasn't a string or a wind instrument or a chime. The breeze wrapped around her throat, just a brush, there and gone. The wordless voice whispered and Ash knew, without knowing how she knew, she was supposed to echo the note.

Help me?

Cecil had said several times, discussing theories of magic, quite often people with a great deal of potential halted and hobbled themselves. Not because they doubted but because they stopped and thought, when they should have simply acted and followed instinctive understanding that couldn't be expressed in words. They should have acted on that brief moment of belief that they *could* do something, before they allowed second and third thoughts to convince them that not only they *couldn't* do it, but it was impossible for everyone and anyone.

Ash opened her mouth and sang, hoping to echo the note. Her throat vibrated, but no sound escaped. At the same moment, she wondered how she could copy a note that hadn't touched her ears. It didn't make any sense.

Yet she was doing it, wasn't she?

The sheer cloth turned solid, just for a second, and became a doorway into a sunlit room. Ash stepped through at the same moment the breeze became a solid hand pushing on the small of her back. She stumbled on her second step and nearly knocked herself off her feet as she turned to look at what she had passed through.

It wasn't there. The room in Filby's warehouse wasn't there. The wall of the sunlit room was white painted plaster, with a thin rectangle drawn on it where Ash thought the door had been.

She sat down, and later couldn't decide if the bench had been there before she sat, or it solidified under her as her legs folded. She dropped the basket. Clothes spilled out. Sturdy, white and pale blue and yellow linen shirts, with all sorts of fanciful embroidery around the collars and wrists and hems. Long trousers in leather and thick, colorful cloth like tapestry. Vests and jackets and hosen and undergarments and breast bands. Made for the purpose, with hook closures, not the makeshift wrappings she had been using. There were more clothes jammed in that basket than Ash thought could fit. And at the bottom were high, metal-reinforced riding boots, ankle-boots, soft indoor slippers, and shoes made for dancing, with glass beads to catch the light.

Shivering, Ash wrapped her arms around herself and just looked at all the clothes. When she had emptied the basket, they made two piles taller than the basket. She knew everything would fit her, without having to pick up a single piece to hold against herself for sizing. Everything was beautifully made, sensible and sturdy, the colors rich. Like clothes made for nobles. These were clothes that would let the world know she was a girl, while letting her travel and ride and work, and not worry about skirts catching and getting in the way.

Maybe she could even let her hair grow, and braid it, for the first time in her life?

"Idiot," she whispered. Such thoughts were for later, when she was sure of herself and what she was doing and what she wanted to do. "Ring … am I in trouble?"

The ring was silent long enough to make her look at her hand, to check that she still had him on her finger.

"Are you all right?"

Yes, Lady Ashlyn.

"Please, don't call me that. These clothes are for a lady, an adventurous lady, strong, a warrior, but I have never felt farther from being one than I do right now."

This is an unusual place. I am thrown entirely off balance by the energies here, despite the reassurances from Lady Filby that you are safe and she will help us. She already has several ideas of how to do that. We are not in the faerie realms, but somewhere in that very thin betweening place that is neither faerie nor human, but both. Our hostess is someone of great power and age … and fortunately, great kindness. I believe we can trust her.

"Believe isn't the same as being sure," Ash whispered.

Then she wondered if that was foolish. This otherness place could be one of those theoretical folds in reality like Blaz's cavern. Worlds on top of worlds, all existing in the same place, just a half-step away from each other. And Filby could be sitting right next to her, sitting on the bench with her, and Ash wouldn't know it. Filby, being very powerful, a half-blood as she had said, could hear every word she said. Maybe know every thought in her head.

Then learn quickly the lessons she offers you and make yourself sure.

That, she had to admit, was common sense.

As if it had sensed she had come to a decision, the breeze returned, tugging on Ash's sleeve so she looked in that direction and saw the doorway into another room. It certainly hadn't been in that wall when she stepped into this room. Ash smelled roses and heard water splashing, and was that steam coming in wisps through the doorway? She followed her nose and stepped into a room with an enormous bathing tub, with rose petals floating on the surface of more steaming water than she had ever seen in her life. A stream of steaming water spilled down the wall into the tub, and ripples of steaming water spilled over in a low spot on the side, and onto a metal grid in the floor. She thought she could lay down in that tub. Why not?

"Thank you." She looked around and found pink-tinged blocks of what she hoped was soap. A pile of towels, scrubbing brushes, and familiar-looking bottles of lotion sat on a long, low table next to the tub. "Do I need to do anything?" she asked the breeze that visibly swirled through the steam rising off the water.

The breeze vanished, and a moment later pushed at her back, toward the tub.

Ash hesitated for a few moments, at the idea of undressing here, when she couldn't be sure she was alone. All the years of cautious bathing, enduring frigid water or brackish water in darkness and before dawn or after dark, to hide her body from any rude, spying eyes, had taught her to fear the very idea of undressing where she could be seen.

Then it occurred to her that the breeze was so different from her. So how could it be offended or think lascivious or shocked thoughts about her when it saw her naked body? Could it see her at all? How could it have a concept of naked when it didn't wear clothes?

She peeled out of her dirty clothes, moving a little faster with every knot untied and buckle undone and layer that slid to the floor. Trembling with eagerness, she nearly laughed at her pale, dirt-smeared leg as she lifted her foot to step into the tub. Ash hissed at the first touch of the steaming water. She put one foot in, then reached for the largest bar of soap. It was soft and the perfume of roses wafted around her as she clutched it to her chest and raised her other foot, to step completely into the tub. Then she slowly knelt, holding her breath until she grew used to the luxurious stinging of hot, hot water rising higher on her body. She slipped as she shifted around to sitting and her head went under. She popped back up, sputtering, then laughing, and didn't flinch when water splashed over all the sides of the tub.

Clean clothes were waiting when she had scrubbed herself and soaked and floated long enough her fingers and toes shriveled. She dressed, and when she bent to pick up the towels and her dirty clothes, she found the clothes were gone. The breeze yanked the wet towels out of her hands. Ash nearly protested that she had to clean up after herself. Or was she insulting the breeze? Filby had called it a housekeeping breeze, so … that was its job?

"Thank you," she said, and turned to follow the towel as it zipped across the room, wadded itself into a ball, and vanished through the door into the bedroom.

She followed it. The door out was open now, and she saw Filby lounging in a massive pile of pillows, reading a book. Beyond her, Fang was head-first in what looked like the rib cage of some large animal. His legs jerked from the exertion of his eating.

Ash muffled a chuckle. Fang was always hungry. Yes, she had fed him, but those sausages had likely vanished the moment he swallowed them. A moment later, her stomach pinched in hunger. Just how long had she walked after eating those sausages? She carefully stepped through the doorway and looked back behind herself to mark where it hung in the air.

"Don't worry, you'll be able to find it whenever you need to go in now," Filby said, without raising her head from her book. "That's your room as long as you stay here." She smiled now and reached for a length of braided threads to slip into the book before she closed it. "After talking with Fang here, I hope you'll feel comfortable enough to stay for a while. At least until that ridiculous man gets impatient and starts flinging magic about, trying to find you. Not that it will do him any good, but it's always wise to avoid catching the attention of nasty forces by being the subject of seeking spells."

"While we are here in this betweening space," the ring said aloud, "you are invisible to Camwell. Thank you greatly, Lady Efilbiana."

"Oh, please." Filby chuckled and stood up. How she managed to rise from that nest of pillows without losing her balance or looking ridiculous, Ash couldn't figure out. "You must call me Filby. Just Filby. I've learned a great deal of your story, but bunnies don't pay attention to the truly interesting, amusing details. Tell me more while we eat?"

They didn't just eat, they feasted. The table that slid into the room from another slit in the air spread out longer than the table in the dining hall at Castle Fairhold, which seated thirty people. It was covered with dishes, and Ash was sure she didn't see any duplicates. She calculated she only recognized about two-thirds of the dishes from the lavish feasts when she waited at the table at the castle. Common sense said to limit herself to things she recognized, so she knew what she could expect. She did hunt for dishes she had only seen and smelled and had the taste described to her. Such special dishes rarely had enough leftovers for anyone in the kitchen to have a taste.

"I'm a glutton," she murmured, as she sat down at the far, cleared end of the table with her heaping plate. Ash was surprised she hadn't lost some of the load of bright colors and the source of the spicy, meaty, luscious smells on her way to her seat.

"You have proper manners, to prevent you diving across the table, jamming handfuls into your mouth as you go," Filby said. "Compared to some who have sat at this table ... well, you show a high level of restraint. Would you mind explaining why you chose those specific dishes, and why you passed up others?"

This was the oddest start to a dinner conversation Ash had known, but she soon realized, and Filby confirmed, her hostess lived for knowledge. She enjoyed glimpses into how people thought and why things happened as they did. The causes for events and what happened when two things that had never been brought together were combined. On and on.

From talking about her food choices, Ash went on to ask about the dishes she didn't recognize. Filby knew all their ingredients and described how they were prepared. She laughed when Ash asked if she had made all that food. While she enjoyed cooking, especially new dishes only described in books, she left much of the cooking and cleaning to the housekeeping breezes. She did have the hostler business to run. There were never enough hours in the day for reading the new books and old documents her couriers found for her in far-off lands. And of course, she needed to talk with all the horses when they returned to the stables, to learn the conditions in those lands the couriers had traveled through.

"Animals observe so much that we humans never even consider. I find it highly useful to see and smell and taste the world through their senses, so to speak, and combine it with what people see and hear and think about. Both sides miss so very much," Filby explained.

"What do you do with that information?"

"She writes it down and shares it with the recluses and philosophers and those who live in the betweening realms," the ring said. "They can see backward and forward in time, and they make recommendations of what to do and not do, both from the good and bad examples in history, and from the possibilities of the future. That doesn't mean anyone listens to them when they send those recommendations to kings and emperors and sorcerers and enchanters, but their consciences are clean. They are doing the work A'theosius gave them."

"That is the most important thing of all," Filby said, nodding. She picked up her goblet full of something that steamed and smelled smoky-spicy. "Would you like to be part of my work?"

Ash nearly dropped her fork. "Excuse me? Doing what, exactly?"

Filby laughed. "Oh, I'm sorry. I have a tendency to jump far ahead in a conversation, because I've spent so much time planning what to say, the order in which to say it, and it feels to me like we already had much of the conversation, but you were left behind ..." She sputtered and shook her head and slumped in her chair, muffling giggles.

"Lady Filby is going to offer you a position as one of her couriers," the ring said. "Am I correct?"

Filby raised her goblet again, still laughing quietly at herself.

"But ... what about Justiciar Camwell?" Ash asked. "He's going to track me. He'll try to look over my shoulder, or through my eyes. I know a little about couriers, and their task requires being swift and unstoppable and avoiding notice. You said someone will notice the tracking spells he'll use on me? That would ruin the whole purpose of being a courier. Wouldn't it?"

"Hmm, yes." Only a small portion of amusement fled Filby's face. "And there are other times when wearing the emblems of my couriers will protect you and intimidate a lot of pompous boors into behaving with some courtesy. My courier web is well known where it needs to be, and invisible where it needs to be. You, with all that lovely magical potential ..." She tipped her head to one side, frowning in thought. "Well, you need training. It's a given your magic will burst out at the most inconvenient time if you're not prepared, or some unscrupulous, greedy dolt will try to enslave you for his own profit, if you aren't trained."

"She's afraid she'll have to agree to be a courier as the price of your help," the ring said.

"Oh, no, no, dear girl, not at all. The more I learn about you, the more fascinating you are, and I want to get to know you. Because I sense we have so very, very much in common." Filby shook her head. "Again, I must apologize. I've jumped too far ahead of myself. Tell me, Ash ... what is your greatest fear, right now? Other than that fool making you move on just when you've gotten comfortable, forcing you to experience places so he can ride on your eyes and ears and nose?"

"The ring. Losing him. The moment I complete the conditions of the quest," Ash blurted in a rapid rattle of words, so she almost didn't understand what she was saying.

"Ah ... that is telling." The woman nodded slowly, an even slower smile tugging up on her lips and narrowing her eyes.

Ash shivered and clutched her hands together in her lap, to keep them from shaking. Fang pulled himself out of the rib cage where he had apparently settled down to sleep. He made shallow hops across the room, pausing every other hop to give a few grooming licks to himself. He was nearly clean of blood by the time he reached Ash and crawled into her lap and wrapped his forelegs around her, purring softly.

"Then that is what we will try to solve first," Filby said, her gaze softening. "Whatever it takes, I will find a way for you and the ring to stay together. Even if I have to put a curse on the ring so it stays on your finger forever, I will find a way."

END

AUTHOR'S NOTE

The Enchanted Castle Archives started with a short story written for the anthology, **When Your Beauty IS The Beast**, full of multiple variations on the trope of Beauty and the Beast. (YeOldeDragonBooks.com)

Daughter of the Beastly Beauty was born from notes I've had in my files for years, for a story called (no surprise here) **The Beastly Beauty**. All I had planned was that the heroine would be beastly, and had a wannabe vampire bunny named Fang for a sidekick.

Since then, four stories have been written (and more to come) following the magical misadventures of Belladonna, known as 'Na, revealing bits about the lives of her parents before and after they met. **Liars' Quest** is the first book in what promises (threatens?) to become a multi-volume adventure of wonky magic.

Liars' Quest first appeared as the featured story in the launch of **Ye Olde Dragon's Library storytelling podcast**. If you care to hear an earlier version of this story, join the podcast. Or you can obtain the revised audiobook version in most places that sell audiobooks. Including Ye Olde Dragon Books.

The next volume, **The Beastly Beauty** (surprised?) should be fully rough drafted by the time this book is published and will appear on the podcast at the end of August 2023.

The Enchanted Castle Archives will switch back and forth with another fantasy series, *Steward's World*, in the **Ye Olde Dragon's Library podcast**. To get updates, excerpts, and more insider knowledge, please join the **Ye Olde Dragon's Library Patreon group**. Supporters will have access to free short stories before they are released for sale, and can order the print, e and audio books at a discount and before they are available for sale.

Think about it? I'm dreaming up all sorts of other goodies to offer supporters of the podcast …

Thanks for reading! I hope you had a good time and are eager for more.

Michelle L. Levigne

About the Author

On the road to publication, Michelle fell into fandom in college and has 40+ stories in various SF and fantasy universes. She has a bunch of useless degrees in theater, English, film/communication, and writing. Even worse, she has over 100 books and novellas with multiple small presses, in science fiction and fantasy, YA, suspense, women's fiction, and sub-genres of romance.

Her official launch into publishing came with winning first place in the Writers of the Future contest in 1990. She was a finalist in the EPIC Awards competition multiple times, winning with *Lorien* in 2006 and *The Meruk Episodes, I-V,* in 2010, and was a finalist in the Realm Awards competition, in conjunction with the Realm Makers convention.

Her training includes the Institute for Children's Literature; proofreading at an advertising agency; and working at a community newspaper. She is a tea snob and freelance edits for a living (MichelleLevigne@gmail.com for info/rates), but only enough to give her time to write. Her newest crime against the literary world is to be co-managing editor at Mt. Zion Ridge Press and launching the publishing co-op, Ye Olde Dragon Books. Be afraid … be very afraid.

And please check out her newest venture: Ye Olde Dragon's Library, the storytelling podcast. Each week, listeners are invited to join Michelle on her blog to ask questions and give feedback and suggestions. Interspersed between the chapters will be interviews with authors of fantastical fiction. Listen to the podcast on your favorite podcast app or listen on the website: www.YeOldeDragonBooks.com, and click on the Ye Olde Dragon's Library link. Then go to her blog to interact: www.MichelleLevigne.blogspot.com

www.Mlevigne.com
www.MichelleLevigne.blogspot.com

www.YeOldeDragonBooks.com
www.MtZionRidgePress.com

Look for Michelle's Goodreads groups:
Guardians of Neighborlee
Voyages of the AFV Defender

NEWSLETTER:
Want to learn about upcoming books, book launch parties, inside information, and cover reveals?
Go to Michelle's website or blog to sign up.

Thanks for reading!
If you enjoyed this book, would you help Michelle by posting a review on Goodreads?

Are you a member of Book Bub? If so, please follow Michelle on Book Bub, and you'll get alerts when new books are coming out.

As a way of saying thanks, Michelle invites you to the Goodies page on her website. It will change regularly, offering you a free short story, a sample audiobook chapter, sneak peeks at new cover art, inside information on discounts and new release dates, etc.

Please go to: Mlevigne.com/good-stuff.html

Also by Michelle L. Levigne

Guardians of the Time Stream: 4-book Steampunk series
The Match Girls: Humorous inspirational romance series starting with **A Match (Not) Made in Heaven**
Sarai's Journey: A 2-book biblical fiction series
Tabor Heights: 18-book inspirational small town romance series.
Quarry Hall: 11-book women's fiction/suspense series
For Sale: Wedding Dress. Never Used: inspirational romance
Crooked Creek: Fun Fables About Critters and Kids: Children's short stories.
Do Yourself a Favor: Tips and Quips on the Writing Life. A book of writing advice.

To Eternity (and beyond): *Writing Spec Fic Good for Your Soul.* A book defending speculative fiction.
Killing His Alter-Ego: contemporary romance/suspense, taking place in fandom.
The Commonwealth Universe: SF series, 25 books and growing
The Hunt: 5-book YA fantasy series
Faxinor: Fantasy series, 4 books and growing
Wildvine: Fantasy series, 14 books when all released
Neighborlee: Humorous fantasy series
Zygradon: 5-book Arthurian fantasy series
AFV Defender: SF adventure series
Young Defenders: Middle Grade SF series, spin-off of *AFV Defender*
Magic to Spare: Fantasy series
Book & Mug Mysteries: cozy mystery series
Quest for the Crescent Moon: fantasy series starting in 2023
Steward's World: fantasy series reboot and expansion, starting in 2023
The Enchanted Castle Archives: fantasy series, Liars' Quest, 1st book in the Ye Olde Dragon's Library podcast